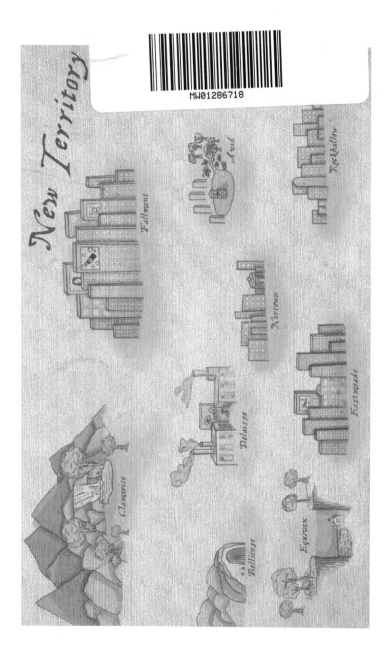

New Territory

Classprite

Fallmont

Avid

Rockhollow

Narrows

Delaisse

Eastmeads

Bellicase

Equeux

Fortitude

Jen Guberman

ISBN: 9781089768241

Any references to historical events, real people, or real places are used fictitiously. Names, characters, and places are products of the author's imagination.

Author photo by: Steep Creek Photography

Printed by KDP Amazon in the United States of America

Second printing edition 2019.

Edited by: Amy Guberman, Kylie McGee, Seth Perry, and Megan Dellinger

www.UberGuberman.com

For everyone who put up with me babbling endlessly about my books whenever I could find a way to work them into conversation.

CHAPTER ONE

I distinctly remember the smell of cinnamon.

I remember the sounds of gunshots and yelling.

And I remember the feeling of sweat on my neck.

When Zane and I escaped Fallmont with the Skeleton Key, we sprinted as fast as we could until we had reached the ruins of a blackened village. We managed to find the Skeleton Key box in Fallmont after finding keys to open it in each of the five exile towns: Avid—the dump town for thieves, Bellicose—the caverns for the aggressive, Clamorite—the waterfall grotto in the mountains for the unruly, Delaisse—the abandoned factories for the druggies and vandals, and Equivox—the lake town hidden in a crater for the liars.

It was growing dark by this point, and we hadn't eaten since before we reached Fallmont. Thinking back to the sweet smell of cinnamon and other spices from the food carts of the city, my stomach began to growl angrily. Squatting down on a mound of rubble, I rummaged through my leather bag, pulling out a piece of crumbling, stale bread. Upon closer observation, the bread had tiny specs of green mold. I picked out the moldy pieces and devoured the slice, holding out a second slice for Zane.

"Thanks, E," he said, taking the bread and sitting next to me. He turned the bread over in his hand for a moment, looking at the green specs before biting.

Not wanting to think about anything, I sat there silently, resting my elbows on my knees and my chin in my palms.

"So," Zane prodded awkwardly.

"What?" I grumbled, exhausted.

"Fortitude?" he asked, a little garbled. His mouth was still blistered from the acid the officials tortured him with when Raine had interrogated me.

"Really, Zane?" I scoffed.

"What?"

"Does now really seem like the right time?"

"Is there ever a right time for anything we do?"

I sighed.

"No. But can't we just rest for the night?"

"Of course, but we have to keep moving in the morning. We don't know if officials from Fallmont are still looking for us."

I nodded sleepily as I stood, making my way toward one of the ruined cottages. I peeked my head inside to inspect it, shrugged, grunted, and flopped onto the floor after pulling my blanket out of my bag. Within minutes, I was asleep.

"Wake up," I heard Zane mutter the next morning, prodding my side with a finger.

I threw the blanket over my face as I moaned.

"We have to keep moving," Zane reminded me. "Not only do we not want to get caught here, but we don't have enough food and water to last us forever."

"What's the plan?"

Zane pulled out a map, stretching out on the floor next to me.

"Skylar said Fortitude was past Bellicose, toward the ocean, right?" he asked.

I nodded.

"Didn't she also say something about a purple light?" I reminded him.

"I think so."

"So, where are we, and where are we headed?"

"We are somewhere in *this* area," he pointed to a blank space on the map near Fallmont. "If we head straight west, we shouldn't run into any cities or exile towns. But at some point, we have to work our way south."

I stared at the map, contemplating. While I focused on the map, Zane nuzzled up against me, kissing my shoulder. I turned and looked at him with a straight face before turning back to the map.

"I mean, the map doesn't show much of what's beyond the cities and towns, so I don't really see what other options we have," I said, folding up the map.

After a quick breakfast, Zane and I started the trek to the west. We were silent most of the day, stopping occasionally for breaks in various ruins. Despite the warmth of the air, puffy clouds blocked the sun and spared us of intense heat.

"Let's make sand angels," Zane spoke up during a silent moment while walking.

"What?"

"You heard me."

"What? You mean like people used to make in the snow?" I asked.

Zane and I have never seen snow, at least not in person. The New Territory never gets snow. Before the war, when the country was populated all throughout, there were people who lived in colder areas, and they would get snow. I thought the concept of wanting to play in frozen water to be unappealing, to say the least.

"Yeah! Oh, come on. We could use a break, and our normal breaks are boring! Let's do it!" Zane smiled warmly.

I rolled my eyes and huffed at Zane as he flopped onto his back, sending up a puff of sand.

He began frantically sifting his arms and legs across the fine sand, stopped, and stretched out his arms.

"Help me up?"

I walked over and pulled him to his feet as he turned to admire his work.

"It doesn't look like an angel," I said, squinting at the ground.

"It looks... like a potato..." Zane said, confused.

I grinned.

"It worked!" He beamed.

"No, it didn't! You said it yourself!" I said, pointing to the potato hole, a smug grin spreading on my lips.

"No, I mean my plan worked! You smiled!"

"Okay, fair enough," I said, my smile fading. "Let's keep moving."

After some time walking through emptiness, we came across some ruins, like the others we had crossed before, except in slightly better shape. Some of the buildings still retained the natural red color of their bricks. A couple of the buildings still stood fairly untouched, with fewer crumbling walls.

Curious, I approached one of the buildings with the door still in place. I went to turn the knob, but it wouldn't budge.

"Zane," I said. "This one is locked."

"Don't you have the Key?" he asked. "See if it'll work on that door."

I dug the Key out of my leather bag, turning it over in my hands as light glimmered off of the silver and through the three pieces of green, purple, and blue stained glass at the Key's head. I inserted it into the lock, twisted the tiny dial on the Key, and turned until I heard a click.

The door opened, revealing a room with faded brown couches, a dusty wooden table, and a few dishes scattered around the room. The walls were a pale blue, and the carpet was a stained cream color with sand tracked throughout the house. Zane followed behind me. I turned into the kitchen while Zane brushed dirt off the couch. I looked at the sink, which had water puddled in it.

"*Zane*," I hissed quietly toward the living room.

A moment later, Zane poked his head in the kitchen door.

"What?" he asked as I frantically signaled for him to lower his voice.

"*I think there are people here,*" I whispered, my eyes wide.

"*What? Where?*"

I shrugged, pointing to the water in the sink. "*It hasn't evaporated yet. It's recent.*"

Zane pulled out his dagger and I pulled out mine as we split up to search the house. Zane and I cautiously opened doors to closets and bedrooms until suddenly, I heard a shriek.

I turned, the hair on my neck standing on end as I held my dagger out defensively, creeping toward Zane, who stood in a doorway, blocking my view.

"Who are you?" I heard Zane demand of someone inside one of the rooms.

"W-we aren't here to hurt anyone! P-p-please!" a female voice whimpered.

We?

"What are you doing here?" Zane asked, still holding out his weapon.

"Wait a minute… You aren't officials, are you?" The girl's voice grew confident. "You aren't carrying a gun."

"No, we aren't officials," Zane answered. "What are you doing here?"

"We escaped from some of the exile towns. We

found each other while looking for shelter in the ruins. We aren't looking for trouble."

"How do I know I can trust you?" Zane asked.

"Why do you *need* to trust us?" a man grunted.

Keeping my distance behind Zane, I could only see beyond the doorframe enough to make out the man who spoke. He was heavy-set, with peppered hair and a bushy beard.

"They don't *have* to trust us, Trent, but there's no harm in allies," the girl chirped.

Trent snorted, crossing his arms.

"Search us! Our bags," the girl continued, and there was a collective *thump* as bags were dropped. "We don't have weapons. We don't have much of anything. The houses here still had some canned food we've been living off of. That's it—I swear."

Zane entered the room, still wielding his golden dagger distrustfully. I could hear him undo zippers and clasps as he searched bags briefly before speaking again.

"Okay. You can't be too sure. I'm sorry for scaring you. My girlfriend and I escaped as well."

Girlfriend? When did we decide this? And why is he willing to trust them so quickly?

"I understand. My name is Cindee—"

"Wait," Zane interrupted, turning to me and beckoning me over.

I stepped into the room, which was clearly an old bedroom, and saw eleven new people staring back at me.

"How…" I trailed off.

"It's a long story," a girl with freckles and two blonde braids replied. *She must be Cindee.*

I looked at Zane, my mouth open in shock.

"I'm Cindee," the girl with braids repeated. She looked about Lamb's age. "I'm from Clamorite."

I looked at the rest of the group. There seemed to be a variety of people—younger and older, male and female.

"This is Bexa from Bellicose, Trent and Persephone from Equivox, Eve, Braylin, and Gwenn from Clamorite, Yulie and Brenur from Delaisse, and Cameron and Astraea from Avid," Cindee introduced.

"I'm Zane, and this is Eos," Zane gestured to me. "We're both from Avid."

"Why'd you leave?" I asked.

"We could ask you the same question," Trent retorted.

"Yeah, but I asked first."

"We didn't like our situations. I'm assuming it was the same for you. Just because we've committed crimes doesn't mean we define ourselves by our crimes, and it doesn't mean we get along with other people just because they committed the same crimes," replied Eve, a short, thin girl with spiked black hair and notable dark circles under her emerald eyes.

Brenur, a dark-skinned man with wide-set eyes, thick arms, and broad shoulders spoke up.

"Yulie and I left because she—" he started before Yulie, a woman with tan skin, a furrowed brow, and silky brown hair, glared coolly at him. The height difference between the two was so huge that I couldn't help but to stare. I was about average height, whereas the top of Yulie's head hardly reached my nose, and Brenur easily towered over me.

"Did you all expect there to be something greater out here?" I spat bitterly.

"Yes," Cindee replied quickly. "Even if there are challenges, sometimes change is necessary. Eve, Braylin, Gwenn, and I all left together. We knew we weren't going to be facing it alone. We came across the rest of the group over time. Some of these people were together, some by themselves. But they all couldn't bear being exiled anymore."

"Being out here," I held my arms out, my eyes wild. "Being out here is *worse*. You're safer in the exile towns."

"Safer isn't always better," Astraea cooed softly. She had long, wavy maroon hair and bright eyes. Her gaze seemed to analyze me as she spoke.

"We answered your question, so answer one of ours. What are your plans, now that you're free?" Trent asked.

Zane looked at me, as if for approval, but without waiting for it, he began.

"We're looking for something," he started.

"*Zane*," I hissed, elbowing his side aggressively.

He cupped his hands over my ear, his voice low.

"I searched their bags—they don't have weapons. I didn't see anything on them, either. They don't even have much food. If they really are who they say they are, isn't this essentially what we wanted to do anyways? Guide exiles to Fortitude?"

"Did he just say Fortitude?" asked a tall woman named Persephone. Before she spoke, her posture straightened with an air of superiority, her ginger bob tickling the pale skin of her jaw. Her wide nose was held upwards, but upon the mention of Fortitude, her snooty appearance transformed into one of curiosity.

There was collective conversation from the group of exiles.

"Zane!" I shouted.

"What?" he cried, holding his hands up as if in surrender.

I groaned in disgust.

"I've heard of it!" Bexa spoke up. She had a frizzy brunette bun and colorful tattoos across her arms and chest.

I had to remind myself not to stare at Bexa's numerous piercings covering her ears, her petite pointed nose, and her thin lips.

Those piercings look painful.

"It's a town of escaped exiles. I've heard about it, but I didn't think it was real. Have you seen it before?" she asked.

"No," I replied.

"Do you know where it is?" she asked.

"Not exactly…"

There were shared grumbles from the exiles.

"I mean we have a general idea. We hadn't heard of it until after we escaped, and at that point, we figured it would be worth a shot."

Fortitude

I decided not to mention the Skeleton Key right now, especially with two other thieves joining us. I also figured it wasn't the best time to mention that we planned on eventually going back to break a bunch of other criminals out of the exile towns.

"So, what's the plan?" asked Eve.

"What do you mean?" I asked in return.

"Well, you obviously aren't going in search of Fortitude without a plan. You said you have a general idea of where it is, and I'm assuming you have plans for getting rations?" she replied.

"Umm…" I struggled, looking at Zane for help.

"We don't exactly have much of a plan. We're heading west until we clear the cities, then we will head south a bit until we near the ocean, which is where Fortitude is supposed to be."

"So, you don't have a plan, is what you're trying to say?" Persephone said with an amused smirk.

"We do," I groaned.

"Where do you plan on getting rations?" she pried.

"None of your business," I hissed, thinking about the Skeleton Key.

"E," Zane breathed, looking at me in disbelief. "Sorry, I don't know what's gotten into her. I was thinking we would stop in cities and towns along the way, snag what we can."

"Excuse me?" I growled. "You 'don't know what's gotten into me?'"

"I didn't mean it like that."

"She's upset that you're sharing all of this with strangers," Astraea observed almost inaudibly.

"Honestly, I think our chances are better if you all join us. Safety in numbers, and all that. More people to help with supplies, too, if you want to come with us to Fortitude," he invited, avoiding my glare.

"May I speak with my group for a moment? Privately?" Cindee asked politely.

"Of course," Zane responded, ushering me back into the kitchen with him as Cindee closed the bedroom door behind her.

"*What are you doing?*" I snarled at Zane.

"They're right! We don't have a plan, Eos! I mean, what are we supposed to do about food and water?"

"We have the Key!" I exclaimed in a hushed voice. "We can get in any town or city we want, and we can get all the supplies we need!"

"We can't carry enough to last us more than a few days. Face it."

"And you think inviting *more* people, who *also* need food is going to fix that problem?"

"Some of their group members look stronger than us and can probably carry more. Plus, with a bigger group, we can have people carry extra supplies and we can switch off in shifts, if we get desperate," Zane argued, as if he had calculated all of this carefully. "Or what if someone has a supply that we need, and we have something they need? A bigger group means more supplies available."

"Fine. But how do you know we can trust them? Especially after what happened in Fallmont!"

"They aren't officials, E."

"But what if they report you?"

"That's a stupid question. Do you really think a group of runaway exiles are going to report other runaway exiles? They don't want to get caught. We don't want to get caught. That means everyone protects each other to some degree by default, as a matter of self-preservation."

"I still don't trust them."

"I'm not sure I do either. It's called a leap of faith. Do you trust me?"

"They might steal the Key, Zane."

"I didn't ask if you trust *them*, I asked if you trust *me*."

"Yes."

He smiled at me softly, placing a hand behind my head and planting a quick kiss on my forehead.

The bedroom door opened, and the group flooded out into the main room of the small house.

The corner of Cindee's lips turned upward in a half smile as she nodded.

"You're in?" Zane asked.

"Yup. We've got at least one person from each exile town, too. We've got everyone we could need to get anything we could need. But first, we have a different plan."

"What is it?" I asked, skeptically.

"We agreed that moving south first, then west, is the best option. South of us is Delaisse, Nortown, and Equivox. If we go south first, we can stock up on supplies, which we might not come across if we head straight toward the west," Cindee offered.

Zane thought for a moment before speaking.

"That's a good point. E?" he asked, turning to me.

"What?"

"I want to know what you think," he said genuinely.

I narrowed my eyes and stared back at him for a moment.

"I—I think that's a good idea," I said, softening my gaze.

"It's settled then. We head south," Zane nodded to Cindee.

"We believe it would be best to visit Delaisse first for a supply run. It's closest. Yulie and Brenur said the rations are easy to access once you're in the town. We just have to find out how to break in, and we can stock up there. If we don't think we have enough to make it to Fortitude with those supplies, we can visit Equivox next. It would probably be safer than trying to sneak into a city, even if that city is just tiny Nortown," Cindee continued to plot.

"Makes sense," I said. "Should we wait until morning to leave? It's getting late, and this is as good a place as any to stay."

"Yeah, that'd probably be best," Cindee answered. "We found some cans of food in the cabinets in the kitchen, if you guys want something for dinner."

"Thank you," I said, staring unblinkingly at Cindee.

What's her motive? She's either planning something, or she's trusting that we can get her somewhere we don't even know exists. Either way, I'm not sure I like it.

Fortitude

The group began to find places to sleep, making themselves comfortable throughout the house as Zane and I dug through the cabinets, picking out a couple cans of beans and vegetables.

"Here," Astraea said, seeming to appear out of nowhere behind me, holding out a metal can opener.

"Thanks," I said, narrowing my gaze at her as her eyes scanned over me.

"You're afraid of us," she perceived, looking into my eyes, her head cocked slightly to the side. "Why?"

"I'm not afraid. I just don't know why you all want to join us."

"We just want freedom. Same as you. We have a better chance of making it to Fortitude if we stick together and help each other. Why do you think we all ended up as such a large group?"

"Look… Astrid," I started.

"Astraea," she corrected under her breath.

"Sorry."

"It's okay. It's a tough one for some people. Ah. Stray. Uh," she sounded out. "You can call me Trae if that's easier."

"Okay. Anyways," I sighed. "We don't even know for sure if Fortitude exists. We've never seen it before."

"So, you're afraid of letting us all down, is that it?" she cooed. "What do 13 criminals really have to lose?"

Their lives.

CHAPTER TWO

I barely slept, but the night was calm. I didn't trust the newcomers, so I couldn't manage to get much sleep. Zane seemed restless throughout the night as well, and woke up next to me out of breath at one point, running a finger along the sores on his tongue and inside his mouth.

Everyone seemed well rested in the morning except Zane and me, as they rose from their makeshift beds and began rummaging through the kitchen for breakfast, chatting excitedly about what they hoped Fortitude would be like. I could hear Eve describing it as a small village, tucked away in some woods that managed to survive the war. Yulie was grimacing, disagreeing with Eve as she described houses along a beach shore, with exotic plants. Astraea stood, her eyes void of emotion, just staring at Eve and Yulie curiously, seeming to imagine the places they described. The two paid her no mind until she spoke up.

"I think Fortitude is just another ruin like this. It's probably in similar shape to this place. There likely aren't that many exiles that have reached Fortitude before, so for all we know, we might just be travelling all that way just to be in almost this exact situation."

Fortitude

"Way to be negative, Trae," teased Cameron, a younger man with pale blue eyes, hair like raven feathers arranged loosely on his head, and a sharp jawbone.

Astraea sighed softly as she clamped a can opener onto a small, unlabeled can.

I gently elbowed Zane. His eyes fluttered open as he grumbled at me groggily.

My mouth felt dry when I woke up, but I wasn't hungry. I decided to pass on the canned food for breakfast, opting for a drink of water instead. When I went to turn the sink on; however, nothing came out.

"It doesn't work," Bexa said.

"I don't understand," I tried again, but still no water came out. "There was water in the sink last night. That's how I knew you guys were here."

"Gwenn accidentally knocked over Cameron's water bottle and spilled some of it when it fell in the sink," she revealed.

"Oh," I said, disappointed.

Once everyone was done eating, we all stuffed as many cans of food into our bags as we could and headed out as a group with Zane, Cindee, and I at the lead. We marched through the sand in awkward silence. After a while, Cameron strode over to me and put his arm around me, draping it over my shoulder.

"What are you doing?" I asked, glaring at him unamused.

"So, tell me a little about yourself," he started casually.

"Get your arm off me," I complained, slouching underneath his arm to slide it off.

He withdrew his arm, and I quickened my pace. He trotted to catch up.

"No, really. What's your story?"

"I don't want to talk about it."

"What? That bad, huh?"

"No. Go away."

"Oh, come on, Stripes."

"'Stripes'?"

"Your hair. Black and blonde like that. Looks like stripes."

I rolled my eyes.

"Come on! Long walks are the best times for stories. I want to know yours."

"If I tell you, will you leave me alone?"

"I suppose, if that's what you want," he answered innocently.

"Fine. My name is Eos Dawn. I lived in Rockhallow with my parents. I stole rum from a bar, and I got caught. I ended up in Avid, and now I'm here."

"There's more than that," Cameron pried, looking at me with a curious twinkle in his sharp blue eyes.

"No, there's not," I argued, looking back to the path ahead of me.

"I can tell there's more just based on the way you carry yourself. You have something weighing on you… Something you feel guilty for."

"What? Are you a psychiatrist now? Stop psycho-analyzing me. I'm fine. You don't know anything about me."

"Maybe not, but I know the look. Eos Dawn, you're hiding something."

"Leave me alone!" I snipped.

"Hey, man, leave her alone," Zane interfered, looking over at Cameron and me.

"I don't mean any harm," Cameron insisted, raising his palms. "I was just making small talk."

Zane nodded and looked ahead again as we continued forward into the sandscape.

Cameron gave me one more inquisitive look before slowing his pace, allowing himself to meld back into the rest of the group.

I've done well to suppress the memories, and the last thing I want is to be forced to talk about how I killed an official in Equivox my first time there while trying to escape. I couldn't talk about how, the second time I was in Equivox, Lamb, one of the only friends I had, was killed trying to protect me. I'd rather believe it was all just a bad dream—something conjured up by the darker parts of my subconscious—not my reality.

People were casually chatting behind me as we marched onwards.

"We're getting close," Brenur called from the back of the group.

"E," Zane called to me casually.

I turned to him to see him beckoning me over.

"What?" I asked, once I was directly next to him as we continued walking.

"Are we going to try to free some of the people in Delaisse while we're there?" he asked in a half-whisper.

"No."

"Why?"

"We aren't ready. We don't know if Fortitude exists. There might not be anything out here for them. We need to know it exists first. We're lucky if we can make it with the amount of people we have already. Extra people would just be an added liability."

"Alright. How do you propose we go in? I mean, we have the Key, but do we want them to know about it yet?

"Heck no," I said. *Why would he even consider letting them see it?*

"So, should we just climb over the fence like last time?"

I nodded.

"I see it up ahead!" Cindee called to the group, who proceeded to elicit excited cheers.

I squinted, making out the chain-link fence of Delaisse in the distance, the decrepit factory buildings just behind it. Delaisse, the town for the addicts and vandals, was beautifully decorated in vibrant graffiti. The deeper into the town you ventured, the more the graffiti covered every surface. I recalled my previous experience there, during which Tanner drugged me and interrogated me, leaving me to believe Zane had abandoned me there.

Once we reached the fence, without hesitation or a moment's discussion, Trent and Cameron began hoisting the group members high onto the fence. Each person scrambled the rest of the way and eased themselves down the other side. When Zane and I were the only two left on Trent and Cameron's side, Cameron waved me over.

"C'mon! What are you waiting for?" he asked impatiently.

"Nothing," I responded, staring back at him with confusion as I mindlessly walked over and put a foot on their linked hands as they raised me from the ground to the fence.

Zane, Trent, and Cameron climbed over the fence and joined the rest of us on the other side.

"Here's the plan," Yulie started. "The storage room is to the west, and we are on the east side. Most people here stay in the buildings or are passed out in the pipes during the day. The only people out during the day are the occasional daytime vandals, but they're nothing to worry about. A lot of them are so far gone mentally that they probably won't even notice you. Just act normal and don't make eye contact. Follow me and Brenur."

No one in the group said a word as she began to march off. I looked at Zane and huffed dramatically as we followed.

The pipe entrance I used when I was in Delaisse in the past must have been in the east side, because the further west we travelled, the less familiar the town looked. Similar to the east side, the west had buildings that were once industrial factories, but were now turned into massive canvases, covered in effervescent paintings of people, landscapes, and stylized names. We continued walking, and along the way, I spotted a painting on a smaller building. The painting had the unmistakable cartoonized figure of Raine Velora, the leader of Fallmont and the overall high power of the New Territory, with her raven black curls and almond-shaped brown eyes. The cartoon depicted

Raine holding a gear in her hand, and had a painted speech bubble above her, saying, "Another cog in the machine!"

I gawked at the painting for a moment, my face feeling flushed, before having to trot to catch up with the rest of the group, who was nearing an old brick warehouse.

Yulie twisted the doorknob of the building.

"It's locked," she grunted, shaking the handle agitatedly.

Zane looked at me and then at my leather bag, which held the Skeleton Key. My eyes widened and I shook my head subtly.

"*Yes*," he mouthed, motioning a hint to me to keep the Key concealed.

I shook my head still and he let out an exasperated sigh and rolled his eyes. He opened his mouth to speak, and just before he did, Cameron squatted down to eyelevel with the knob and began to pick the lock.

Snap.

"Shi-" Cameron grumbled to himself, retrieving his broken pick. "Anyone else have a lock pick or something?"

No one spoke.

"Let me try. I've got a pick," I said.

It's not a full lie, I rationalized.

Cameron stepped back and allowed me to kneel at the doorknob. I pulled the Skeleton Key out of my bag subtly, keeping it hidden in my sleeve as I brought it up to the keyhole. Turning the dial on the Key through my sleeve, I pretended to be fidgeting with a lock pick until I heard the bolt make a *thunk*. I slipped the Key back into my bag, careful not to let anyone else see.

"This is your home," I said, motioning Yulie and Brenur to the door. "Do the honors?"

"Don't call this place our 'home.' It's anything but," Yulie grimaced.

"Mmh," Brenur grunted in agreement, reaching for the doorknob.

He pulled the door open, revealing a wide room full of shelves. Many of the shelves were empty, but the shelves along the far right wall were stocked with food, medical supplies, and unlabeled boxes. Suddenly, everyone in the group began to rush toward the shelves, grabbing what they could and shoving it in their bags.

"Move!" Persephone growled at Gwenn, a curvy girl with thick blonde curls and large green eyes, as she reached for a packaged cupcake.

"Find your own, jerk!" Gwenn said, stuffing the cupcake in her bag while beaming snarkily at Persephone.

"Ugh," Persephone snarled in disgust, her face as bright as her ginger bob as she moved to a different area on the shelf.

I decided to pick the far edge of the full shelves, where the only other person rummaging was Braylin, a young-looking Clamorite with silver hair that revealed black roots. He silently rummaged through supplies, turning to face me briefly when I joined him. His round face was spotted with tiny freckles, and his arms were decorated in simple black tattoos.

"Hey," he smiled meekly at me as I poked through the options on a shelf beside him.

I pursed my lips and nodded, turning back to face the shelf.

"Braylin," he said, holding out a hand. "I'm Cindee's brother."

I turned to face him again, pausing before shaking his hand.

"Eos," I said plainly.

"Do you have a favorite food?" he asked politely.

"Chocolate pudding."

"Huh," he said, thinking for a moment before rapidly digging through food on his shelf. "I think I saw some a minute ag—oh! Here we go."

He pulled out a cup of chocolate pudding and handed it to me with a shy smile.

"Look, Braylin," I said, squinting at him pensively. "I'm not looking to make friends right now, okay? The people I care about only seem to end up hurt. It's in your best interest to stay away from me."

"I'm not trying to be your friend. I just know that we've all been through a lot, and sometimes the simple comforts—like your favorite food—can go a long way. Take it. I'm not subjecting you to friendship through the taking of a pudding cup," he laughed.

"Thanks," I mumbled, tucking the cup into my bag. "What's your favorite food?"

He chuckled.

"What?"

"You aren't going to find my favorite food in an exile town," he answered.

"Why not?"

"Waffles. Mine and Cindee's mom used to make us waffles before school every morning. She'd put so much syrup on them that every little square on them was full."

"I've never had a waffle," I said plainly.

"You've—you've never had a *waffle?*" Braylin stared at me, his mouth open. "Oh, we *have* to change that!"

"How?" I asked, a smile growing on my face.

"I don't know. Maybe once we are in Fortitude, we can find a way to make everyone waffles," he proposed halfheartedly.

"Yeah," I said, my smile fading as we both turned in silence to resume looking through the food on the shelves.

I stuffed a few raw vegetables in my bag, as well as a couple boxes of crackers, a jar of peanut butter, some water bottles, and a loaf of bread. The bread didn't want to fit in my bag with all of the other food, as well as my blanket, a change of clothes, and the medical supplies I grabbed—rubbing alcohol, bandages, and a few random bottles of medicine. I kept pushing down on the bread, determined to fit it, until I eventually squished it underneath everything else. At this point, my sturdy bag was bulging at the seams. *That's enough. I can't fit anymore.*

As everyone began to finish stuffing their bags and pockets full of supplies, we began slowly filing out of the warehouse. Astraea was the last one out, after Cindee had to go back in to let her know that everyone was done. Astraea looked back at Cindee, momentarily confused as she put down the bottle she was observing.

"Should we lock it back up?" Bexa proposed. "That way no one alerts any officials?"

"I'm pretty sure someone's going to notice that there are rations missing. Thirteen people just raided their storage," Eve stated. "Don't bother."

Bexa shrugged, and Brenur and Yulie began to lead the way back out of Delaisse. We all walked briskly down the street and toward the fence. Once we grew closer to the fence, a group of about three Delaisse men spotted us and eyed us suspiciously.

"Don't look at them, just keep moving," Yulie hissed back at us as we quickened our pace.

"Brenur, is that you?" called one of the men, with a stubbly face and a bald head, his speech slurred as he stumbled toward our group.

Brenur kept his face down and remained silent. He took long, purposeful strides, but the man kept trotting after him.

"Bren, hey, bro… Slow down!" the man shouted with a raised voice, stretching out his arms for balance as he wobbled toward us.

"Where've you been, man?" he continued to shout, his voice booming. A few other people began to poke their heads out of doors in response to the noise. One older looking woman who peered out from behind a door stared back at us, her eyes wide as she called out to us.

"They're escaping! Look! Help! Before they get away!" she called, her eyes searching frantically for someone to stop us.

"*Go!*" Yulie commanded us as she took off in a full-speed sprint toward the fence.

We stampeded toward the fence, which rattled as everyone began scurrying over it. I was one of the last ones to climb, and just before I did, I spotted the woman from the door calling for the attention of a lanky young man covered in tattoos, with a bad slouch and a snapback.

"Do something!" she croaked. "You're in charge—you're supposed to stop them! If I can't leave—no one should."

"Listen, lady, I've got things under control," he spat, straightening his posture as he got in her face. "Don't tell me how to do my job."

Before I could see anything else, the people in front of me had cleared the fence, so I began to pull myself over it to join them, with only Trent and Zane behind me.

"Quick!" Yulie beckoned us to continue running past the fence.

"Why? They can't do anything from in there," Gwenn observed.

"Yeah," observed Trent as we all finished climbing over. "Why don't they just climb the fence, too?"

"I wouldn't worry about them leaving, but even if they did—that man in the hat is the supervisor over Delaisse. As far as exile life goes, his is more than just a little cushy. If any of those people left and he knows who they are, he can report them. Every official in the New Territory would be looking for them, because he faces consequences when he doesn't report escapes," Yulie explained.

"How would the officials even know that anyone escaped if he never told them anyways?" I asked.

"I'm not sure. I always assumed they did like a secret headcount or something, or made sure all of the jobs were done in the towns," she answered.

"Jobs? What kind of jobs did you have in Delaisse? I mean, I had a job in Avid, but it was gardening related, and I didn't see gardens here."

"Unfortunately, mine and Brenur's jobs weren't nearly as glamorous as gardening," Yulie scoffed. "We actually met because we were assigned the same job. It was the most revolting job possible... Keep in mind, Delaisse has a lot of druggies, and sometimes druggies overdo it and... get... ill. Somebody had to keep the town vomit-free. Lucky us."

I grimaced.

We continued into the sandscape in the direction of Nortown and Equivox until the Delaisse fence was no longer in sight. The sun was beginning to set, and the sky filled with cotton candy clouds as my eyes began scanning for some sort of ruins to stop in for the night. The horizon was completely clear of anything but sand, with the occasional patch of dried up plants.

There's got to be something. There's never not something.

"Cindee?" called Gwenn from the back of the group. "Where are we going to stay? We're running out of light."

"It looks like we might just have to set up camp here," she answered, looking at our surroundings, and then at Zane and me.

"Not sure what other options we have," I shrugged, dropping my bag in the sand at my feet.

"We should set up a watch system, since we're out in the open," Zane suggested. "I'll take first watch with Eos, then Gwenn and Persephone."

Zane continued to list off pairs, ending with Trent, Astraea, and Cameron in a group of three. Everyone nodded in agreement, settling down in the sand to eat before going to sleep. The number of conscious people began to dwindle. Once everyone was asleep, Zane and I got situated, sitting back to back, daggers in hand.

"What happens if we don't find Fortitude?" I whispered to Zane.

"I'm not sure. I was thinking about that earlier. I guess we would have to eventually head back and find ruins near an exile town so we could get rations."

"Do you think we will honestly have enough food and water to last us the trip there and back though?"

"No. But there has to be something between us and where Fortitude is supposed to be. There used to be people all over before the war—I'm sure we will come across ruins along the way with supplies still left in them."

"That's dangerously optimistic, but I hope you're right."

I could feel Zane shrug behind me with a sigh.

"I heard some of the girls talking about Fortitude earlier," I started after a moment of silence. "They were talking about what they think it's going to be like."

"Yeah?"

"Mhm. If it does exist, what do you think it'll be like?"

"I'm not sure. I think I'd rather not try to build some kind of expectations. I hate that I even believe it exists. Deep down, I think I know that it doesn't, but there's just this bit of hope that I have that Fortitude does exist, and that this is all going to work out."

I raised an eyebrow inquisitively before speaking up.

"How do you do that?"

"Do what?"

"Stay so positive. After everything."

"I don't know. I mean, I guess if I didn't, there'd be nothing to keep pushing me forward. Think about it… if I let all of this crush every ounce of hope I have, there'd be nothing worth fighting or living for. I have to believe there's something more—something to move toward. If I stop thinking about Fortitude, all I can think about is Lamb, and what Raine did to me, and I don't want to. I don't want to remember that stuff."

"Me neither, but I don't feel right forgetting what happened to Lamb. It was my fault, and if I just brush it off… it's just… that's not fair to her memory."

"And dwelling on her death *is*?"

"I—"

"No. It's not. You may not have known Lamb as long as I did, but what's not fair to her memory is to only think about how she died."

"*Actually*," I started angrily. "It *is* fair. She didn't die protecting *you*. You don't have to feel any kind of burden about it. If I were to forget what she did for me…"

"Instead of torturing yourself with that, why don't you just focus on how she was selfless? Remember her as her happy, bubbly self, and appreciate that she was a selfless person. Stop thinking about her death, Eos."

"I *can't*. Every time I close my eyes for even a moment… if it's not that, it's the official I killed, or more recently it's the thought of Raine's men torturing you."

"*Stop*," Zane groaned impatiently.

"I *can't*," I repeated.

"Yes, you can. Just shut it off!"

"You're in denial, Zane."

"No, I'm not. I'm just better at coping than you are."

I scoffed.

"What?" he asked belligerently.

"You literally just denied being in denial, and I thought it was kinda' funny."

"Oh, shut up," he laughed.

After that, he was still.

I want to say something. I want to talk to him. I just don't want to talk about what happened. He says to shut it off as if it's a light switch. How can he be in such denial after what Raine did to him?

We sat back to back without speaking for what felt like ages, until Zane finally spoke up.

"Do you think it's about time we woke Gwenn and Persephone?" he asked. "I'm struggling to keep my eyes open."

"Yeah, probably. You wake Gwenn, I'll get Persephone."

I stretched my stiff legs and stood slowly, patting the sand off of my pants. Persephone was asleep next to Trent, so I snuck over to her, her mouth wide open in her sleep.

"Hey, Persephone," I whispered throatily. "Your turn for watch."

She blinked her eyes a few times, smacking her lips together as she gained consciousness. With a grunt, she stood to her feet and moseyed after me. We joined Zane and Gwenn, who looked only relatively awake.

"Here," said Zane, handing Gwenn his dagger. "Just in case. They're the only weapons we have, so please be careful."

"What good is a dagger going to do if someone were to come after us right now?" Persephone snuffed. "Officials have guns. You've only got a couple inches range with that letter opener."

"It's the best we've got. What do *you* suggest?" I glared at Persephone until she begrudgingly took my dagger and sat against Gwenn's back.

Zane and I shuffled over to a place in the sand, lying down. I dug my blanket out of my bag after shifting around some of its contents, and I threw the blanket over us. After a matter of moments, Zane's arm draped over my waist and he nuzzled his nose against my arm, both of us dozing off without a word.

It was pitch black when I woke up to a loud scream, piercing through the darkness.

CHAPTER THREE

I scrambled out from under the blanket, patting my jacket pockets for the dagger, remembering I gave it to Persephone.

"Eos," I could hear Zane call to me under his breath from our spot in the sand. "What happened? What's going on?"

"I don't know. There was a scream, but I don't know who it was or what happened."

I squinted in the darkness, struggling to make out the figures of the members of our group, who were all waking from their sleep. Squinting through the darkness, I could identify Gwenn with an unidentifiable figure behind her, pressing a gun to her temple. I could feel my body go cold as I spotted three other figures in the sand around us, one of which had a gun to Persephone's head, another with Cindee, and the fourth with Braylin. Behind the figures were two trucks.

"*Don't move!*" boomed the figure with Gwenn.

Officials. The supervisor in Delaisse must have reported us, and that's how they knew to look for us.

I stood there, frozen.

"You're all under arrest for theft and for unlawfully escaping your exile town," the official continued in his thunderous voice.

The official with Braylin began to move toward one of the trucks, dragging a reluctant Braylin with him. Throwing him into the truck, the official slammed the door shut and began to move toward Bexa, who snarled like a cornered animal staring back at him. The officials focused on the man approaching Bexa as they held their captives, when suddenly there was a yelp.

I turned to the source, seeing the official that held Persephone. He was hunched over, both of his hands on his leg. Persephone stood next to him, my dagger in her hand. *How—?*

Without a moment's hesitation, she lunged at the next closest official—the one with Cindee, and jabbed at his arm before he could appropriately assess the situation. Just as Persephone pulled the dagger from his arm, I heard a *crack* as Bexa punched the official in front of her square in the nose. I could see blood ooze from his nose as he clutched it. There was a loud *bang*, but it didn't appear as if anyone had been hit. Realizing three of the four officials were preoccupied, I pointed to the fourth and shouted.

"Get him!"

Just then, everyone scrambled to the official, who released Gwenn instantaneously and darted into the truck with Braylin. The other three officials sprinted to the trucks, and before anyone could reach them, they accelerated and took off, sending up a cloud of sand behind them. Cindee screamed, chasing after the truck that held Braylin.

"No! No!" she cried after it, slowing her run and falling to her knees as the truck grew smaller and smaller in the distance.

Cindee burst into tears where she sat. I jogged over and squatted down next to her.

"Cindee, we have to go. Before word gets out of where we are. If they come back, there will be more of them. Come on," I urged, turning back to the group.

Everyone looked at me as I cleared my throat.

"We keep moving! Get your stuff—let's go!" I ordered, retrieving my bag and shoving my blanket back down into it.

Cindee stood, wiped her eyes with a sniffle, and joined the group as we all took off running the same direction we were heading before night. It was still dark, and incredibly difficult to see with only the moon and stars lighting the sandy plain. After a while, some of the group members could no longer keep pace with us, and we had to slow down. Up ahead, I could make out a splotchy dark area growing on the horizon.

"There's something up there," I pointed out. "We should have gone south of Delaisse. What's directly south?"

There was silence for a moment before Cameron spoke up.

"Equivox," he said, tucking a map back into his knapsack.

"*The woods*," I muttered to myself. "Guys! Equivox is surrounded by tons of trees. We can hide out there until we figure out what to do next, but we have to keep moving!"

The stragglers picked up their pace upon the news of a hiding place, and before we knew it, the smudge on the horizon turned into identifiable silhouettes of trees and other greenery.

"Almost there," I grinned, feeling a slight sense of security as the trees grew larger and larger the closer we drew to them.

Thump.

I turned around at the noise, spotting Bexa crumpled up, unconscious in the sand.

"What happened?" I asked, panicked as I looked around for unseen attackers.

"I don't know!" Eve exclaimed, her eyes wide with fear as she looked from me back to Bexa. "She was walking one minute, and then she just collapsed!"

Zane trotted over and crouched down beside Bexa, nudging her. When she didn't respond, he put his hand on her neck.

"Her pulse seems a bit slow," he observed with eerie calmness. "Let's move her into cover and we can decide what to do next."

He rolled her over flat on her back to pick her up when I spotted it.

She was shot in the arm.

"Her arm," I spouted quickly. "She was shot. I heard a gun go off earlier when we were attacked, but I didn't see anyone get hit. I thought they missed!"

"They did," Astraea breathed. "I doubt they meant to shoot her in the arm."

"Does anyone have anything I can use to tie her arm to slow the blood?" Zane asked.

"Yeah! I've got some ribbon," Cindee offered, undoing her braids and handing Zane one of her pink ribbons.

She fixed her wavy blonde hair into a single braid along her back with the remaining ribbon as she watched Zane tie the other snuggly on Bexa's upper arm. Zane scooped up Bexa and rose unsteadily to his feet, struggling to gain his balance in the sand with the added weight.

"Let me help," Brenur offered, taking Bexa in his arms.

"Let's get her under some cover before the sun comes up," Yulie reminded the group as we continued briskly toward the trees.

I wonder if Braylin was injured when the officials took him. I don't think there was much of a struggle with him. Hopefully, wherever he is, they can give him medical attention if he was hurt.

Once we reached the trees, I pulled Zane to the side.

"How do you plan on helping her?" I hissed under my breath.

"What do you mean?"

"Well, not to be blunt, but the last time we were in charge of dealing with a medical emergency, somebody died."

"Lamb, I know," he sighed. "But this is different. The wound is much smaller, and it isn't as fatal as a stab to the stomach. We just have to find a way to get the bullet out, and then stop the bleeding."

I clicked my tongue in thought for a moment, turning toward Bexa, who was still unconscious, now lying in the grass in the shade of the trees.

Cameron shoved his way from the back of the cluster of people around Bexa, making his way to her side.

"We have to get her arm elevated!" Cameron growled. "Do *none* of you have a clue what to do if someone is shot? Eleven criminals and I'm the only one who's been shot? I don't believe that. Someone hand me their bag."

Eve passed her bag toward Cameron, who stacked it on top of his own and Bexa's, propping Bexa's arm on the pile.

"I'm going to give you all a lesson," Cameron spoke slowly, with a hint of condescension. "If someone is shot in the arm or leg, prop it up, add pressure to stop the bleeding, and if possible—leave the bullet *in*."

Well, I guess it's good Zane didn't try anything.

"The bullet could be preventing worse bleeding," Cameron answered, spotting Zane as he was about to speak up.

"What else do we do?" I asked. "She's going to get better?"

"She'll be fine," Cameron answered. "She probably passed out from a mixture of exhaustion, dehydration, blood loss, and pain. We need to stay here for a while so she can rest, we need to get her to drink when she wakes up, her arm needs to stay lifted and we need to keep pressure on it. We should find some kind of pain medication for her."

"Great," I nodded with relief.

"See if anyone grabbed any pain meds from Delaisse."

I approached each of the group members, asking to see the bottles of medication from their bags. Gwenn dug through her bag, pulling out a tiny bottle of white pills labeled as painkillers.

"How about these?" she offered them to me.

"Perfect," I said, thanking her.

I tossed the bottle to Cameron just as Bexa was beginning to wake.

"Wh—" Bexa muttered, squinting at us all standing around her.

"You're fine," Cameron said quickly. "Did you know how bad your arm was?"

"You mean that the bullet is still there?" she asked weakly, nodding her head.

"Yeah. You passed out while we were walking, but you're going to be fine. Take these, they'll help," Cameron unscrewed the cap of the bottle, pouring a couple of pills into Bexa's open palm.

He passed her a bottle of water, which she slurped from noisily while lifting her head from the ground.

"Where are we?" she asked after swallowing the pills.

"Equivox," Zane answered. "Sort of. We are just outside it."

The trees began to gradually illuminate in a stunning gold light as the sun started to rise.

"How about we send people for additional supplies, and a few others can stay with Bexa?" Cindee suggested.

I nodded in agreement, pointing to Cameron, Zane, Brenur, and Persephone.

"You four stay with Bexa. If something happens, you guys should be able to carry her somewhere safe. If you have to move locations, make sure one of you finds us to guide us back."

Cameron, Zane, Brenur, and Persephone made themselves comfortable around Bexa, who was sitting up at this point.

The rest of the group turned to Trent.

"You're from Equivox, Trent," Cindee said. "What's the best way in?"

"Well," he thought for a moment. "The only time I ever saw officials enter and exit Equivox was through the storage room."

"I just jumped in the lake," I said without thinking.

No! I can't believe I just said that…

"What do you mean you 'jumped in the lake'?" Eve asked me incredulously.

I stuttered for a half second before speaking up.

"What? I said I *would* just jump in the lake," I corrected.

Eve continued staring at me with suspicion for a moment before disregarding the confusion.

"How'd you know there's a lake?" Trent asked.

"We learned about it in school," I answered. *It isn't a lie. I did learn about some of the signature features of the towns in school when I was growing up. They don't have to know I have had personal experiences with them.*

"Okay, so let's say we jump in the lake. How do we get back out?"

I decided to keep quiet to prevent myself from speaking up without thinking again.

"If we can get in, I can get us out," Trent said confidently. "Just one problem—there's a ring of trees blocking the cliff around the entire town. It won't be a problem for us when we are leaving, but we can't get to the lake unless we can get past the trees."

The group members' eyes scanned the area for a gap in the trees, but of course they had no luck.

"The trees are too thick and close together, and the ones we could fit between have briers everywhere. Can we just climb one of the trees and work our way to the other side of it?" Gwenn proposed.

"Sure," Cindee answered with a shrug as the rest of the group nodded in agreement.

The group members began helping each other up the trees, working as a team to boost people onto higher branches.

I began to follow after the group, reaching out to the tree to climb when I heard Persephone calling after me.

"Eos!" she shouted, holding out my dagger. "I forgot to give this back to you. Thank you for letting me borrow it. If you hadn't, I'm not sure where we'd be right now."

She grinned proudly.

I squinted seriously at her, taking my dagger with a nod and tucking it away in one of the pockets inside my jacket before turning to catch up with the group.

Everyone except Yulie and I had already worked their way up the trees, shimmying around toward the other side.

"Do you want me to give you a boost?" Yulie offered.

"It's okay. I used to be terrible at climbing trees, but I've gotten a little better. I'm still not great at it, but I can manage. What about you?"

"I might just stay back and help with Bexa."

"Everything okay?"

"Yeah," she said, her voice shaky. "I'm good."

"What's wrong?"

"Nothing. I'm just not too keen on heights," she chuckled nervously.

"But you were able to climb the fence around Delaisse?" I questioned.

"It was a fence, and there were countless spots in it to grab at. This is a tree. There are a few branches and that's it. It just seems less secure, I guess."

"The thin, chain-link fence around Delaisse seems more secure than a tree?" I laughed.

"Well, I guess not," she smiled. "I don't know. I've never had to climb a tree and I have no idea how to."

"Fair enough. It's about time you learned, though."

"Wait, what?" she asked, as if expecting me to let her just stand there.

"Let's go. We have to catch up to the rest of them," I said, looking the tree over for the lowest branch.

"I—," she hesitated, a worried look on her face.

"Here," I said, pointing to a branch. "I can give you a boost if you need someone to coddle you, or you can learn how I learned."

"How's that?"

"Trial and error," I said, jumping and latching onto the branch.

I clung to the thick branch, pulling my legs up and around it. I maneuvered myself until I was right side up, straddling the branch.

"I'm going to move to another branch. I want you to follow my lead," I instructed.

She looked up at me, mortified and frozen as I moved up to a higher limb.

"Go on," I prodded.

She approached the tree, her eyes wide. She bit down on her bottom lip as she surveyed it for a moment. With a slow inhale, she leapt up and wrapped her arms around the branch. She hung there for a second before flailing her legs around, trying to get them up. With a groan, she released her grip and fell into the grass and leaves below the tree.

"I can't!" she hollered up at me.

"Yes, you can. Try it again. If you can't get your legs up, walk them up the trunk."

Yulie huffed and nodded, shaking her hands loosely. She jumped and latched onto the branch again, this time walking her legs up the trunk until she could twist herself on top of it. She sat there for a moment, closing her eyes and breathing deeply.

"Told you." I scoffed, continuing up the tree until I could work my way around to the other side of it.

"Wait for me!" she called.

"Why? You've got this. I'll meet you on the other side."

I heard her exclaim in a mixture of shock and fear.

Once I was on the inner side of the ring of trees, I lowered myself onto branches below me until I was close enough to the ground, careful to pick a landing place free of the prickly briars. Arms around the branch, I dropped my legs over the edge and released my grip. When my feet hit the ground, I stumbled backward but managed to catch myself before I fell.

I brushed the dirt and dried leaves off of myself and turned, looking over Equivox. *The fall is farther than I remember.* I stood, toes at the edge of the cliff, the slightest breeze motivating me to quickly step away from the cliff.

I could see the rest of the group working their way closer to the edge of the cliff nearest the lake while I waited on Yulie, who was stumbling through the branches on her way down. She toed nervously at the lowest branch, clinging to the trunk of the tree. With a sharp yelp, she dropped onto the branch. She giggled in relief, exchanging glances between the forest floor and me. Once she joined me on the ground, we jogged to catch up with everyone else.

"You okay?" Eve asked, pulling a leaf out of Yulie's tangled hair.

"I'm good," Yulie huffed exhaustedly.

"Right here," Cindee called, pointing at the lake below us.

"So, we're just supposed to jump?" Yulie asked, her eyes wide.

Fortitude

"That's the idea," I replied.

"Why jump?" Yulie continued to ask, her hand on the back of her neck as she stared down into the pit. "There isn't a better way down?"

"Without one of the official's trucks and control pads, there's no way down through the elevator on this side. The only other way is to climb, but if we try to climb down, one misstep and we could land on hard ground… break a leg… a neck… the water is more of a guarantee. It won't feel good, but it's better than slipping, falling into this literal pit of a town, and breaking something—or worse," Trent reasoned.

We stood in silence for a moment before Astraea spoke up.

"Trent," she said softly. "You know for sure that you can get us out, once we are in?"

Trent nodded confidently.

"Okay," Astraea breathed, taking a few steps away from the cliff.

She smiled half-heartedly at us before taking off full speed at the cliff, leaping from the edge. Cindee covered her mouth in shock, watching in horror as Astraea seemed to soar below us, crashing into the lake with a distant splash. Everyone gathered to the edge of the cliff, holding a collective breath as we waited for Astraea to resurface. A few seconds passed and we saw her head poke above the water as she swam toward the shore. Cindee and Gwenn erupted in cheers and applause, to which the rest of the group joined in celebrating. Astraea turned and gave us a display of excited gestures from below.

"Keep quiet when you get down to the bottom. They probably won't hear much of what's going on up here, but be careful at the bottom," Trent advised.

"Who's next?" Cindee grinned enthusiastically.

"I'll go!" Gwenn bounced in place before taking off toward the cliff with a squeal as she jumped.

She flapped her arms as she fell, as if trying to fly, but instead she looked like a baby bird falling from a tree. Once we could see her blonde hair as she swam to the surface, we all whooped and cheered from the top of the cliff.

One by one, people began to join Astraea and Gwenn at the bottom until only Yulie and I were left.

"You go ahead," Yulie motioned to the cliff, her hands twitching even as she stood far from the edge.

"I don't trust you to jump," I said bluntly, cocking an eyebrow.

"I will. I'll just go last. I need a minute," she said, breathing heavily.

"Nope," I said, grabbing at her hand and tugging her as I ran at the edge of the cliff.

"No! I can't! Stop!" Yulie screamed at me, digging her heels into the dirt.

I stopped and looked at her, unamused.

"You're holding everyone back. It's just one jump. Close your eyes if you have to—I'm leading us anyways."

"I can't—I can't," she said between shaky breaths.

"You escaped an exile town, have been on the run for I don't even know how long. You avoided an ambush of officials, and you climbed a huge tree. Let's go," I said, squeezing her hand.

She stared back at me with terror in her eyes as I began to run again. This time, she ran with me, her hand crushing mine as we threw ourselves off of the cliff. I could hear Yulie let out a mixture of a stiffled scream and a whimper as we tumbled through the air, a whooshing sound filling our ears.

"Hold your breath!" I reminded her over the wind with a gasp, just before we collided with the lake.

I could feel Yulie release my hand as the sharp cold of the water hit my skin. Almost instantly, I pulled myself above the water, gulping at warm air. Yulie popped up with a quiet splash beside me and coughed up some water. I reached for her wrist and guided her to the shore, where everyone was trying to keep the volume down as they celebrated our dive. Cindee and Eve smiled, stretching their hands out to us to pull us onto the dirt. Yulie flopped over on her back, her chest heaving as she tried to catch her breath until she began laughing.

Everyone looked at Yulie with amusement as she lay there sniggering.

"Yulie?" I grinned. "Something funny?"

"That was intense," she giggled timidly, sitting up.

"Let's get moving," Trent urged as everyone's smiles faded. "The noises probably haven't gone unnoticed, so we're gunna' need to be fast."

"Which way?" Cindee asked.

"Storage house is that way," Trent pointed to the room with the vehicle tunnel that Zane, Lamb, and I had used when we were in Equivox retrieving my belongings and the Equivox key to open the Skeleton Key box.

We ran on tiptoes toward the storage house. I kept a hand on the hilt of my dagger inside my jacket as we ran, darting behind bushes and houses at every chance in order to stay hidden. When we reached the storage house, Gwenn went straight for the door.

"Don't bother," Trent hissed from behind a bush. "It's going to be locked. Eos and Astraea are from Avid. Let one of the thieves unlock it."

"Oh," Gwenn said plainly, walking toward a bush dejectedly.

"I'll get it," I volunteered quickly.

They don't have to know I'm using the Key. They won't be able to see it from the bushes, but we can get in faster if I just do it with the Key.

I scrambled out from the bush concealing me and walked confidently to the door. Looking to either side, I slipped my hand into my leather bag, feeling blindly for the Key. When I finally felt it, I pulled it out and pushed it into the lock with one swift motion, turning the dial until I heard a click. Upon hearing the door unlock, there was a familiar child's voice behind me.

"Elle?"

CHAPTER FOUR

No, I thought. *Please, please, please no.*

I stood there frozen as the girl continued to speak.

"What are you doing?" she asked.

Subtly, I removed the Key from the door and let it drop back into my bag before turning to look into Eloise's wide eyes. Upon making eye contact, her wide eyes began to well up with tears as she spoke.

"You lied to me," she whimpered. "You told me not to lie like my mom did, but you lied to me."

"What do you mean?" I asked, genuinely confused.

"When you broke into our house and my mom was taken away instead of you…you broke into our house and stole that little key after everything my mom did for you. She made you dinner and let you stay in our house, and then you lied to me and you ran away! You told me my mom was coming back. She never came back. You're a thief *and* a liar."

Irritated, I stared back at Eloise coolly.

Her mother killed Lamb. She's going to end up just like her mom eventually. Why spare her feelings?

"Your mom killed my friend," I growled at her as her bottom lip quivered.

"What?"

"Your mom is a liar and a *murderer.*"

Eloise grimaced at me, her brow furrowed in silent anger for a moment before letting out a blood-curdling scream.

What is she doing? She's going to get me caught, and maybe everyone hiding in the bushes!

Without thinking, I threw myself at Eloise, slapping a hand over her mouth to muffle her screams. Her eyes stared back at me, panicked, as I pressed my hand over her mouth with more force.

"*Shut up!*" I growled, staring into her eyes angrily.

It's too late anyways—somebody was bound to have heard her. We have to go before someone calls the officials. I can't let her see that I'm not alone though.

Eloise squirmed as I pinned her down, still muffling her screams. Thinking quickly, I forced her against a side wall of the storage house, taking away her view of the bushes and the door. As I kept her there, I turned my gaze toward the bushes.

"*Go!*" I silently mouthed to my group, waving my hand frantically

The others darted out of the bushes and filed into the storage house, closing the door behind them just as a couple of concerned people came out of their houses to see me with my hand over a child's mouth, pushing her face against a wall. *Lovely*.

Thinking on my feet, I spun Eloise away from the building, quickly pulling out my dagger and holding it to her, turning her face a bright red as she began whimpering, staring helplessly at her neighbors.

"Don't take another step!" I warned the onlookers, staring them down.

"The officials have already been called," said a tall man with short brown hair and copious freckles. "Let the girl go before you make this worse for yourself."

I stood for a moment, frozen in thought. I hesitated before pushing Eloise away from the wall as I slipped into the storage house, slamming the door shut behind me and locking it. No one was left in the house. I turned toward the vehicle tunnel in the back of the house, remembering when I had to treat Lamb's stab wound in this same place. I felt a chill run down my spine as I began to sweat, my throat feeling tight.

Keep moving.

I could hear voices nearing the door as I took off sprinting up the tunnel, the lights along the sides blurring as I ran. When I reached the end of the tunnel, I remembered the elevator, which was controlled by buttons inside the trucks the officials drove.

I'm trapped.

I frantically began running my hands along the dirt dead end. "Please, no!"

I started hyperventilating while searching for something—anything—to help me out of the tunnel.

The rest of the group got out somehow. There has to be a way.

I began to paw at the walls when suddenly my fingers slid over a panel, camouflaged against the paneling of the open elevator shaft. I picked at it with my fingernails and opened it, revealing a small blue switch.

Desperately, I flicked the switch and felt the ground below me rumble as the spacious elevator began to rise, pushing me to the surface. The elevator was the same Zane, Lamb, and I had escaped Equivox through after the incident with Lamb. It felt larger than I last recalled, but rather than riding up inside a bulky truck, I was standing there, alone.

The lift crawled slowly upward, and the closer I got to the top, the more the sunlight filled the hole in the ground. Just before the elevator reached the top, I spotted two officials waiting for me over the hole. I pulled out my dagger and shifted my weight with one foot behind me, ready to run. Once the elevator lifted me into their reach, both of the officials began to claw at me, trying to pin me down. I pushed off with my back foot, barreling past them as I disappeared into the thick woods. I could hear the crunching of the leaves under their feet as they took off after me.

I kept at full speed, dashing as far from the officials as I could, but they kept fairly close behind. Looking back, I could see that they were both wielding pistols as they trailed after me. Just as I tried to spontaneously turn a corner to throw them off, one of the officials pulled the trigger, hitting the tree I slid behind and knocking off a chunk of bark.

"This way!" a man called to me in a hushed voice, poking his head out from behind a tree in the distance.

I stared at him, hesitantly, unable to make out his features.

Fortitude

Is he an official? An escaped exile?

The man frantically waved me toward him.

I stood, staring at him for a moment longer until I could hear the officials nearing me.

What other choice do I have?

I sprinted toward the man, who began making decisive turns around trees, leading me deeper into the forest and further from the cliffside and the ring of trees. He grabbed my hand as we ran, directing me around a sharp turn.

"*Down!*" he warned, tugging my hand, causing me to fall as we slid down a steep hill on our backs.

The ground was covered in a thick layer of leaves and thorny plants that left burs in my jacket as we slid to the bottom. The bottom of the hill held an even denser forest, through which the man continued to guide me.

"I think we lost them." I huffed in exhaustion, throwing glances behind me as he continued to run, pulling me along with him.

"They're just a bit behind us. We have to keep moving a little further to really lose them," he advised.

I nodded in complacent agreement as I followed alongside him until we reached a wide concrete building, concealed by all of the foliage. The building looked old and worn, with crumbling chunks of concrete littered around the area, webs built up in the few windows, all of which had rusting metal bars across them, and there were splotchy patches of darker and lighter grey all over the building.

"Let's hide in here until we know they're gone," the

man suggested, wrenching my arm forward toward the building.

"I don't want to end up cornered in some building," I said, resisting him as he urged me to follow.

"There's a door on the other side, too. I've hidden in here before. If they even find us, we can run out the back entrance before they have a chance to spot us, and they'll be stuck searching the building—giving us a head start."

I thought for a moment before nodding my head in agreement, following him into the building, where he shut the door behind us. He flipped a switch on the wall, illuminating the dark interior of the structure in the whitish-blue of overhead florescent lights that flickered on with a soft buzz.

"The power still works here?" I asked, dumbfounded.

"Mhm," the man nodded.

This was the first time I could really make out his features. He looked about 30 years old, with shoulder-length, nappy brown hair tucked back behind his ears. The dark circles under his eyes emphasized his sunken cheeks, and his tattered grey hoodie and grass-stained jeans looked a couple sizes too large for him. Looking back at me, he scanned me over.

"Where are you from?" he asked with plain curiosity, scratching at his neck beard.

No sense in lying. He knows I'm on the run, obviously.

"Avid," I answered. "You?"

"Fallmont."

"Wait… you're from a city? Not an exile town? What are you doing outside the gates?"

He shrugged, a bored look in his dull brown eyes.

I squinted back at him in confusion, cocking one of my eyebrows up.

"What's your name?" he asked.

"E."

"E. Strange name."

I blinked, unamused.

"Asa. Asa Powder," he introduced himself.

"And you thought E was a weird name…" I muttered.

He shrugged.

"The name Asa means 'healer.' What does E mean?" he asked.

I mockingly shrugged.

"What is this place?" I asked.

"An old hospital. It's small, but it seems like it used to be well-equipped."

"How do you know?"

He beckoned me to follow him as he ambled down a wide hallway and into one of the rooms. The room had an examination table, a faded painting of an orchid, a few weathered medical supplies, and a biohazard bin.

"Oh," I sighed, scanning the room over.

I dropped my bag on the counter, scavenging through it until I retrieved two cans of soup. I hopped up on the exam table and pulled out my dagger, stabbing a hole through the top of the can. Turning the can upside-down,

I drank straight from it hungrily. I picked up the second can, holding it out to Asa.

"No, thank you," he replied.

"Come on—you look like you haven't eaten in a month," I pushed, wiggling the can at him.

Without another word, Asa scooped up my bag and casually but swiftly left the room, shutting and locking the door behind him.

"Asa! That's not funny!" I yelled, sliding off the table and hurrying to the door. "Come unlock the door and give me my bag back!"

I jiggled the doorknob in frustration.

"Asa!"

No answer.

What's he doing with my stuff? Why'd he lock me in here? I can tell he's not an official. Why is he even here?

"*Hey!*" I screamed, pounding on the door. "Let me out!"

The next time he opens that door, I swear I'm going to kill him! I twirled my dagger around in my hands.

I paced across the room, trying to think of ways out.

What if he steals the Skeleton Key?

I opened the window, but there were bars outside.

What if he doesn't come back?

I checked the medical supplies for things that could be used as lock picks, but found nothing.

What if no one finds me?

I grabbed at the bars outside the window, rattling

them desperately, growling as they remained unmoved. I paced back and forth, rage growing inside me before I released it in a burst, kicking the door with every ounce of my strength, to no avail.

Irritated and drained after repeatedly jarring the window bars, I sat down in defeat.

I kept the window open, enjoying the occasional cool breeze in the exam room as I sat there, waiting. There was a jar of old tongue depressors in a jar on the counter, and I proceeded to dump the jar out on the countertop, moving the sticks around to make various shapes and designs in my boredom.

"Asa—" I called out in a singsongy voice. "Let me *out!*"

No answer.

Of course.

I let out an irritated sigh as I leaned against the wall.

This is your own fault, I reminded myself. *You decided to trust the stranger rather than handling things yourself. Does this count as kidnapping if I voluntarily came here? Even if I escape, I can't do anything to stop Asa from doing this to someone else— I'm as much of a criminal as he is, so reporting him to officials isn't an option.*

I crawled up on the exam table, laying there in thought and in wait. It seemed like hours had passed before I heard a sound outside the door—a different door slamming shut.

"Asa! I know you're there! I hear you!" I hollered between the door and the doorframe.

Again, there was silence.

I groaned dramatically, throwing my empty soup can at the door.

Hours passed without another sound. The sun was beginning to set, and bugs began fluttering through the window, attracted to the light in my room, so I shut the window. No longer able to tell how much time was passing, I curled up on the exam table, trying to get comfortable. I lay there, staring up at a plump moth, throwing himself repeatedly against the light, making a faint *tink* sound every time he touched it. Eventually, everything began to go out of focus as I fell asleep.

When I woke up, my window was open again and there was a bowl of what resembled oatmeal sitting on the countertop across the room. Frantically, I pushed myself up and hopped off the table, running to check the door.

Locked.

Can't say I truly expected otherwise.

I turned to the bowl of oatmeal and walked toward it skeptically.

Crunch.

I looked down at my foot, picking it off the ground. Pieces of moth wings stuck to the bottom of my shoe, and the rest of the moth remained on the ground, mushed. There were a few other, smaller dead bugs sprinkled on the ground. I used my foot to brush them to the far end of the room and then picked up the bowl of oatmeal, sniffing it suspiciously.

I wasn't that hungry anyways, I thought, putting the mysterious oatmeal back on the counter and sitting back on the exam table.

Suddenly, the door opened quickly and Asa entered, shutting the door behind him.

I scrambled off the table and made a beeline for Asa, punching him square in the face with all of my strength as he crumpled on the floor, blood oozing from his nose and mouth.

"*Move*," I growled, kicking him out of the way and pulling the door open.

"You're not safe!" he sputtered through the blood, his eyes wide and teary as he clutched his nose.

"Neither are you," I muttered, feeling my dagger in my jacket pocket. "Don't try anything."

I left the room, slamming the door behind me furiously. I walked down the hallway, turning around a corner toward the main door when I spotted her.

On a gurney blocking the door was Bexa, her arms and legs strapped down as she sobbed. When her eyes met mine, she gasped in relief as she giggled nervously between sobs.

"Eos!" she cried excitedly. "Please help me!"

I stared back at her, confused.

"Eos—please!"

I shook my head, refocusing.

"Of course," I said, running over to her, grabbing for the straps around her arms.

"Don't—" I heard Asa say from behind me.

Quickly, I turned to face him.

"Who do you think you are?" I spat at him.

"I'm helping her," he breathed, holding his empty but bloody palms out. "I'm not armed. I'm not going to hurt you. I just want to help."

I pulled out my dagger, tapping it threateningly against my thigh as I spoke.

"Don't take another step," I said.

"She needs medical attention," said Asa, extreme concern in his voice.

"What are you talking about?" I asked, wondering if he knew Bexa was shot.

"Her arm. She's been shot," he said. "If you don't believe me, take a look for yourself. See that I'm not lying."

"I know she's been shot. But she doesn't need *your* help."

"You know her," he said with more of a tone of observation than question.

"Yup. And I know you aren't taking another step closer," I reminded him as he tried to creep forward, his palms still out. A droplet of blood fell from his chin to the floor, splattering.

"*Please*," he begged desperately. "She needs help!"

"Just because you're holed up in some abandoned doctor's office doesn't mean you have a clue what you're doing. You aren't a doctor, and she doesn't need your help."

"I was," he said.

"Was what?"

"A doctor. In Fallmont. I was a doctor."

"Then why are you here? You're lying."

"No, I'm not."

"Why are you here?" I repeated.

"I just want to help people," he responded vaguely.

"Not a good enough answer," I said, tapping my leg again with the blade.

"You know what?" he said, deepening his voice as he dropped his hands to his sides. "Go ahead. But she won't last long without my help."

"She's fine. I can take care of her. It will just take a little time to heal."

"Wrong," Asa said plainly, pointing to Bexa. "Take a closer look."

I turned to Bexa, still strapped to the gurney. I peeled back a bandage on her shoulder, revealing a pus-covered wound. Bexa flinched as I pulled on the bandage.

"What's wrong with it?" I asked, growing concerned.

"It's infected. She's got a fever, too. If it goes untreated, it's only going to get worse."

"So, what? She needs some antibiotics?" I asked, turning back to face Asa.

"That's part of it, yes. She needs to be properly patched up and carefully monitored to make sure the antibiotics work."

"Show me where you keep the antibiotics," I demanded.

"No."

"Excuse me?"

"She'll die if you try to treat her, and I'm not going to let that happen."

"That's not up for you to decide."

"You need help too, E," he said with a tone of concern.

I raised an eyebrow and stared back at him angrily.

"You're showing signs of depression, anxiety, and PTSD."

"So now you're psychoanalyzing me?" I grumbled, rolling my eyes. "A doctor and a psychiatrist? *Wow*, you must have been a busy man. There's nothing wrong with me except the fact that I've been abducted by a creep who *thinks* he's a doctor. My only problem right now is *you*."

He shook his head as he stared back at me.

"Who's Lamb?" he asked.

I felt my heart sink into my stomach.

"I don't know what you're talking about," I lied, gritting my teeth.

"Yes, you do. What happened to Lamb?" he pried.

I shook my head and Asa simply kept watching me.

"I heard you in your sleep last night," he said. "It was hard not to. You kept screaming 'Lamb' in the most bloodcurdling screams. It was painful to listen to, really."

"Eos?" Bexa asked me, her voice weak behind me. "What happened to you?"

"Eos?" Asa repeated. "Is that your actual name? I was wondering what 'E' was short for."

"How did you find her?" I asked Asa, changing the subject as I motioned to Bexa.

"She was in the woods, and I could see that she was hurt, so I took her here."

"I know she didn't just volunteer to come here," I said.

Asa remained silent.

"She wasn't alone," I continued. "What did you do?"

Still, he stood there speechless.

"*Asa*, what did you do to them?" I began to panic.

"I didn't hurt them. They're safe."

"How do I know you're telling the truth?"

"You don't."

At this, I stormed over to Asa, pointing the tip of my dagger against his throat as I stared him down. His eyes remained calm as he lifted his chin.

"You better be telling the truth because if I find out you're lying and something happened to any of those people, I swear I'll make you *wish* I'd slit your throat and end it, but I won't make it that easy," I hissed without hesitation.

Asa blinked.

"Then your friend here will die. Besides, I'd have no reason to do anything to your friends. I *help* people. They didn't need my help."

"How did you get her away from them?"

"Why do you ask unimportant questions? Your friends are fine. That's all that should matter to you."

I turned to Bexa, keeping my dagger trained on Asa's neck.

"How did he get you away from them?" I asked.

"I—" she thought for a moment. "I don't know. I don't remember?"

"What do you mean you 'don't remember'?"

"I mean I don't know what happened. I was with them one minute... Cameron and Zane were talking. Brenur was a little ways away, keeping watch. Persephone wasn't there. I don't know where she went, but she said she'd be right back. That's the last thing I remember before waking up in the woods, strapped to this bed, being wheeled here," she said, taking short and sharp breaths.

"What did you do to her?" I threw my gaze back to Asa, pursing my lips. "Did you drug her? You say you help people, but you know what? *You're* the sick one."

"I did what needed to be done to save her," he replied genuinely. "She's hurt, and she's only getting worse. How much time do you honestly think she has if she doesn't get the help she needs?"

"She's not that sick," I said, turning to look briefly at Bexa, only to have Asa rapidly grab at my wrist, twisting it and forcing me to drop the dagger before I could react, though the movement caused the blade to nick his throat. A tiny droplet of blood trickled down his neck as we simultaneously threw ourselves at the knife on the floor. He snatched it up and wielded it awkwardly, pointing it between my eyes.

I squatted there as he stood cautiously, keeping the blade tip between my eyes.

"Aww..." I teased mockingly. "I'm so scared!"

I laughed.

"If you're a doctor, and you claim you just want to help people, isn't it a little counterproductive to hurt a patient?" I asked, a smirk creeping across my lips.

"You're not my patient," he stated matter-of-factly.

"You just said you wanted to help me because I'm a psychological mess," I reminded him.

"You don't deserve my help."

"Good! I don't want it. I don't need it. Now give me back my stuff and get the hell away. And stay away."

He pressed the dagger lightly into the skin above the bridge of my nose.

"I *have* to help her," he said urgently. "Stand."

I sat there, looking back at him indignantly.

"*Stand*," he repeated, pushing the dagger into my skin.

"Agh—" I groaned painfully, standing.

"Walk," he commanded, holding the dagger in both hands and motioning with his head toward the exam rooms.

I could try to grab the dagger, but he's got both hands on it and likely isn't going to release it. I could try to run, but then I'd have to leave Bexa. I could try to negotiate, but I think we are beyond that. If I just do what he says and go back to the exam room, he will treat Bexa and maybe then he will let us both go.

I submitted and walked reluctantly toward the initial exam room down the hall. He followed behind me, holding the dagger straight out in front of him. When we approached the exam room, I began to turn into it when he stopped me.

65

"No. Not that room," he said.

"Wait, what?" I asked, confused.

"Keep moving. Down the hall."

I turned again, my back to Asa, and rolled my eyes as I walked.

"Right," he directed me down another hall.

There was a faded sign suspended from above a wide doorway into a different hallway. I squinted, trying to make out the letters.

General Surgery.

CHAPTER FIVE

"Why not just keep me in the same room?" I asked, a hint of concern in my voice.

"I need to be sure you don't attack me again," he sniffed, as if reminding me that I punched him.

I grumbled to myself.

He has a point.

"How are these rooms supposed to keep me from attacking you? If I'm supposed to trust that you're going to help her, how about you just trust that I'm not going to attack you again?"

Asa scoffed.

"Room 116," he said plainly.

I read the numbers of the rooms as we walked, passing underneath the hall sign.

119… 118… 117…

I stopped at the door of room 116 and stared in, noticing what appeared to be an observation room of an operating theater. I sighed under my breath in relief.

It's just an observation room. It's not too creepy, I guess.

He nudged me forward and I stepped into the observation room, looking over the equipment. There were dusty computer monitors, panels of buttons, a swivel chair, and a clipboard with wrinkled and faded patient notes hanging from the wall. The wall along the entire right side of the room was a thick glass window.

"In," he prodded, motioning toward a door along the far edge of the glass wall.

"What?"

"*In*," Asa repeated impatiently.

I felt my heart sink a little as I opened the door to the operating room. The room still smelled of chemicals, and the equipment was deceptively dust-free for an abandoned hospital.

"Why can't I just stay in the observation room?" I asked, paranoid.

"Because. It's hard to sit in the same room as someone who wants to hurt you."

I felt uneasy at the way that his response could easily be turned around as if *he* was the one who wanted to do the hurting. *Even still, I'm sure I want to hurt him far worse.*

"On the table," he directed.

I looked from him to the operating table, and back to him.

I chuckled with a mixture of sarcasm and nerves.

He shifted his weight on his feet, steadying the blade in front of him.

"*No*," I replied firmly, turning to face him completely.

Fortitude

He stepped closer to me with the dagger.

"I said *n*—" I snapped my hand toward his wrist in an attempt to force him to drop the dagger, but in a quick response he sliced the knife in the air in front of him, slashing my wrist.

I let out a pained shriek as I dropped to my knees, clutching my bleeding wrist.

"*Great*," he sighed. "Now I have to patch that up, too. Just get on the damn table, Eos."

"Why can't you just leave me alone?" I wailed, my vision growing fuzzy from the searing pain in my wrist.

I began to slump over slowly. Asa bent down, scooping me up and dropping me carelessly on the table.

"*No…*" I mumbled, my eyes fluttering and the room spinning around me as everything went dark.

When I began to come to, I had to blink back the bright lights in front of me. I tried to sit up but was abruptly stopped by a band across my chest, tethering me to the table. I lifted my head, letting out quick and nervous breaths as I looked down toward my wrists, my arms also bound to the table. I peered at my injured wrist, noticing a thick cloth bandage wound around it.

I began to hyperventilate, frantically scanning the room for inspiration on how to escape.

I can't get up. I'm stuck. What'd he do to me?

"Asa!" I screamed, trying to keep my voice from wavering too much.

While peering around the room in my panic, I noticed Asa observing calmly from behind the glass wall of the observation room. He nodded in acknowledgment as my eyes met his.

"*Please*," I begged sincerely. "Let me go."

"I can't do that," he responded, as if I should know that by now.

"What if I say you can drug me and drop me off somewhere in the woods where I won't be able to find you again? I'm giving you permission to drug me! Just please let me go!"

"And your friend?"

"Do the same with her," I hesitated, knowing that Bexa needed some treatment.

"I can't do that."

"What if you just let *me* go?"

I can get the rest of the group together and we can work out a plan to find Bexa here and get her back.

"Nope."

"What?" I asked, stunned.

"It isn't just about her."

"Why do you need me here?"

Asa didn't respond, and instead he entered the operating theater, a bag of clear liquid in his hand. He approached me and began fiddling with a tall metal stand beside my head, hooking the bag onto the top. He clipped a long, clear tube into the bag and fidgeted with it for a moment before reaching for my uninjured wrist. I began thrashing against my restraints, trying to free my arms.

"What is that?" I panicked. "Get it away!"

"Hold still. You're only making this worse for yourself," Asa warned, squeezing my good wrist to steady my hand.

"Stop!" I shrieked as he tied a rubber strip tight around my arm.

He grabbed for a tiny white cloth, using it to wipe the back of my hand.

"What are you doing? Please don't do this!"

Asa unwrapped a sealed object with a needled tip. He brought the needle toward my hand and I screamed, flopping my hand around in vain. He grabbed my hand, squeezing it to keep it still as he inserted the needle while I cried out. Grabbing the end of the long tubing, he affixed it to the exposed end of the needle device.

"What is that?" I whimpered, eyeing the bag.

"It's a saline drip," he said calmly. "You're dehydrated."

"Oh," I said with a shaky sigh. "Why not just let me drink some water?"

"This is faster."

I stared back at Asa.

"Why do you need me here?"

"I told you already. You need my help."

"My wrist is fine now. It's bandaged up."

"You don't just need help with your wrist, Eos."

"I don't get it," I admitted.

"Something happened to you."

I looked back at him, confused.

71

"I can tell you have some degree of PTSD, as well as some anxiety and depression."

I blinked, as if to convey that I still didn't follow.

"PTSD is Post Traumatic Stress Disorder."

"I know that, but why do you think I have that?"

"You have nightmares, don't you? You talk and even cry in your sleep."

"So? Even when I was little, I had nightmares. Everyone has nightmares sometimes."

"Not like that. People don't usually cry in their sleep."

"I'm fine," I assured him.

"Who's Lamb?"

"You've already asked me that and I told you I don't know what you're talking about," I lied, my face feeling flushed.

"Yes, you do. What happened with Lamb? Did he or she hurt you?"

I looked back at Asa for a moment before submitting.

"No."

"What happened with Lamb?"

"She was my friend."

"What'd she do?"

"She saved me."

"Saved you?" he repeated.

I nodded.

"Saved you from what?" he asked.

"That's not your business."

"Okay. What happened to Lamb?"

My eyes began to sting as I stared back at him with hatred.

"What happened to Lamb?" he raised his voice as if demanding an answer.

I continued staring, my eyes burning as I refused the tears.

"What ha—"

"—She died," I interrupted, looking at him unblinkingly.

"Oh," he paused, looking away with discomfort on his face. "Did she die trying to save you?"

"Enough questions," I warned.

This time, Asa nodded in agreement, pursing his lips as he thought.

"I'll get you something to eat. Are you hungry?"

I looked at my restraints and turned my head to glare angrily at Asa.

"I'll undo your restraints during meal times, but you'll be under a mild sedative," he explained.

I groaned crankily.

"No, I didn't," Asa mumbled, turning away from me.

"You didn't what?" I asked.

"She won't," he muttered.

"What are you talking about?"

Asa turned to me again, a blank look on his face.

"I didn't say anything," he sighed, leaving the room.

That's not creepy, I scoffed as the door shut.

Once I was confident that Asa was out of earshot, I began thrashing under my restraints, trying to stretch and loosen them. They allowed for almost no wiggle room, and I could feel them rubbing my arms raw as I moved.

They wouldn't budge.

I swore under my breath as I relaxed my muscles. Moments later, Asa reentered the operating theater, a bowl in one hand, the Skeleton Key in the other.

"What's this?" he asked, holding up the Key.

"It's nothing."

"If you want food, you'll tell me what it is."

"I'm not that hungry," I lied.

"Suit yourself," he said, tucking the Key into his pocket and reaching for the spoon sticking out of the bowl.

He began eating from the bowl, throwing occasional glances at me.

"It's spiced rice," he said, holding out the bowl for me to see as he continued to eat.

He finished the rice in uncomfortable silence before leaving the room again.

I squirmed beneath the restraints with even more intensity, letting out a frustrated scream.

What does he want with the Key? If he doesn't know what it is, he might not try as hard to keep it, so it might be easier to steal back when I finally get out of here. If he learns what it does, there's no way he's letting it out of his sight. What can I tell him it is that would be believable, yet not worthy of him keeping?

After a while, the saline bag began to empty, and eventually the machine began to beep before shutting the IV off. The IV continued to beep for hours without another visit from Asa. I spent some of my time trying to wiggle my restraints loose, but they were too stiff and tight.

Just try it one more time, I kept encouraging myself.

Frustrated, I thrashed with all of my strength against the restraints until I felt a sudden sharp pain in my bandaged arm. My fingertips began to tingle as my arm seared. Picking my head up to get a look at my wrist, I noticed a growing red patch on my bandage.

I felt my heart drop as a cold chill went over my body.

"*Asa!*" I cried. "Help!"

I continued to scream for help until I heard the door open as Asa popped his head into the room.

"My arm," I breathed, answering the look of confusion on his face.

His gaze focused on my arm and the corners of his lips immediately turned downwards as he rushed to the bedside. I began whimpering, unable to hold back my reaction to the pain in my arm.

"You popped a stitch," Asa informed me with a tone of urgency as he began peeling away the soaked bandage.

He opened a metal drawer from beneath the bed, pulling out a needle and some kind of thread. Without hesitation, he squeezed my arm as he pierced the skin around my wound with the needle, pulling the thread along through the hole. I let out an ear-splitting scream, throwing my head back against the bed. Biting down on my lip, I turned away from my arm, my chest heaving as I took rapid and shaky breaths.

"Almost done," he said calmly after a moment.

I let out a pained moan as I nodded my head.

"There," I could feel him begin to bandage my arm tight again.

Turning to face Asa, I reluctantly thanked him.

"*This*," he said, motioning to my arm, which still stung and began to throb. "*This* is why you need to stay here."

"You're the reason my wrist was even cut in the first place!" I reminded him.

"It's about more than just your wrist, but even if you don't understand the other reasons, this is at least a reason you should understand." He turned and left, shutting the door behind him without another word.

Unlike the exam room, the operating room had no windows. There wasn't a clock. There was no way for me to tell how much time had passed. Eventually, I drifted into unconsciousness, letting the exhaustion overtake me. When I awoke, I had no idea if it was night or day, even though it felt like a lifetime had gone by stuck on an operating table before Asa returned again, this time with a plate of food and a syringe.

"How are you getting food?" I asked, squinting at Asa.

"The hospital is conveniently located near Equivox. Fortunately, I know my way in and out, so I go on supply runs when needed."

"So, what's the special today?" I joked groggily, half-asleep.

"A peanut butter sandwich with a side of kidney beans."

"Interesting combination."

Asa shrugged.

He stood there, staring at me without either of us saying a word.

"Well?" he asked.

"'Well' what?"

He sighed, setting the plate and syringe down as he pulled out the Key.

"I'm not telling you what it is."

"Suit yourself," he said, picking up the sandwich.

"Wait!" I stopped him.

He stared back at me with intense curiosity.

"It was Lamb's."

"But what does it do?"

"She never told me. She just carried it with her and said her sister gave it to her when she was little. When she was exiled and had to pick which personal items to bring with her, she wanted something that reminded her of her sister because they were really close. When Lamb was killed, I took it to remember her."

Alright. That's convincing, right?

"You really have no idea what this does, do you?" he huffed with a subtle grin. "You've been carrying *this* with you and didn't even know what it was!"

He laughed, turning the Key over in his hands.

"I don't get it. What's so funny?"

"You found the Skeleton Key."

I felt like my heart stopped beating for a moment before I spoke.

"The what?" I asked, pretending to have never heard of the Key before.

"It unlocks literally *any* lock you put it in."

"That's impossible."

Asa scoffed.

"I wasn't sure it existed, myself, but when I saw it in your bag, it seemed an awful lot like the one rumors talked about. Not many people have heard of it, but when I used to work in the hospital in Fallmont years ago, some kid ended up in the ER needing immediate treatment because some gunshot wounds he ended up with. When I asked the officials who brought him in what happened, they told me they caught him sneaking *into* an exile town. Turns out he escaped one, only to go to another. After the kid began to recover, some officials were sent to interrogate him, and I overheard the conversation. He had heard of the Skeleton Key from someone and went looking for it but was caught along the way. I didn't think it was real, but I remember the kid describing it. A silver body, three circles of stained glass at the head—green, purple, and blue, holes along the stem, and a little dial."

"This," he turned the Key over in his hand, his chuckles dying down and his eyes full of excitement, "is exactly what he described. So, I had to test it out, see if it really did what he said it did. Sure enough. It works on every lock in the hospital—every one of the doors with a lock… Even the storage cabinets! And you mean to tell me you never used it? You didn't know you were carrying the Skeleton Key with you?"

I shook my head innocently.

I'm already in my lie now, no sense in fessing up and making him angry with me for lying. I'll just play along with it.

He erupted in laughter again.

"That's a damn shame." He smiled, tucking the Key into his pocket. "You've earned this."

He motioned to the plate of food, and I sat my head up eagerly.

"Whoa, now," he said. "I've gotta' sedate you first. I'm not about to get punched in the face again. It's a light sedative though—you'll be fine."

Asa picked up the syringe, ambling over and emptying it into my IV. The corners of his lips turned upwards in a subtle smile—he was enjoying this too much. Moments later, I could feel my muscles relax, and I began to feel mildly sleepy. Asa undid my arm and chest restraints, handing me the plate.

I sat up rapidly, devouring the sandwich without looking up from my plate.

"Have you thought about your dead friend recently?" he asked bluntly.

I glared at him before I resumed eating. When I had finished every crumb of the sandwich, I went to move onto the kidney beans.

"Can I have a spoon? Or a fork?" I asked, eyeing the beans hungrily.

"I don't have any."

"I have a hard time believing that you have all of these supplies but no fork or spoon. I know you used one for your rice the other day," I muttered, too fatigued to truly argue.

I put my lips to the edge of the plate and used a finger to slide the beans toward my open mouth. After I finished the last bean, Asa took the plate from me.

Suddenly, I started uncontrollably convulsing.

"What's happening to me?" I cried weakly as I shook.

Asa stood there silently, reaching for a clipboard at the end of my bed. He began scribbling leisurely, tossing occasional glances my way.

"Please, help me!" I howled.

As I jerked violently, I felt acid rise in my throat, and I began to drool helplessly until my convulsions died down. I fell back against the bed, exhausted, stomach acid and little chunks of kidney beans dripping off my chin.

Defeated, I began to sob.

Asa continued to jot notes down on his clipboard, a plain and observational appearance on his face. When he had finished writing, he hung the clipboard back up and rummaged around in one of the metal drawers in the room. He fetched out a wipe from the drawer's contents and he proceeded to clean my face before securing my restraints again. He left the room and returned only a moment later with a glass of water and a straw.

Without speaking, he steadied the straw by my mouth as I sipped, swishing the cool water around in my mouth before swallowing it.

"Why?" I managed to ask, my body completely weak.

Fortitude

Asa mumbled incoherently to himself, turned, and left the room.

Now alone, I allowed the exhaustion to set in, and the room faded to black.

CHAPTER SIX

I have to get out of here.

When I awoke, I was even more confused about the time than I had been before. There was a new bag of fluid connected to my IV, and I felt sore and groggy. I blinked back a bright light, and the more my vision cleared, the more I could make out Asa's shape leaning against a wall with his clipboard.

"Please," I managed to say in my weakness.

"You're not done yet," Asa replied. "There's so much work left to be done."

I squinted at him in confusion.

He sighed and pulled out a syringe full of a pale-yellow liquid. Disconnecting the IV tube, he injected the syringe through the end of the IV on my hand.

"What—" I breathed, struggling to keep my eyes open as I turned to look at Asa.

Within seconds, I felt my arm growing cold, and my fingertips began to tingle. The numbing sensation travelled up my arm, across my chest, and continued until it overwhelmed my entire body. Then, it stopped completely.

Fortitude

What is this? I tried to speak up, but my mouth refused to move. *Am I really that tired that I can't move my mouth?*

My eyes burned with dryness from my lethargy. *I can't blink*, I realized as I tried to cure myself of the stinging. *What's happening? Why can't I blink? What was in the syringe?*

"If you can move... blink, or wiggle a finger for me," Asa instructed.

I stared back at him, unable to do anything else.

"Lovely," he said, scribbling on his clipboard.

What could he possibly need that stupid clipboard for?

"I know what you must be thinking," he started. "What did he do to me? Am I paralyzed forever? No, Eos, you are fine. The effects are temporary. You can still feel, and you are going to stay conscious—this won't put you to sleep. But this step is incredibly vital to your treatment."

There he goes again... Talking about "helping" me. He's only making things worse.

"As I've said before, you have depression, anxiety, and PTSD. You're a colorful case," he sniffed. "I've got a theory on how to cure you, but it's very experimental, and I need your full cooperation. Based on how you've interacted with me thus far, this is my best option for the time being. Frankly, I understand why you've acted the way you have; however, I'm going to help you, so I have to start with this."

If I could roll my eyes right now, I would. I want to. I almost want to roll them more than I want to blink, which is saying a lot because they really burn.

I stared back at Asa, fuming beneath the paralyzed exterior.

He briskly crossed the room, dragging a tall light on a wheeled stand over to the side of my bed, situating it above me. He flicked it on, and the stunning light blinded me for a moment, but I couldn't blink. My eyes seared until they eventually cleared enough for me to see my reflection through a metallic bit in the center of the light. My eyes were bloodshot and my skin was pale as I stared back at my expressionless reflection.

"Let's get started," he said as he squatted. I could hear metal instruments clattering in a drawer beneath the table.

Started? We haven't started yet?

"What happened yesterday was part of the process. You're probably thinking I'm a monster… I didn't put you through that for nothing though—I promise. It's going to help you in the long run. This is all a process. I ask that you be patient with me."

He chuckled.

"*Patient.* Get it?" He smiled at me as he stood to his feet. "Because I'm a doctor, and you're my patient."

This guy is an idiot.

After pulling wrappers off of the wires in his hands, he took one of the wires and stuck his hand down the front of my shirt.

Oh, heck no, I thought, wishing more than anything to have the ability to punch him.

Asa scoffed.

"Don't flatter yourself. It's a heart monitor."

He fiddled with the wires as he flicked a switch on a

machine. As the machine whirred to life, I could hear a steady and repetitive *beep*.

"I'm going to ask you a series of questions. Of course, I know you can't answer them... At least not verbally."

Asa switched pages on his clipboard before speaking again.

"Did you really not know about the Skeleton Key?" he started.

Why won't he lay off about the Key? He's got it now. Why does he care if I knew?

The beeps grew faster.

"*Oh!* I *knew* it! You're a clever liar, but not incredibly convincing. Don't worry—it doesn't really matter. That one was just for me."

He waited for a moment until the beeping steadied again.

"I want you to think about your friend, Lamb, for a moment. Think of the memories you have of her."

Involuntarily, I began picturing the knife plunging into her stomach in Equivox. I thought about the way she tried to play games back in Avid, before all of this mess caused by the Skeleton Key. I remembered the story she told me about her nickname, and how her little sister, Tessy, couldn't pronounce the name Leanne when Lamb was young.

The machine began to beep more rapidly as my heart rate quickened.

"Good, you must be thinking of Lamb," he observed.

Without a second's pause, he lifted the bottom of my shirt, exposing my pale abdomen. He revealed a scalpel in his hand and pressed it gingerly into my skin, leaving a short and shallow slice. I wanted to scream, but nothing would come out. My eyes stung, and I could hear the rapid beeping of the machine as my heart began pounding in my chest.

Asa stood there, watching me intently as little beads of blood rose from the cut. Watching helplessly up at my reflection, I saw the droplets grow closer together until they trickled slowly down my side, leaving behind a streak of deep crimson.

Help me, I thought, though I wasn't sure to whom I was pleading. *Why hasn't anybody come looking for me? I'm going to die in this place. Asa is actually going to kill me.*

Unable to move, my heart rate and the beeping eventually steadied—faster than they had started, but consistent.

"Now think about the friends you have now. They're out there. They're probably looking for you, too. They care about you. You're lucky to have friends. You're lucky not to be in an exile town."

Zane wouldn't let the group leave without me. Even if they did leave, Zane has to be out there looking for me. We've come too far together for him to just leave me behind. Unless he thinks I ran off on purpose, like I thought he did when we got separated back in Delaisse while we were looking for the keys to the Skeleton Key box. Zane knows me better than that by now though, and he's caring. Zane's caring and protective and he's the best thing I've got—he's out there looking for me.

Gradually, the beeps grew more separated, and Asa grabbed at my jaw, opening my mouth and placing a thin strip of something on my tongue. Within a second, I could taste something sweet and minty. Half expecting the strip to cause some painful and adverse reaction, I sat in nervous wait, but nothing happened. It was just a mint of sorts. The cut on my abdomen still stung, but my body began to slightly relax as Asa let me rest for a moment while he took notes on his clipboard.

"You're done for the day. See? That wasn't so bad, was it?" He took out a wipe and began blotting at my wound before patching it up with a small bandage and some kind of antibiotic gel. "I'll bring you a meal. You'll regain your movement soon."

He left the room, closing the door behind him. I sat in wait when suddenly the tingling from earlier returned. It started in my extremities and crept its way across my body. When it finally reached my face, I could blink—albeit, with some difficulty at first.

My eyes are so dry.

When I blinked, it felt as if I was scraping sandpaper against my corneas.

I groaned as I squeezed my eyes shut and held them like that until I heard the door open again.

"I hope you like vegetable rice," Asa said.

My eyes fluttered open and I could see Asa hovering over me with a bowl of rice.

"Wow! You look like sh—"

I furrowed my brow at him impatiently as he set the rice down.

"Never mind. I have some eye drops that might help. I'm sure your eyes don't feel good right now. They're seriously bloodshot."

I must have looked at him with extreme suspicion because he threw his open palms out as if demonstrating his innocence.

"I promise. Nothing bad. They're just basic eye drops. We're done with treatment for the day. The rice isn't going to make you sick. The eye drops might sting, but only because your eyes are so dry. The only other thing is that I'm going to give you a light sedative before you eat. That's just for my safety."

I nodded in complacent agreement.

He pulled out a syringe, injecting it in my IV as he did the last time. While the sedative began to weaken my muscles, Asa retrieved a tiny white bottle. Undoing the stopper, he steadied the bottle over each of my eyes, releasing two drops into each. When the liquid dripped into my dry eyes, I blinked back the stinging sensation and felt the cooling relief just moments later.

Asa undid the restraints across the top half of my body and handed me the bowl of rice and a spoon.

"I knew you had a spoon," I murmured.

He chuckled.

I really want to know why he's here and why he's this insane.

"So," I started as I munched on a spoonful of rice. "What's your story?"

"Meaning?"

"Why are you here?"

"Oh," he huffed.

I stared curiously at him as I scooped more rice.

"It's a long story."

"Apparently I'm not going anywhere, so I have time."

He grunted in affirmation.

"I already told you I'm from Fallmont."

"But why did you leave?"

"I was a doctor," he said. "I had a patient with terrible depression after her mother passed away. She was a regular patient of mine anyways—she had a disease that affected her lungs, but it wasn't anything too serious. She just needed checkups sometimes. I came up with a treatment for her depression, but it was a bit… experimental, I suppose. My supervisors didn't approve of it, but I knew it could help her. If you knew you had the ability to make somebody's life better, wouldn't you try?"

"What was the treatment?"

"Have you ever heard of operant conditioning?"

"No," I answered.

"It's a system of essentially training somebody through means of rewards and punishments. I would hook my patient up to a heart monitor, and after a while, I'd mention something about her mother. Naturally, this made her upset. I never said anything hurtful about her—I would simply ask her about memories of her mother… things like that. When she'd get upset, her heart rate would spike, and I would issue a punishment. When she eventually calmed down and her heart rate slowed, I would reward her with a piece of candy or a mint strip. Something simple."

"Why?"

"See, the intention was to train her to stop feeling sad about her mother. Ideally, the patient would begin to associate the idea of feeling sad about her mother with physical pain, which scared her. People avoid things they are afraid of, so she would begin to avoid feeling sad about her mother. She would have no choice but to think about her mother because I made her think about it, but it was up to her how she responded and felt. I didn't get to finish with my experiment, however, after my supervisors found out what I was doing."

"So, you don't know if it worked?"

"Oh, it was beginning to work. I could see improvements after just a few days of treatment. I wanted to make sure the treatment was lasting though, and I didn't have the opportunity. My supervisors were going to take me to court to try me for lying and for violent malpractice, but I didn't give them the chance. The night before my trial, I slipped out of the town gate and went in search of shelter. After some time searching, I eventually happened across this place. Isn't it funny? An ex-doctor finding an abandoned but fully equipped hospital as a shelter?"

Hilarious.

I looked at Asa in silence.

"Is that what you're hoping to do to me?" I asked after a moment of silence.

"Is what?"

"The treatment you used on your patient. Is that what you're hoping to do to me?"

"Yes. It works—I know it does. You'll stop feeling sad about your friend. Think of it as grief counseling, but with faster results. I told you—I'm trying to help you."

"I don't need your help… Grief is natural."

"Not the level you experience. You've been through a lot, but it seems like this is weighing heaviest on you, and I think it's because you feel responsible for Lamb's death," he observed.

Actually, you're *weighing heaviest on me right now. Torture isn't a way to treat PTSD or depression,* I thought about responding. *I am responsible for her death, and that's my burden to carry. Some freak-show doctor runaway isn't going to change anything. Asa's nothing more than a monster hiding behind a mask of contorted philanthropy.*

I could feel my heart thumping in my chest angrily as I glared back at Asa.

"Stop pretending like you understand what I've been through," I said, putting the spoon in the empty bowl.

"I *do* understand, Eos. I ran away, too. I'm alone. You at least have friends by your side, and you should be grateful for what you have."

"Don't tell me how I should feel, Asa. You don't know the half of it."

"Is there something you aren't sharing?"

"I've killed someone before," I started. "I've gotten a mother arrested, forcing her to leave behind her little girl. My parents wouldn't even let me say goodbye when I was exiled. A man in Bellicose assaulted me. I had to watch the one person I still care about get tortured by Raine Velora. My childhood best friend betrayed me and almost got me sent off to Ironwood. So, before you pretend like you understand anything about me, maybe try to learn the whole story first."

"I can help you with all of that!" Asa announced enthusiastically, a smile lighting up on his face. "This treatment could fix all of that. You aren't beyond fixing!"

"I hope you burn in hell," I spat. "I'm not some leaky pipe that needs to be 'fixed.'"

"I know that," Asa defended. "But you need help."

"I don't need anything from you except to be let go."

"I can't do that."

"I'm really getting sick of you saying that."

Suddenly, there was a crashing sound from another part of the hospital.

Asa turned, panicked, to look at the door.

"Be right back," he said, rushing out the door.

I sat there on the table, my legs and ankles still restrained. Unfortunately, I could tell the sedative was still in my system. My muscles were weak as I tried to unlatch the restraints quickly, my heart racing.

I don't know the next time I'll get a chance like this.

Just when I thought I figured out how to release my leg restraints, Asa burst through the doors again. I froze in position, my hands still on my restraints as I stared wide-eyed back at him.

"The hospital's on fire," he wheezed shakily. "I don't know what happened, but I can't find any fire extinguishers."

He dug through the storage cabinets in the room for a fire extinguisher, flinging metal instruments behind him as he searched.

"I can't find anything!" he panicked, moving to the next cabinet.

Unsure of what to do, I looked around the room as I thought out my options.

Fortitude

I could try to undo my restraints while he's distracted, but I don't know how well I can run or escape a fire if my muscles are this weak. But if I just sit here and Asa doesn't find a way to put out the fire, I could burn alive.

I turned toward the observation room as I sat in urgent thought, seeking alternatives, when I spotted a set of eyes staring at me through the glass.

Zane.

CHAPTER SEVEN

"What are you doing?" I mouthed, eyes wide.

Zane looked back at me, putting a finger to his lips as if to hush me. He lifted his other hand, revealing a red container.

Gasoline. He set the hospital on fire!

"We have to go!" Asa shouted, turning to me.

I quickly looked away from Zane and instead stared back at Asa, who began to reach for my restraints.

"Go where?" I asked, confused.

"It doesn't matter! We have to leave! You're not cured yet, and we aren't safe here."

"You're not taking her anywhere," Zane said, appearing behind Asa.

As soon as Asa turned to face him, Zane sent a fist soaring into Asa's nose with a crack. Asa clutched his nose as blood trickled through his palm, and Zane hurried to my side, fiddling urgently with my restraints.

"Zane!" I shouted as Asa came at Zane with a syringe, undoubtedly full of sedative.

Zane reacted swiftly, ducking down and pushing Asa's legs, causing him to tumble over, grabbing Zane's shirt and pulling him and the red jug down with him, sloshing gasoline on Zane and the ex-doctor.

Leaving the empty jug on the ground, Zane hopped to his feet and moved to my side, but Asa held tight to Zane's shirt, yanking Zane back and biting his arm.

Zane let out a slew of profanity before slamming Asa into the cabinets forcefully with a loud crash.

"She needs my help!" Asa pleaded as Zane raised a fist to hit him.

"She's fine. I'll take good care of her," Zane reasoned, keeping Asa pinned to the cabinets.

Asa shook his head frantically, his eyes wide and urgent.

"Has this man been helping you?" Zane called back to me, keeping his eyes trained on Asa.

"No. Quite the opposite," I said shakily, watching helplessly from the table. "He's *sick*."

At my words, Zane threw Asa to the side, the ex-doctor tumbling to the ground, away from Zane. Before he could stand again, his expression melted into one of terror and bewilderment as his eyes met a match pinched between Zane's fingers—a match that must have been previously concealed in his palm.

"Please stop!" Asa shrieked as tears began pouring from his bloodshot eyes. "I'm helping h—"

Zane swiftly lit the match and flicked it at Asa before he could finish, and suddenly Asa was engulfed by a wave of fire. Zane rapidly tugged at my restraints as he began to free me, but all I could do was stare at Asa's burning body as he wailed in unimaginable pain.

"Can you run?" Zane asked urgently, his wild eyes focused on me.

"I—" I stuttered, my gaze bouncing from Zane to Asa. "I don't know. He hit me with a sedative a while ago and …"

I reached for the clipboard at the end of my bed, pulling off the papers and shoving them halfway into my pocket. Without hesitation, Zane scooped me up and bolted toward the door, kicking it open with his foot. In the hallway, I could see flames undulating a short distance away.

Zane ran toward the opposite end of the hospital and away from the entrance through which I was taken what felt like ages ago.

Zane's shoes squeaked against the white tile floor as he ran with me bouncing in his arms with every step.

Bexa is still here.

"Zane! Stop!" I shouted.

"We have to get out of here—what's wrong?" he asked, continuing toward the exit.

"Bexa," I breathed. "She's here."

"Bexa's here?" he asked, a look of shock on his face as he stopped in his tracks. "We thought the officials got her outside Equivox! What's she doing here? Where is she?"

"I don't know. He was treating her gunshot wound and we got separated. I don't know where he put her. We can't leave her here though!"

"We won't, but I have to get you out first," he said, sprinting toward the exit.

He threw his shoulder into the double door entrance and I could immediately feel cool night air wash over me. Zane dropped my feet to the ground, steadying me as I tried to gain my footing.

"Stay here," he urged, guiding me to the base of a tree.

I nodded as I fell against the tree, trying to gain control of my legs before deciding to sit.

"I'll be right back," he said, darting to the entrance. "I promise!"

Exhausted, I slumped over on the ground, resting my cheek against the tree trunk. I slowly breathed in the crisp air, closing my eyes and feeling the rough bark against my cheek. It was in that moment that I broke down completely. I felt my chest begin to heave until my entire body shook with my sobs. I was relieved, but broken. The air felt extra frigid as it brushed against the tears streaking my face and trickling down my neck.

Time passed slowly until Zane appeared through the doors again, with my bag over his shoulder—alone.

"I can't find her," he breathed shakily. "She's not in there."

"She has to be!" I sniffed, wiping my eyes before turning to Zane.

"She isn't—I looked everywhere. Maybe he let her go?"

"I don't think he did. She has to be in there!" I screamed at Zane desperately.

"She isn't! I wouldn't lie about that!"

"She is! She has to be!"

"E, we have to go—we can't stay here. The fire is getting bigger and it isn't safe."

"Go where? Where is everybody else? Cindee? Brenur? Yulie? Where are they all?"

"They're safe. We joined a camp a few miles away. I've been searching for you for days."

"A camp? And how many days? How long have I been here?"

"Four days. And yes, a camp. Other exiles. We found them while looking for you and they've been helping us. We share resources and they help protect us."

"Protect you?"

"We have more people on watch," Zane clarified. "Come on—I'll help you up."

Zane wrapped his arm around my waist and lifted me from the ground. I stumbled over my own feet as I tried to gain my footing.

"You okay?" Zane asked, steadying me and keeping his arm around me.

I nodded, allowing Zane to guide me away from the hospital and the growing fire.

When we were out of sight of the hospital, I could feel my legs regaining a little strength, but I still felt weak and a bit lightheaded.

"Do you have any food?" I asked feebly.

"Uh—" he thought for a second, caught off guard. "I

didn't think to bring any. I'm so sorry! Have you had anything to eat while you were missing?"

"A little."

"Oh, wait!" Zane exclaimed, grabbing at my bag against his hip.

He dug frantically with his free hand until he retrieved a cup of chocolate pudding.

"Your favorite, right?" Zane smiled, hopeful. "Chocolate pudding makes everything better!"

I smiled softly, taking the cup and peeling back the lid. I tipped the cup upside down above my mouth, letting the thick pudding slide bit by bit into my mouth.

"What did he do to you?" Zane asked, a look of sadness and fear expressed on every inch of his face.

My eyes flicked to meet his and looked back toward the cup of pudding.

"Eos? Please tell me what happened."

I ignored his question.

"Please," he pried.

As I finished the last of the pudding, I began to tap on the bottom of the cup to empty it completely. I licked the last bit off of the lid and tossed the cup to the ground.

"E... You can trust me."

"I know I can."

"Then why aren't you telling me what happened?"

I glared angrily at him.

"What did he do?"

"What aren't you getting?" I asked, narrowing my eyes.

"What?" he asked with innocent confusion.

"I don't want to talk about it, Zane."

"I'm sorry, I just… I want you to know I'm here for you, and I just want to make sure you're okay."

"I'm fine. You don't need to know what happened to know that I'm fine."

"Okay," he said, dropping the subject. "I found the Key."

"What?"

"That guy from the hospital… he must have looked through your bag. The Key was sitting on a desk in some office. I found it while I was looking for Bexa, and I put it back in your bag."

"Thank you," I said, feeling a sense of relief wash over me.

I'm safe now, I reminded myself. *Asa is dead, Zane is here, I have the Key. Everything is going to be okay.*

I knew the sense of security was a lie, but I couldn't afford to let myself think like that.

Just then, there was a loud rustling through a gap in the trees. Zane grabbed my shoulders forcefully and directed me behind him as he stood facing the rustling, pulling his dagger out and wielding it before him.

We patiently waited, watching the darkness in front of us.

"Help me," cried a weak and scratchy female voice.

Fortitude

Zane prepared himself, steadying his dagger as we watched the bushes rustle before Bexa emerged.

"Bexa," I breathed, stunned and relieved.

"Please!" Bexa squeaked. "You have to help me!"

I could see her squint in the darkness of the night, trying to make out Zane's face and mine.

"Eos, Zane, guys!" she exclaimed, a smile growing on her face. "How did you—"

"How did *I* get out?" I laughed breathily. "Better question is how did *you* get out?"

"The hospital was on fire. Asa let me out and told me I was free to go."

"What?" I asked in disbelief.

"Is that not what happened to you?"

"No," I sighed.

"But then how—"

"Zane. He set the hospital on fire and saved me. He tried looking for you and couldn't find you."

"And Asa?"

"Zane burned him."

Bexa let out a surprised expletive under her breath.

"I'm sorry," she murmured. "I just didn't peg you as the type to burn a guy alive. Either way, I'm exhausted and I'm starving, and quite frankly I'm just glad to be out of there."

I smiled half-heartedly.

"Thanks for the fire, Zane! Asa must have just gotten to me first to release me," she reasoned.

"He said he was going to relocate me."

"What?" Bexa asked, curiosity replacing the fatigue on her face.

"He said we had to go, and that I 'wasn't cured yet.' He wasn't done with me."

"Wasn't done what?" Zane chimed in, the tone of immense concern growing stronger.

"He just… wasn't done with me. I guess."

"What did he do to you, E?" Zane asked again.

"I don't want to talk about that."

Zane sighed dramatically.

"Where's everyone else?" Bexa asked.

"At a camp. It's a long story—I'll tell you on the way. Are you good enough to walk?"

"Yeah," Bexa replied. "Good enough. Just take it slow—I haven't been able to walk around since I got there, so my legs feel a little funny."

Zane led us through the woods, still helping keep me balanced. Occasionally, he had to catch Bexa when her legs wobbled, causing her to stumble. While walking, Zane explained that the group looked for us for a day before expanding outside of the woods surrounding Equivox. Outside of the woods, they came across a group of escaped exiles. Consisting of about two-dozen people, the campers were living out of a truck full of food, and they sent shifts of people in search of more supplies on a regular basis. No one individual leads them, but rather they all give commands when they see fit. Zane and the others joined them as a temporary arrangement under the agreement that we would help them search for supplies.

Zane told us that he didn't tell any of them that we were looking for Fortitude—he simply told them that two of their friends were missing and that they wanted to find us.

We began to reach the edge of the forest, continuing into the open plane of sand outside of the wooded region circling Equivox. After nearly an hour, I could see a flickering orange light in the distance, and I could smell smoke.

"They have a fire?" I asked. "Why? That literally just points a big flashing arrow at them for the officials."

"That's what I told them. They didn't listen. They said they've been doing this for nearly a year, and that every official that's ever come close, they've 'dealt with.'"

"Yeesh," Bexa said.

We approached the campsite, which turned out to be a circle of sloppily assembled tents arranged around a large fire. There was a truck like the one Zane, Lamb, and I stole when we left Bellicose, and I could see a pile of cans and packages inside. Some of the campers were outside of the tents, and they turned to face us, looking at us as if we were trespassers. I could see Cindee, Brenur, Trent, and Persephone at the far end of the site. As soon as Cindee made eye contact with Bexa, she came sprinting toward her, throwing her arms around Bexa with a wide smile.

"He found you guys!" Cindee exclaimed, her excited voice cracking before she turned to me and hugged me.

"Welcome back, guys!" Brenur said, hugging us both.

"Guys!" Cindee shouted. "They're back!"

Just then, Cameron, Yulie, Astraea, Gwenn, and Eve poked their heads out of some of the tents. When they all realized what was happening, they clamored around us with smiles on each of their faces.

"Glad you aren't dead," Cameron grinned, wrapping his arms around Bexa and me at the same time in a bear hug.

"Let me in on this!" Gwenn piped, throwing herself into the hug.

One by one, the group joined the massive embrace, looks of relief on each of their faces.

"Does that mean you guys will be leaving now?" asked one of the campers, a muscular man with a bushy brown beard and permanent creases on his forehead.

"I was thinking we might stay the night and leave tomorrow morning. These two need rest," Zane answered.

"You know what the deal was," the man reminded Zane. "For each night you stay, you have to bring back resources as payment."

"We brought back a ton of supplies yesterday," Zane argued. "We completely restocked your medical supplies."

"That was to pay for last night. You have to pay for tonight if you're going to stay."

"Fine. I'll get more stuff while these two get rest," Zane submitted.

The man nodded in agreement, but I could feel my face growing hot.

"Wait a second," I interjected in the short-lived silence. "That's not fair. He said he *completely* restocked your medical supplies. I think that's more than enough to pay for another night. We aren't requiring much of you— just some space and a little protection."

The man turned back to face me, giving me an expression as if he had just been slapped.

"I'm going to go easy on you because you're new here, but don't think that just because you have the pity of some people that you get off with a free pass. We can't afford to just let anyone stay and mooch off of us."

"We aren't. We aren't taking any supplies. We just want to stay the night and leave in the morning."

"And that doesn't come free."

"Look," I said. "I'm asking nicely. If you make us search for supplies in the morning, we lose valuable daylight we could be using to go set up our own base. The sooner you let us leave, the sooner we are no longer your problem."

"That's not how this works," he warned. "You follow the rules, or you get punished. *That's* how this works."

"*Eos*," Zane called under his breath. "Just drop it. You and Bexa go get some sleep and I'll get supplies. It's fine."

"It's not fine!" I replied indignantly. "This guy's being a greedy d—"

Crack.

My vision flashed red as the bearded man sent his fist soaring into my jaw. I landed in the sand, sending up a puff of sand around me.

There were collective gasps, and I could hear Zane pleading with the man as I sat in the sand, rubbing my jaw.

"Please! She doesn't mean any harm. She's been through a lot. I'll go search for supplies now, and we will be gone before you wake up in the morning—I promise."

I scoffed.

The man stormed over to me, but Zane hopped between the two of us.

"Sir, please."

"Move."

"Sir!"

"*Move.*"

He forcefully grabbed Zane's shoulders and jerked him to the side, making him to lose his footing and stumble. The man grabbed a handful of my hair with his huge hands and dragged me across the sand toward the campfire. His fingers tangled in my hair and he shoved my face close to the flames of the campfire. I could feel beads of sweat immediately form on my face, my eyes stung with the heat, and I began to cough.

"You don't talk to me like that," he boomed. "You treat me with respect!"

I coughed, pressing my eyes shut to stop the stinging and block out the blinding light.

"Got it?"

I groaned and continued coughing.

"You respect your providers. We protect you. We offer you a place to stay. What do you do? You outright disrespect us when you should be thanking us."

I began flailing, my face feeling dangerously close to blistering. One of the stray strands of my hair dipped into the flickering flames and the tip ignited.

I let out a panicked scream, and the man tossed me to the side and into the cool sand. Frantically I began patting out the tiny flame in my hair until it turned into a blackened tip of hair with a thin stream of smoke. Looking around, I could no longer see the bearded man, but instead saw the terrified eyes of my friends.

Without saying a word, Zane stormed off, beckoning Cameron, Trent, Astraea, and Brenur to follow. The five of them disappeared, leaving me to sit in the sand with my swollen jaw and singed hair.

"Are you okay?" Cindee asked, too stunned to move.

"I'm fine," I lied.

"That was a stupid question," she said, disheartened. "I'm sorry."

I shrugged, easing myself to my feet and brushing off the sand.

"They're from Bellicose," Eve informed me.

Bexa turned to look at Eve, who was standing beside a sleepy looking Gwenn.

"What's that supposed to mean?" Bexa asked defensively.

"Nothing! Not all Bellicose are bad. It's just… they're aggressive. That's all."

Persephone scoffed, and Bexa rolled her eyes.

"Wait… they're *all* from Bellicose?" I asked.

"Yeah. One of them said they all stormed the gates one day when a supply truck came with the rations," Eve answered.

"How long ago did they escape?" I continued, thinking about Paren, a friend I had made while I was trapped in Bellicose looking for the Bellicose key to the Skeleton Key box.

"They didn't say," said Eve. "They said they've had the camp for almost a year, but I don't know how long ago they actually escaped."

"It's been a while, I'm assuming," Yulie added. "The one I talked to said something about going back for some friends who were still stuck there and being unable to get them because the cities had put up additional security bars at the mouth of the Bellicose caverns."

"Oh," I sighed.

Zane and the others returned, their arms full of medical supplies and food, which they proceeded to chuck into the fire.

"*Run*," Zane said to us in a hushed and urgent voice.

I stood, confused for a moment as I watched the flames wrap around boxes of bandages and packets of food, mesmerized by the way the products blackened and curled under the extreme heat. I felt Zane grab my hand and tug me along after him as the group of us rushed through the campground, darting past tents and confused campers.

"HEY!" boomed a voice from behind. "They burned our supplies!"

"*Go, go, go!*" Zane urged as we pushed through the edge of the campground and into the darkened plain of sand ahead of us.

Darting blindly through the darkness, I could feel the toes of my shoes sink into the soft sand with every push, making running difficult. For a short while, I could hear the bearded camper hollering after us, hoping to chase us down. It sounded like he was followed by a couple of other campers, but their voices were lost after a short time. Eventually, the bearded camper grew silent as he resigned from the chase, but we continued to run away until we could no longer see the light of the fire behind us.

"Stop," I pleaded, out of breath. "I can't."

Zane grabbed my hand, and everyone stopped in place. I could hear everyone's heavy breathing as they collected themselves.

"I'm sorry, E. I know you haven't been able to rest or anything. I would have been fine with going out for supplies," Zane admitted. "I didn't want to, but it wasn't a huge deal. But after the way he treated you… I didn't feel safe with us staying in the campground another night. We'd be better off on our own."

"Well, you got your wish. We're on our own now," Persephone huffed crankily.

"And we're better off," said Cameron.

"Are we though?" Persephone spat. "We can hardly see two feet in front of us, we are completely in the open, and Mr. Gel-for-brains over there burned a ton of supplies we could have used!"

"But he didn't burn all of them," Astraea cooed. "A bunch of us filled our bags with supplies first. He only burned enough to make them think he burned them all. We saved food, a few basic medical supplies, and this!"

Astraea pulled a small metal pot from her bag.

"What are we supposed to do with that?" Persephone grumbled snarkily.

"It could come in handy," Astraea retorted. "Even if it's just as simple as using it to make a hot meal. Zane has matches, so we could start a fire and cook over it if we wanted."

Persephone was quiet for a moment before speaking up.

"He should have had us all take supplies. It was a waste to burn even some."

"If we would've taken them all, the campers would realize we have them and wouldn't have given up so easily on chasing us," Astraea said.

"Let them chase us! At least we'd have enough supplies to last us more than a week! Who knows how long we will still be wandering through the freaking desert until we find Fortitude? *If* we even find anything at all!" Persephone began to raise her voice.

"She has a point," Trent agreed. "How far is Fortitude?"

"We don't know," Zane sighed.

"Exactly!" Persephone crowed. "We don't know how long we're going to be out here, so the more supplies the better! If we have to keep heading the same direction, eventually we will be too far from the cities and the exile towns to restock our supplies. Soon, we are going to be completely on our own for supplies!"

"We will figure something out, Persephone, chill!" chimed Gwenn.

"Shut up, tubby," shot Persephone.

"Excuse me?" said Gwenn.

"Why do you think they didn't ask you to help them grab the supplies?" said Persephone. "They thought you'd eat them all! That's why no one trusts you with the food!"

"We trust her with food just fine! Stop being a bully!" Yulie barked.

"Yulie, let's just stay out of it," Brenur said calmly.

"Now we're going to have over-emotional pregnant women butting in?" Persephone snorted.

"Wait, Yulie's pregnant?" Zane asked.

"I—" Yulie started.

"Yup!" Cindee said cheerfully. "She's only about four months in, I think. If we were in a city, she could be figuring out if it's a boy or a girl pretty soon…"

"Thanks for reminding me that I can't figure out until the baby's born," Yulie grumbled sarcastically.

"Sorry."

"Don't worry, Yules, Persephone is just jealous because she wishes she was in a happy relationship like you and Brenur. But instead, Trent is only with her because he was separated from his wife after he was exiled! You and Brenur are perfect together though!" Gwenn chirped.

"What did you say about me?" Trent yelled furiously. "Persephone and I are *not* together. We're just friends because the two of us are the only two here who are actually logical thinkers!"

Persephone huffed.

"Look," she started. "Brenur and Yulie are *not* perfect just because he knocked her up. They may be stupid, but I don't think they'd want to raise a child in an exile town."

Yulie let out an indignant noise.

"I didn't 'knock her up,'" Brenur coolly retorted.

"So what? Either the baby isn't yours or you're really

selfish and stupid enough to want to bring a child into an exile town. Which is it?" Persephone continued.

"Delaisse really isn't that bad," Yulie said. "We had a makeshift house together, and we convinced our town supervisor to contact the cities for an old crib."

"I think what Fertile Myrtle is trying to say is that they wanted to start a happy little family of criminals," said a new female voice.

Just then, everyone was silent.

"It's too dark," Cindee spoke up. "Which one of you said that?"

There was hushed chatter between members of the group, but nobody spoke up.

"Guys?" Cindee pried.

"We don't know," Eve said, a hint of fear in her voice.

"Wow!" The voice spoke up again. "If I was an official, you'd all be dead as doornails!"

"Who are you?" Zane asked, deepening his voice as if trying to project a tone of defense.

The newcomer giggled.

"Please," Cindee begged. "Whoever you are—"

"Mmm?" the voice pried.

"Don't hurt us," Cindee finished. "You're from the camp, aren't you? We're so sorry about your supplies!"

"I'm not from the camp," the voice revealed.

"Wait a minute," I said in a hushed voice, squeezing Zane's hand. "I know who she is."

"What?" Zane asked in a husky whisper.

"Her name is Skylar," I spoke up.

"*Bingo.*"

CHAPTER EIGHT

"Wait," Cindee began, confused. "You two know each other?"

"Sort of," I said.

"Her and her band of merry exiles literally left me in the dirt."

"You threatened us."

"I'd like to think of it as persuaded."

"You pointed a gun at us and demanded our truck."

"You guys had a truck?" Gwenn asked.

"Better question to ask," started Cameron. "You had a *gun?*"

"*She* had a gun," I clarified.

"Yeah, and *you* had a truck. Imagine what a team we could've made!" Skylar said with a snarky tone.

"'Team?'" I scoffed. "You threatened us, demanding that we give you the truck!"

"Eh… Potato, tomato."

"Why are you here?" Zane asked.

"Well," Skylar said. "You guys aren't exactly the quietest bunch. If you were trying to hide, I can tell you now that you were doing a dirt-poor job of it."

"That doesn't answer my question."

"I'm still looking for Fortitude. I happened to be within earshot when I caught word that you are all headed to Fortitude, and I want to join you."

"Fat chance," I snorted.

"I've got a gun—"

"You don't have to use it," Cindee chimed nervously.

"—So I can provide protection if you share supplies," Skylar finished.

"Oh," Cindee whispered, embarrassed.

"No deal," I answered.

"What?" Skylar asked, stunned. "I come over offering better protection than any one of you could offer, and all I ask for is a small ration of food while I tag along, and you have the nerve to turn me down?"

"I don't trust you," I said. "Simple as that."

"I'm not giving you much of a choice," Skylar replied. "Simple as *that*."

"Look," Cindee said. "How about we let her join. I mean, there are twelve of us, one of her. You say all you want is enough food to get by, and you just want to get to Fortitude, right?"

"Yup."

"See? But she's willing to protect us!"

"Fine," I submitted, my lips melting into a frown as I crossed my arms.

"Goody," Skylar said plainly. "It isn't like I *want* to join a lot of exiles who don't even know to how keep their voices down, but I haven't had much luck finding Fortitude on my own."

"If *you* couldn't find it," said Cameron. "What makes you think *we* can?"

"Do you have a map?" she asked.

"Yeah," I replied.

"There you go."

"Wait… You've been wandering for *how* long without a map?" Persephone asked.

"Long enough."

"Alright. Well, we have two group members who have had a really rough past few days, and they need sleep before we can go anywhere in the morning. I'll take watch with Skylar, Cameron, and Eve," Zane suggested.

I felt him release my hand as he went off to join the night watch, leaving me with my bag. I pulled Asa's notes from my pocket, burying them deep within the bag before digging through my belongings, feeling the softness of my blanket buried in my bag. I pulled it out, curled up in the sand, and covered myself with it. Realizing my complete exhaustion, I fell asleep within a matter of minutes.

That night, I dreamt of Asa dragging the scalpel across my abdomen again and woke up to Zane pinning me down as I screamed and thrashed in the sand.

"Eos!" he called. "Calm down! It was just a bad dream! You're okay! You're safe!"

Fortitude

I could feel my heart pounding in my chest as I tried to process where I was.

"Where am I?" I asked, my voice cracking.

"You're with your friends. You're safe, E," he said soothingly.

I went limp, my chest rising and falling rapidly as I breathed.

I could hear Skylar grumbling in complaint about the noise to some of the others as Zane tried to calm me.

"It's okay. You can go back to sleep. I traded with Brenur for watch. I'm here now and I'm not going to let anything bad happen to you," he promised.

I nodded weakly and sniffled.

He climbed off of me and ran his hand gently through my hair.

"Just try to get some sleep, okay?"

I nodded again, closing my eyes and rolling onto my side as Zane covered me with the blanket again. Exhausted, I dozed off again after a while.

That morning, I woke up to a gentle and persistent nudging in my side. Blinking back the sharp orange light of the sunrise, I began to make out Skylar's face, with her long chestnut hair, petite nose, and subtle cleft chin. She tapped my side with her foot again.

"Get up," she pestered, her olive-green eyes narrowing at me.

I grunted.

"Everyone's having breakfast and then we're leaving. They were going to let you sleep through breakfast because they said you 'needed the sleep.' I figured I'd do you a favor—you probably need food more."

"Thanks," I grumbled sleepily as I stretched.

"Yup."

Skylar walked off, joining the rest of the group members a few yards away. Everyone was chitchatting peacefully, munching on snacks from their bags. I saw Zane toss Skylar a packaged muffin and she caught it in her right hand.

I sighed, forcing myself to sit upright. I sat there, still for a moment before rummaging through my bag for something to eat. Pulling out a granola bar, I peeled back the wrapper and munched drowsily until Zane sat beside me.

"How'd you sleep?" he asked.

I shrugged.

"After you fell back asleep, you were pretty still the rest of the night," he observed.

I gave an acknowledging nod as I snacked on my granola bar.

"Skylar had a good idea," Zane started. "She thinks we have enough rations from the campers to continue toward the coast. We sat down with the map and figured out where we are. Based on how far we've gone, it seems like we are only a day or two of solid walking away from where Fortitude should be... *Ish*... But factoring in breaks and nights, it'll take a little longer. We aren't far though."

"Lead the way," I muttered, crinkling the empty granola bar wrapper in my fist.

"You okay?"

"Good as I'm gunna' get," I stood, brushing the sand off of myself.

"We're leaving!" Skylar called from the group. "If you two are joining, you should probably get moving!"

"Are you ready to head out?" Zane asked.

I arranged the strap of my bag across my shoulder and threw Zane a quick glance as I trotted to catch up to the group, which was now headed out as a small pack into the desert.

"How do you know we're headed the right way?" I asked.

"The sun rises in the East. The coast is to the West. It's early, so the sun is supposed to be behind us," Astraea answered.

"Ah."

Skylar and Zane were at the head of the group for a majority of the trek, whereas I was toward the back with Bexa. Every time I looked up toward Zane, I'd hear him laughing at Skylar, and she always seemed to have a sweet smile on her face as she ran her fingers through her hair, occasionally flipping it. I rolled my eyes, trying to ignore her.

"What are you brooding about?" Bexa teased.

"Nothing," I groaned.

"Lies!" she chuckled.

"It's nothing."

"What is it? It's something. You look like someone pooped in your shoe."

"What? No."

"Come on. Amuse me. Whatever is on your mind is probably far more entertaining than what's on mine anyways."

"It's just *her*," I glared at Skylar.

"Who? Sky?"

"You're calling her Sky now?" I huffed.

"Why does that matter?"

"Are you guys friends or something?"

"What?"

"'Sky.'"

"So what? Just because I shortened her name doesn't make us friends. It makes *me* lazy. Don't change the focus. Why is she on your mind?"

"Look at her!" I breathed in disbelief. "Could she make it more obvious that she's flirting with Zane? She's practically begging him!"

Bexa laughed.

"E, I don't think she feels that way about him. I think they're just having friendly conversation because walking through the desert is as boring as... well honestly I don't think I can compare it to anything that would do this level of boredom justice."

"It isn't that they're talking. I don't care if they talk— at least then, no one is asking me questions anymore. She's just putting on a show for him and it's sickening."

"Why?"

"Why what?"

"Why do you think it's sickening?"

"Because she's trying too hard."

"Why does it matter?"

"I don't know! It's just annoying!"

"Is it annoying, or do you feel threatened?"

"Threatened? Bexa, I have killed a man before and I have faced a sadistic torturer. Do you really think I'm threatened by a girl who's flirting with my boyfriend?"

Bexa smirked and shook her head.

"You have nothing to worry about, E."

I could see Skylar playfully poke Zane's shoulder as she threw her head backward in warm laughter.

Make her stop.

We continued for a while before eventually stopping for a lunch break.

Everyone spread out and sat in the sand, picking through the rations in their bags for water and something to eat. I took a finger and drew an arrow in the sand to keep track of the direction in which we were headed. Walking along the outside of the group, I spotted a furry spider burrowing itself in the sand. The hairs on my arms rose as I shuttered.

Just then, an idea struck, and I could feel a smile spread across my lips. Without thinking twice, my hand shot down into the sand, scooping up the spider. I let out a muffled whimper as I cupped my hands, trapping the eight-legged monster as I made a beeline for Skylar, who was along the edge of the group with her back to the outside. The only one sitting with her was Zane, who sat beside her, unable to see me as I flicked the spider at Skylar's hair. I rapidly continued walking, so as not to arouse suspicion before I sat next to Zane and pulled out a packaged cup of precooked pasta.

"And then she told my mother! She was so mad she didn't talk to me for a week!" Skylar continued whatever story she had been telling Zane before I had joined.

"Hey, E," Zane said with a smile, turning to greet me.

I smiled half-heartedly back, looking into Zane's eyes as he stared back at me with a mixture of genuine friendliness and concern for me. Behind him, I could see Skylar's mouth contort into a terrified expression as she spotted the furry spider stepping across her hair.

"Help me!" she squeaked pathetically, staring at the spider, paralyzed.

Zane turned and, upon seeing the spider, proceeded to try to smack it from her hair. The spider's little legs got tangled in her hair, and Skylar let out a helpless wail as Zane tried repeatedly to whack the spider away. I suppressed a grin as I watched the comical fiasco ensue until, eventually, Zane succeeded in ridding Skylar's hair of the spider, who was looking worse for wear as it twitched in the sand with only six remaining legs.

"Thanks," she muttered, trying to play it cool.

"Of course," Zane said, eyeing the spider before grinding the toe of his shoe against it in the sand.

"That reminds me of this one time with my brother, when—"

I got up and walked over to Bexa, leaving Skylar's voice to trail off.

"You look guilty," Bexa crossed her arms.

"What?" I asked, sitting with my pasta cup.

"The spider. I saw that."

"Wha— no!" I lied.

Bexa scoffed.

"Was it obvious?" I asked.

"Well, to me it was. I don't think anyone else noticed you *flick* a spider into Sky's hair, if that's what you're asking."

I groaned, stuffing a fork full of pasta in my mouth.

While everyone was still eating, I dug my map out of my bag, tracing my finger along the paper as I worked out a rough estimate of our location. We still had quite a distance to travel, but based on the speed at which we were travelling, I gathered that we were right near the edge of the New Territory. Once everyone had finished eating, I searched for the arrow I drew in the sand and called for the group's attention.

"Hey!" I called to everyone, one foot on either side of my sand arrow. "I looked at the map, and we are about to reach the border of the New Territory!"

Everyone in the group began to excitedly chatter.

"This is a good thing, and a bad thing," I continued, raising my voice even louder.

The noise died down and the group members looked at me with curiosity and concern.

"It's a good thing because it means we are getting closer! We're probably only a few days away from the coast. If Fortitude is where we think, that means we are only a few days from Fortitude as well. However… beyond the border of the New Territory is pretty outdated on the map. We don't know what there is out there. There could be towns or villages with other people. There could be forests, or more desert, or who knows what else. We have to be alert. I kept reference of which direction we were headed," I pointed behind me. "So we just have to push on for a few more days if we keep up this same pace and we have no other incidents."

"What about rations?" Persephone asked.

"We have enough for everyone to eat for probably a little under a week," Zane answered.

Satisfied, Persephone nodded.

"Water?" Cameron asked. "My bottles are pretty much empty."

"Mine too," Yulie said.

"Okay. That's understandable—we've been walking through the desert for quite a while. Everyone keep an eye out for water sources," Zane said.

"Alright!" cheered Cindee. "Let's go!"

We began walking, stretching out the longer we walked until everyone had their own travel group. Zane and Skylar were toward the front of the group, Yulie and Brenur walked together not far behind them. Cindee, Eve, and Gwenn clustered together, and I could tell Cindee and Gwenn did most of the talking in their group. Cameron and Astraea stayed together, but didn't seem to say a word to each other at any point. Close to the back of our train of people were Persephone and Trent, and every time I caught a snippet of their conversations, it seemed to be Persephone complaining about somebody or something. Bexa and I lagged behind as the tail end of the group.

"Are you and Zane okay?" she asked me.

"What do you mean?"

"Like, has he said much to you since the hospital?"

"Not really, but I don't think it's because anything is wrong. I think he's just trying to think of the group and focus on getting us to Fortitude."

"When did he become the leader?" Bexa chuckled.

"I don't know."

"Are you okay with that?"

"With what? Zane being leader?"

"Yup."

I shrugged.

"I mean, it doesn't bother me. I don't care one way or another if I'm leader."

Bexa cocked an eyebrow at me.

"I don't!" I defended. "I know he's capable of leading. Maybe I'm not capable right now."

"You're plenty capable, E."

I snorted.

"You handle things really well."

"Oh *please*. Like what?"

"Like the campers. You stood up for the group when you thought we weren't being treated fairly."

"That doesn't mean I handle things well. That guy almost fried my face."

"That's not the point. And the hospital! You're handling it really well."

"*Handling?*" I repeated, dragging out the last syllable. "Present tense?"

"I mean, you said Asa wasn't done with you and wanted to relocate you. So my guess is he was doing some weird stuff to you, since you didn't even need treatment for anything. What exactly was he doing to you? You didn't have any injuries. He was just treating my gunshot wound and making sure it didn't get infected. He was really weird about everything, and he wasn't very gentle with me considering I was injured… He asked a lot of personal questions that were really weird. He also didn't really feed me much. He was a jerk, but he was helpful. He wouldn't let me go even when my shoulder started healing up, just because he said that if I was still there, he could convince you to stay. What did he do to you?"

"He just did some sick experiment."

"Experiment? Like what?"

"He said he was trying to help me get over the death of a friend."

"That doesn't sound too bad."

I scoffed.

"How did he plan to help you get over it?" she asked.

"He basically caused me pain every time I thought about her."

"That doesn't sound like a healthy way to grieve."

I shot a look at Bexa as if to say, "duh."

"Do you mind me asking how he caused you pain?"

I was silent for a moment, feeling my heart rate increase before I spoke. I told her about how Asa had cut me with a scalpel when I thought about Lamb, how he rewarded me with a mint strip when I calmed down, and how he basically poisoned my food. She listened intently, with a look of horror and disgust on her face the entire time.

"He deserved to burn! I mean, while we were there, I assumed he had some twisted plans for you. Otherwise, why would he want to keep you there when you weren't hurt or sick? He didn't do much to me. Treated my wound, talked to himself a lot, forgot to feed me sometimes, messed up my pain meds pretty bad one night, but nothing too serious. To me, he was just some weirdo kidnapper who liked to play doctor. I didn't realize how bad it was. God, E, I'm so sorry," her voice trailed off in thought.

I shrugged as I nibbled on the inside of my cheek.

"You're handling it even better than I initially thought."

"Thanks."

"Does Zane know what Asa did to you?"

I shook my head silently, staring at Zane at the front of the group, chatting with Skylar.

"Are you going to tell him?"

"Why bother? What good is it going to do?"

"He should know what happened so he can handle it better."

"Handle what? He already burned Asa. What's left to handle? Me?"

"I didn't mean it like that."

"There's no reason to tell him. I can handle myself. That reminds me," I said, pawing through my bag as we walked. I pulled out the notes Asa left on the clipboard in the hospital—the ones I took before Zane rescued me.

"What's that?" Bexa asked, eyeing the papers.

"His notes."

"Asa's?"

I nodded.

"Huh. I didn't even think to grab mine. I should've. Could have been an interesting read."

I scoffed, unfolding the notes and smoothing them out the best I could as we trailed behind the rest of the group. I held them between Bexa and I as we walked side-by-side reading.

Patient: Eos

Diagnosis: Post-Traumatic Stress Disorder, anxiety, depression

> *Day 1:* Acclimation day. Treatment to begin after tomorrow. Patient experiencing nightmares—screamed throughout the night in irregular intervals about "Lamb." Lamb will be first focus of treatment.

> *Day 2:* Patient lashed out violently. She was restrained and admitted to General Surgery. Patient suffered a laceration to the right wrist—stitched the wound and applied antibiotics. Issued a saline IV for dehydration. Patient popped a stitch. Stitched the wound again and applied additional antibiotics. Patient showing reluctance for treatment.

> *Day 3:* Chief physician ordered the beginning of treatment. Patient questioned about Lamb. Lamb is deceased female friend of patient. Patient responsible? Patient given a meal

with 600mg trexametaphine. Induced convulsions and foaming at the mouth.

<u>Day 4:</u> Patient sedated. Heart rate monitor used during questioning. Patient reacted adversely to statements about Lamb, and punishment inflicted.

After that, I stopped reading. I could feel my heart thud in my chest angrily as I crumbled the papers up.

"'Chief physician?'" Bexa quoted from the notes. "Wouldn't Asa technically have been the chief physician, as well as literally every other job in the hospital?"

"Yeah," I said. "If there was another person in that hospital running things, we would have met them, or at least heard about them. I think this was just part of him playing the role of doctor. He used to be a doctor in Fallmont, so he was probably just pretending he was back at his old job. Only, he wasn't allowed to perform his idea of treatment when he was at his old job. That's why he ran away."

Bexa grew quiet for a moment before changing the subject.

"I have an idea," she proposed.

I turned to her as we walked.

"An idea for what?"

"To help with your Skylar problem."

CHAPTER NINE

"I'm listening."

"It's silly."

"I don't care. I don't want to think about Asa or the hospital anymore."

"Tonight, steal her shoelaces. Mess with her rations a little. But don't make it super obvious. Maybe just poke holes in one of her packaged snacks she has so it gets stale."

"You're secretly a terrible person, Bexa," I snorted.

"I'm serious!" She grinned. "If you do anything too obvious, she will know it's you, and Zane will find out, and it will just cause all sorts of problems. It's the stupid stuff that gives you a little sense of satisfaction."

"Valid point."

Bexa and I continued to make jokes as we walked. Eventually, we spotted a cluster of green in the distance.

"More woods?" I asked Bexa, squinting at the green spot.

"I guess. It looks really small, if it is."

Fortitude

The closer we walked to the green spot on the horizon, the clearer the shapes grew. There were some trees, but mostly smaller plants.

"This would be a good place to rest," Zane suggested to the group, pointing at the greenery ahead.

There was a chatter of agreement as everyone trekked onward.

Once we reached the greenery, I noticed the pool of water in the middle of it all.

We found an oasis.

"Water!" I called, taking off running toward the pool of still water.

The realization hit everybody like a wave, and they sprinted after me. At the water's edge, we began taking our empty water bottles from our bags when Astraea shouted.

"Stop!"

We stared at her impatiently, the cool water grazing my fingertips as I was about to dip my bottle into it.

"We don't know if the water's safe."

"We're going to die of dehydration if we don't drink," Persephone argued.

"I know. We will drink. We just have to be a little patient," she said, digging through her backpack and pulling out the metal pot she stole from the campers outside of Equivox. "We can boil it."

Everyone set their water bottles in the sand beside them, thirstily eyeing the oasis as Astraea scooped up a pot full of water.

"Zane," she called. "You have matches. Can you start a fire with some of the drier brush?"

Zane nodded, standing and collecting bits of dry plants from the farther edges of the oasis. When he returned moments later, he piled the brush together, pulled out a match, flicked it against its box, and tossed it onto the brush. The small pile ignited, and Astraea carefully steadied the pot over the fire.

I hadn't noticed how thirsty I was until I had to sit and watch a pot of water boil in front of me. After the water boiled for a minute, Astraea set the pot in the sand and let it cool before pouring it into our bottles. She repeated the process until every bottle was full again, including after some of us drank a full bottle while waiting.

When everybody had their share of water, we resumed our journey for a short distance until we approached some blackened ruins less than an hour's walk away from the oasis. They seemed similar to the many ruins I've come across before.

Does the rest of the world look like this?

"We probably only have an hour until it starts to get dark. Any objections to staying here for the night?" Zane asked, turning to face the group.

Nobody spoke, and there were a couple of neutral shrugs.

"Alright," he said. "Let's check the buildings, make sure we're secure. Then we can pick the one that looks the most sound."

Everyone dispersed to different buildings. This town had about a half dozen charred houses that were still standing, with barely more damage than blackened walls, but there were almost a dozen more that were hardly more structural than a pile of ash. I approached one of the smaller, single-story buildings alone and reached for the doorknob.

Locked.

I checked over my shoulder before pulling the Skeleton Key from my bag, wedging it into the lock. Seconds later, I was in the building. The inside was eerily intact. The walls were lined with untouched photos of a young boy of about two. There were a couple pictures of the boy with who must have been his parents, posed on a couch. I looked into the living room of the house, spotting the same couch from the photo. The couch was a simple tan color, and there were a couple of royal blue throw pillows placed nicely in both of the corners. I cautiously stepped through the living room and into the kitchen. Pulling open the fridge, my eyes grew wide as I spotted plastic containers full of moldy food, and there was an overwhelmingly pungent stench that reminded me of sewage and rotten eggs. I covered my mouth and nose, suppressing my gag reflex as I quickly shut the fridge door.

The cabinets had a few cans of vegetables, soups, and even a can of something labeled *pineapple*. I grabbed the cans, dropping them into my bag, which felt significantly heavier. I turned the faucet of the kitchen sink.

Nothing.

Can't say I expected anything different.

Next, I checked what must have been the master bedroom and bathroom. There wasn't much of interest in either. There were some clothes in the drawers, an empty planter in the windowsill, and some random accessories. There was only one room left to check, so I made my way toward it, still leery being in the strange house alone. This door was only cracked open slightly, so I pulled out my dagger, using the blade to gently nudge the door open. As it swung open, I began to process what I was seeing.

It was the little boy from the photo's room. The walls were navy blue, with little cartoon cars painted in a line around the room. The room was carpeted in a simple cream color. There were building blocks in a bucket next to a dresser and multiple stuffed teddy bears throughout the room. It wasn't the sight of the toys that bothered me. It wasn't the photo of the boy's mother on his dresser. It wasn't the tiny shoes placed carefully to the side of the door. It was the sight of the wooden crib on its side on the floor.

I felt my heart sink as I wondered what had caused the crib to fall. *Have other exiles been here, and maybe accidentally knocked the crib over? Or could it have been something far more sobering than that? Could the crib have been knocked over in an explosion? Or while the mother or father quickly scooped the child up to get him to safety?*

Chills crept over my body as I stood in the room. I tiptoed toward the crib, picking it up by the side and leaning it upright again. The blanket from the crib still lay on the floor, and I reached down to pick it up, revealing a bloodstain on the carpet.

I dropped the blanket immediately, my eyes welling up with tears. I took a few steps backward, my eyes trained on the blanket on the floor. As I stepped back, I bumped into someone.

I let out a terrified scream, followed by blubbering whimpers.

"Hey! What's wrong? Are you okay?" Zane asked, steadying me.

I shook my head, my eyes shut tight.

"What happened?"

I pointed at the blanket without a word.

"A blanket?" he asked. "Eos, everything's fine."

"It's what's under the blanket. The crib was tipped over. I picked it up. And the blanket."

I opened my eyes as Zane casually walked towards the blanket, picking it up.

"Oh," he sighed as he spotted the blood. He laid the blanket out neatly, covering the stain. "We'll stay in a different house, don't worry. Skylar found one that's in pretty good shape, and it has four bedrooms. It's a much bigger house, so some people can actually sleep in beds tonight!"

I took deep breaths, wiping my fingers underneath my eyes to clear any buildup of tears.

"What's going on with you, E?" Zane asked.

I looked at him, uncertain.

"It isn't like you to get spooked that easily."

"'Spooked?' Are you serious right now?"

"I just mean… you've been through a lot. I didn't figure a blood stain would get you this freaked."

"It isn't the fact that there's a blood stain. It's the fact that these ruins used to be somebody's home. A little boy used to live in this room, and the crib was tipped over and there was blood on the ground. It must've fallen over and he probably hit his head on the crib! Who knows where his parents were! What if they weren't able to help him? What if something happened to them! Or even if they found their little boy—what happened to him in the end? Did they all escape the attacks?"

"I'm sorry, E. I didn't realize how passionate you were about this stuff."

"It's not that I'm passionate—I'm human. I used to babysit for my neighbors back in Rockhollow once in a while. They had a little boy, too. His name was Julius. He was such a sweet kid, and I can't imagine anything happening to him."

"Come here," Zane said, wrapping his arm around my waist and pulling me into a hug.

I kept my fists balled up, resting them on his chest as he squeezed me tight.

"We'll never know what happened to this family. Maybe the little boy's parents found him right away, patched him up, and got out in time before the attacks. Maybe they found somewhere safe to stay."

I closed my eyes as I stayed in his arms. I felt Zane gently rub a hand against my back.

"Come on," he urged. "Let's get out of here."

I nodded, letting him lead me out of the room and out of the house.

The sun was nearing the horizon when we returned to the rest of the group. It seemed like everyone was done inspecting the houses and had congregated in the middle of the ruins, talking amongst themselves.

"Hey, E, you okay?" Bexa asked upon noticing my return.

"Yeah, I'm good."

Bexa looked to Zane, clearly unconvinced.

"She's just exhausted," he lied for me. "I think the house Skylar found is our best option."

"Of course it is," mumbled Bexa, looking at me and rolling her eyes.

I smirked.

Zane appeared not to have noticed, as he led the group toward a tall house on the far end of the ruins. We all filed into the house, which was significantly larger than the one I had inspected.

"I already checked the kitchen," Skylar stated. "There isn't much of interest that isn't covered in ancient mold."

Everyone began pulling out food and dropping their bags, spreading out throughout the house, getting comfortable as they ate dinner. Carrying my bag with me, I made my way to one of the bedrooms to sit on a bed while I ate. When I opened a bedroom door, I noticed Astraea sitting at the edge of the bed, picking at a packet of pre-cooked rice.

"Sorry," I said, starting to close the door again.

"It's okay. Sit with me," Astraea said sweetly, patting the bed beside her. "I don't mind some company."

"Alright," I said plopping down beside her, digging through my stash of food.

Astraea watched me dig through the contents of my bag, and suddenly, she threw her hand across mine to stop me.

"Is that pineapple?" she asked, gaping at the can of pineapple in my bag.

"Yeah," I answered. "You want it?"

Astraea enthusiastically nodded her head, accepting the can from me with a grateful smile.

"I've never had pineapple," she grinned excitedly.

"Then why do you want it so bad?"

"I've heard of it before, and I didn't think there was any left out there. The country stopped getting shipments of pineapple a long time ago because of the war."

"Do you need to borrow my dagger?" I asked.

She looked at me, confused.

"To open the can," I clarified.

"Oh," she giggled. "No, I'm good. I've got one."

She reached for her bag on the floor, fishing out a simple metal can opener. She latched it to the can of pineapple, and began twisting it until the can was open. Eagerly, she peeled back the metal lid, revealing bluish grey chunks floating in a dingy yellow juice.

"It's rotten," she sighed, the excitement fading from her eyes. She set the can down on the floor and resumed picking at her rice.

"Sorry about the pineapple, Trae," I said.

"It's okay. I just figured it would have been nice to maybe be the only person who has had pineapple in a long time," she looked at me and smiled half-heartedly.

We finished eating, and everyone began dispersing throughout the house, arguing over who got to have which bed, and who was willing to share a bed. There were four beds—Brenur and Yulie got one and invited Eve to share with them. Persephone and Trent claimed a bed and refused to allow a third to join them. Cindee, Gwenn, and Astraea all squished in together on a smaller bed. Skylar and Cameron took the two couches in the living room, and Bexa shared the last bed with Zane and me. I lie there, wide-awake until Zane finally dozed off. I rolled over, facing Bexa.

"Bex," I whispered. "You awake?"

Bexa rolled over to look at me, squinting in the dark.

"Mm?" she muttered.

"Let me out, but be careful not to wake Zane up."

"Bathroom?" she asked plainly.

"No," I said, sliding off the bed after her, slowly. "You'll see tomorrow. I'll only be a second—don't get comfortable."

"Whatever," she grumbled sleepily, standing next to the bed in wait as I dug my dagger out of my bag and tiptoed to the living room.

Skylar and Cameron were dead asleep on the couches. Skylar's backpack and shoes sat next to her couch. I felt a smile tug at the corner of my lips as I made my way to her shoes. She turned in her sleep ever so slightly, and I froze in place, waiting for her to settle back down a moment later. As soon as I was sure she was fully asleep, I rummaged around in her bag, pulling out a couple of packaged foods. I used my teeth to rip the packages open just the tiniest bit before placing the food back in her bag. Then, I pawed around on the floor until I made contact with her shoes. I unlaced one of them halfway and used my dagger to saw at the unlaced string. I could feel the lace begin to fray as I cut it. Once I had completely separated the piece of her shoelace, I took it and dropped it down the drain of the kitchen sink. Suppressing laughter, I snuck off to the bedroom again and put my blade back in my bag.

I crawled back into bed and Bexa followed suit. It didn't take me long after to fall asleep.

~

"Calm down, Eos!" Bexa yelled. "You're safe!"

I could feel someone pinning down my wrists. When my eyes shot open, I saw Zane and Bexa's concerned stares looking back at me. I lie there, breathing heavily. I could feel sweat all over my body. Cameron, Cindee, Eve, and Gwenn were all poking their heads through the bedroom door, gawking at me as I tried to calm down.

"What happened?" I asked. "Why is everybody staring at me?"

"You had another nightmare," Zane answered. "You were screaming."

I felt my face grow warm with embarrassment.

"It's okay though, you're fine. Nobody is judging you—you've been through a lot," Bexa sympathized.

Bexa and Zane got off the bed, standing to the side to allow me space to breathe.

"What exactly happened to you guys at the hospital?" I overheard Zane ask Bexa.

"It's complicated," she answered. "I'd rather Eos tell you when and if she feels ready to talk about it."

"I'll tell him," I offered, sitting up slowly. "Let's go outside, please. I need some air."

"Of course," he said, coming to my side and helping me as I stood.

We left the house while everyone was having an early breakfast. The air was fairly cool that morning, and the sky had a thick layer of puffy clouds for the first time since we had started our journey.

Once we got outside, Zane handed me a flattened packaged muffin.

"Thanks," I said, ripping open the package.

We began to walk for a little while, just taking laps around the ruins while I silently ate my muffin. I felt my heart racing as I processed what I was going to say to him.

"He tortured me," I said plainly, still looking straight ahead.

"What?" Zane paused.

I proceeded to tell him all about how Asa experimented on me by hurting me and making me ill. Zane clung to my every word, and I could see his eyes turn glassy as he sniffed, trying to maintain his composure. He sucked his tongue over his teeth as he looked into the distance and nodded, trying to wrap his head around everything.

"You don't have to worry about him anymore," Zane reminded me.

"I know. I don't know why I keep having these nightmares. I'm sure they'll go away eventually."

"Probably," Zane nodded, a look of uncertainty creeping across his face.

I squinted at him.

"Let's go back to the house and get ready to head out," I suggested.

Back at the house, people were finishing their breakfasts and getting ready to leave.

"What the hell happened to my shoe?" Skylar shrieked furiously from the living room.

I bit my lip to hide my smile. My eyes met Bexa's, and she returned the look with a satisfied grin and a nod.

"Something chewed off my shoelace!" Skylar raged, holding her shoe up to show Zane as we entered the living room.

"It's fine. It was probably just a mouse or something. You can still wear the shoes, right?" he asked.

"Yeah, but—"

"So you're fine," Zane encouraged, accidentally letting out a singular chuckle.

Skylar groaned in disgust as she tried to tie her shortened shoelace.

The group began to exit the house, walking toward the same direction we were headed the previous day. Not an hour into the walk, Skylar buried her hand into her backpack, pulling out a granola bar. She turned it over in her hands, her eyes narrowing as she looked at it. With an enraged scream, she threw the granola bar as hard as she could into the sand in the distance.

"Stupid mouse got into my food!" she wailed, giving up on the notion of a snack.

Bexa elbowed me as we walked.

"Ouch," I said. "What was that for?"

"That was clever," she smirked. "You're welcome for the inspiration."

"Just wait," I teased, pulling a bottle from my bag.

"What's that?" she asked.

"I got it from Delaisse. I grabbed a bunch of random boxes and bottles of medicine without looking at all the labels. I already put a bunch in her water bottle."

I turned the bottle over, displaying it to Bexa.

Laxatives.

Bexa covered her mouth to hide her giggling.

"You're a monster, you know that?" she said.

"I don't trust her. You didn't meet her when Zane and I did. She threatened us and tried to steal the truck we were using. Now, she's playing cute with Zane, acting like they're as close as can be. I don't trust her, and I don't want her coming with us to Fortitude."

As we were walking, I spotted Skylar offering her water bottle to Zane.

No! No, no, no—don't drink that!

He tipped his head and the bottle back, chugging for a moment before handing the bottle back to Skylar, who took a swig after him.

Crap.

CHAPTER TEN

"Oh no," Bexa breathed, watching in horror alongside me. "How much did you put in her water?"

"A lot," I said, shaking the laxative bottle, hearing the remaining liquid slosh inside.

Bexa groaned.

"Nothing we can do about it now," I sighed.

We trekked onward. The air felt wonderfully cooler than usual, and the occasional crisp breeze sent a shiver across my body. I stopped walking, crouching down to untie my shoes.

"What are you doing?" Bexa asked, stopping ahead of me and looking back.

I smiled subtly as I kicked off my shoes and peeled my socks off. I stuffed the socks into my bag and tied the laces of my shoes around the strap. Barefoot, I jogged to catch up with the group.

"Any reason you're barefoot?" she asked.

"It's cool outside, so I figured, for once, the sand would be cool too."

"Is it?" she asked.

By now, some of the other group members from the tail end began to peer backwards, eyeing my bare feet. Astraea snickered, pulling off her socks and shoes. One by one, everyone began to take off their socks and shoes—all except for Skylar. She continued to throw judgmental glances at people's bare feet, letting out irritated huffs and sighs, as if she was subjected to babysitting a dozen children in the desert.

"Prude," I heard Persephone mutter, clearly audible enough so Skylar would hear.

"Practical," Skylar called back to Persephone.

We walked in peaceful silence for a while. Everyone seemed to be at ease as we felt the soft, cool sand between our toes with every step. While we were traveling, the pockets of ruins grew closer and closer together. As we were passing through the last bit of a ruined neighborhood, I noticed Skylar tap Zane's shoulder, motioning for him to continue walking as she handed him her bag, and she took off running in the opposite direction of the group and into one of the buildings, slamming the door shut behind her. I exchanged glances with Bexa. Sure enough, a few minutes later, Zane stopped in his tracks, dropped his and Skylar's bags, and turned to face the rest of the group.

"You guys keep going. I'll catch up in a minute!" he said, trying to sound collected, but seeming urgent as he dashed to the nearest standing building.

"Should we keep going? We're two short now," Cindee questioned.

"How about we take a break?" Yulie suggested.

Everyone agreed, and we all took a seat. I pulled out

my map, tracing my finger along our path, trying to predict our location.

"We're getting pretty close. I know we still have another couple days of walking, but we are definitely outside the New Territory at this point," I shared with Bexa, Cameron, and Astraea.

"So, it could be anywhere in this region?" Cameron asked, circling a section of the map along the coast with his finger.

"Basically."

He let out an exasperated puff as he lay back in the sand.

While waiting, everyone started to put their shoes back on, including myself. My feet felt dry and dusty from the sand, and that feeling was amplified once my feet were back in my shoes.

As everyone kept distracted with their conversations and snacks, I began to toss around an idea in my head.

"I just thought of something," I grinned at Bexa.

She cocked an eyebrow at me.

With a subtle smirk, I stood, casually making my way to Skylar and Zane's bags. Checking over my shoulder, I crouched down and sifted through Skylar's bag, immediately feeling the cool metal of the gun in her bag. Being extra cautious to make sure no one was watching, I slid the gun out of her bag and into Zane's.

She will either think he's playing some stupid cute game with her, or hopefully, she'll get mad and stop flirting with him.

I left the bags alone after the swap, and I rejoined

Bexa. She stared back at me with curiosity and concern, but didn't ask any questions.

This break was by far our longest, as we all began to lie in the cool sand after chitchatting and snacking. I dipped my hand into the sand, scooping it up and letting it slowly sift back down to the ground. Eventually, Skylar rejoined the group, a deep scowl on her face.

Everyone was silent, and when Cindee tried to speak, Skylar injected.

"Don't," she growled, making her way to the front of the group.

She paced angrily for a moment.

"Where's Zane?" she asked.

"He went into one of the houses," Cindee answered.

Skylar continued to pace, tracing a shallow trench in the sand the more times she walked over the same stretch. When Zane rejoined our group, he began leading the group again without saying a word. I trotted to the front of the group until I was walking next to Zane.

"Hey," I started. "You okay?"

"Yeah, I'm good," he answered, looking straight ahead. "I think I just ate some spoiled food or something."

"Yikes," I said softly. "I'm sorry."

In more ways than you know.

"It's whatever. Gotta' keep moving."

"Have you noticed how many more ruins there are now?" I asked, changing the subject.

"Yeah. I wonder if that means we're on the right track, or if it means anything at all. You'd think Fortitude would be near some ruins or something, if some exiles have found a way to make their home there."

"How many people do you think are in Fortitude?"

"You mean if it exists?"

"You pick now to be doubtful?" I asked.

"I've been doubtful this whole time. It's hard not to be. But what other choice do we have?"

I shrugged.

"I guess maybe a hundred people," he answered, looking around us and admiring the vast ruins surrounding us.

"That many? That's a lot of exiles that had to have escaped first."

"I'm sure they've escaped over time. Plus, you've got our group, the campers, and I'm sure there are other exiles out there. The campers alone had about two-dozen people. Is it so crazy to think that Fortitude would have about a hundred?"

"That makes sense. I initially pictured maybe about half that, but I think your logic makes sense."

"I hope we find it, E."

"Me too."

"Are you two lovebirds done talking about your feelings and dreams together?" Skylar complained.

Zane scoffed, and just then, there was a *smack* sound in the sand behind me. I turned around and saw Cindee lying in the sand, unconscious.

"Cindee?" Gwenn gasped, dropping to her knees

beside her friend, shaking Cindee's shoulders. "She won't wake up!"

I turned on my heels and quickly made my way to Cindee's side. I checked her pulse and was reassured that it seemed only slightly slower than it should be. I placed my hand on her forehead. *She's burning up.*

"*The air,*" I heard Astraea whisper to herself behind me.

"She's probably suffering from dehydration and exhaustion. Let's get her in some shade, and get her some water," I commanded.

Cameron scooped Cindee up and carried her toward the closest remains of a building. We all joined them indoors as he laid her across a couch. Cindee began to come to, a look of extreme confusion on her face.

"What happened?" she asked groggily.

"You fainted," I answered. "You're okay. We brought you inside to get you cooled down. You feel like you have a fever. Drink."

I handed her water and she sipped weakly.

"*The air,*" Astraea muttered again across the room.

I threw a confused look her direction briefly before looking back down at Cindee, who was now shivering.

"Hey," I called, concerned. "Are you cold?"

"Freezing," she responded, her teeth chattering uncontrollably.

I looked back at Zane, panicked. Shaking my head in confusion, I spoke to Cindee again.

"Cindee… It's warm out. It's warm in here. The breeze outside today is a little chilly, but overall, it's fairly warm. Drink more water, then close your eyes and get some rest for a while," I advised.

"It's the air," Astraea tried to speak up, still too quiet to be heard by a majority of the group.

"Trae, what are you talking about?" I asked, a bit frustrated by her mumblings.

"The air is bad. It's making her sick."

"What do you mean 'the air is bad?'"

"We've been walking through ruins all day. During the war, some cities had instances of chemical warfare. The enemies used chemicals and toxins that would be harmful to the people living in the cities. Are we so sure those chemicals have expiration dates?"

"Nobody is tossing around chemicals right now," I replied.

"No," she replied thoughtfully. "But the toxins are probably all around us. In the air, in the sand surrounding the affected areas, in the water, in the remains of the buildings."

"So, you mean to say we're in the middle of a toxic wasteland where any and all of us can be infected?"

Just then, Cameron went limp and fell to the floor.

"Basically," Astraea's voice cracked in fear, her eyes huge as she looked down at Cameron's pale body crumpled on the ground.

"How do we stop it?" I asked urgently, squatting down beside Cameron.

She shrugged.

"I don't know if we can. We might be able to stop others from getting sick though."

At this point, everybody who was conscious was staring at Astraea in terror.

"How?" I prodded.

"The most common chemical they used was a new development. Highly experimental. Its symptoms were a lot like this. If that's the case, we need iodide pills, and everyone needs to take them as soon as possible."

"Everybody check to see if you picked up iodide pills!" Zane instructed, searching immediately through his belongings.

I rummaged through my bag, fishing out a small white bottle marked "IODIDE."

This must have been one of the medicines I grabbed when we were filling our bags in Delaisse.

"Here!" I shouted, holding up the bottle.

I poured out a pill for myself, passing the bottle off. Everyone proceeded to swallow a singular pill and wash it down with water.

"Is that it?" I asked Astraea.

"I—" she hesitated. "I mean, it isn't a guarantee. Some people might still be susceptible if they didn't take the pill early enough. Cindee and Cameron need to take a pill each, too. It won't cure them, but it will keep more chemicals from entering their systems. We don't know how much toxin already has, so they might just start to get worse. The human body can correct some of the damage over time, but not if it takes in too much. I only studied this stuff briefly. I went through a phase where I was

151

obsessed with war history, and that's when I read about the chemical warfare involved."

"We need to leave the ruins as quickly as possible," Zane said, his eyes bouncing between unconscious Cameron and shivering Cindee.

"Should we carry Cameron and Cindee and keep moving?" I asked. "We can give Cindee her pill before we leave, and we can give Cameron his pill as soon as he's awake, but I don't think either of them will be walking anytime soon."

"I think that's our best bet," Zane nodded. "We need to get out of here as soon as possible."

Cameron began to stir on the ground, blinking back the light as he stared back at us all.

"Why's everybody looking at me?" he asked, a pained grimace on his face as he attempted to sit up. A trickle of blood began to roll from his nose as he gaped at us.

"Cam," Astraea cooed, motioning with her hand under her nose in a wiping motion.

Cameron wiped his nose with the back of his hand, smearing the blood. He looked down at the blood on his hand and back up at us, his mouth opened slightly, his thick black brows furrowed, and his pale blue eyes wide.

"Oh God," he breathed, putting his palm on his forehead, feeling for a temperature.

We stared unblinkingly and silently at him as he shook his head.

"What's wrong with me?"

"We need to go," Zane urged the group.

"Take this," Astraea said, handing him an iodide pill,

which he swallowed without hesitation. She turned to Cindee, instructing her to do the same.

"Who's going to move Sickly Sally and Bloody Bob out of here?" Skylar asked, crinkling her nose.

"It doesn't matter," Zane answered. "We just have to move quickly. The sooner we're out of these ruins, the better."

"I think you're missing the point, Zane," she continued. "Cameron was fine. Then he carried Cindee. Now Cameron's not fine. Got it? We can't carry them. If they're infected with whatever nasty toxins are in this place, coming into contact with them is only going to increase chances of getting sick."

By then, everyone was nervously communicating amongst the group.

"I'll carry Cameron," Brenur volunteered.

"Brenur!" Yulie disagreed.

"We aren't leaving them behind, and they can't walk! But we can't stay here. I can't let you get sick."

"I'll carry Cindee," Bexa offered.

"I'll help," said Eve.

"That settles it," Zane said. "Let's move out. Things will only get worse if we st—"

Zane's eyes fluttered as he stumbled and collapsed.

Skylar stared at him on the floor beside her, horrified.

"There are too many people out," Astraea announced. "Everyone should be fine, as long as we keep moving. Cameron, Cindee, and Zane all took the tablets, so they shouldn't get any worse."

"We aren't going to be able to carry everyone out if people keep falling ill like this," Eve worried.

"We can't stay here though!" Skylar growled at Eve.

"Trent can carry Zane," Persephone hollered.

"I— what?" Trent stuttered.

"We need to leave," Persephone grumbled threateningly at Trent.

"What if I catch it?" he argued.

"We all have equal chances of getting sick. It's in the air. There's nothing we can do but take the iodide pills and get out of here," Astraea advised.

"How do you know that?" he retorted.

"This chemical caused fainting spells, high fevers, confusion, chills, breathing problems, sometimes hallucinations, internal bleeding, and eventually death if prolonged exposure occurred. These three are already showing some of the symptoms, in which case I can at least tell you with complete confidence that the chemical is in the air."

"Death?" Cindee whimpered from the couch. "How do we treat it?"

"There weren't any studies really done, but there were some recorded accounts of survivors making it out of the affected cities and healing over time, if iodide pills were taken early enough to prevent an irreversible amount of the chemical from entering the system."

"So as long as we take iodide pills, we'll be okay?" I urged, my body shaking as I watched Zane, waiting for him to wake.

"Essentially. If we took them early enough, at least. Most of us aren't even showing symptoms yet."

There was a collective sigh of relief, and the fear on everyone's faces began to melt. Everyone except Skylar.

"How long until it was no longer reversible?" she asked.

"What?" replied Astraea.

"How long until the chemical poisoning can't be cured once you show symptoms?"

"Oh," Astraea responded, dropping her shoulders with a sigh.

Everybody turned their eyes towards her as she answered with a worried inhale.

"12 hours."

CHAPTER ELEVEN

"Is that 12 hours from the first symptom?" Skylar asked for clarification.

"12 hours from the moment the fever hits."

"How do we know how long they have then?" Skylar shouted angrily at Astraea. "For all we know, they could've had the fevers for hours and not noticed until they got sick enough!"

"Well... like I said... the tablets should, in theory, prevent them from getting any worse, at least for a while. And we can assume they were exposed in *this* city. We've been walking in ruins all day, so contact may have happened late this morning, at the earliest."

"That might only give them a few hours!"

"I know..."

"Why aren't we all sick?" Yulie asked, her hands wrapped across her slightly enlarged belly, mostly concealed by a flowing shirt.

"It takes longer for some people's bodies to react, and some people are more susceptible to the effects. Children and pregnant women are at the highest risk, whether or not they directly show symptoms right away. However, my guess is that Cindee, Cameron, and Zane's bodies are the least hardy against the chemical. Everyone else is due to follow after. It could take minutes, or for those of us who are lucky—hours."

"Great. So no one will be left to carry us all out of the ruins," Skylar replied sarcastically.

"Not if we move quickly," Astraea pressed. "The tablets should keep us all safe long enough to get out of here if we get moving."

I nodded, a solemn look on my face just as Zane woke.

"*Zane*," I breathed, kneeling by his side. "Are you okay?"

I felt his forehead for a fever. His head felt just as hot as Cindee's, if not worse.

"I'm good," he answered shakily, his face a pale yellow.

I turned back to the rest of the group, panic spreading on my face.

"Let's go," Skylar said, leading the way out of the door of the house. Behind her, Brenur followed with Cameron limp in his arms, and Bexa and Eve came shortly after with Cindee in theirs. Trent looked down at Zane hesitantly, a hint of disgust creeping across his face.

"I can walk," Zane said, shakily trying to rise to his feet, only to stumble and fall face-first on the floor with a groan.

"Just pick him up, you wuss," Persephone griped.

"Wuss? Would *you* like to carry him?" Trent retorted.

Persephone scoffed and trailed after the group as they filed out the door, leaving just Zane, Trent, and I in the house.

Trent grumbled in complaint and hesitation as he stared down at Zane in contemplation.

"Just go," I told Trent, aggravated.

I grabbed Zane's hand, using it to wrap his arm across my shoulder. With a deep inhale, I pushed with my legs, lifting his weight with my own.

"You don't have to do this, E," he groaned weakly.

"Yes, I do. I'm not leaving you, and no one else jumped up to help."

"Thank you," he said, looking into my eyes with a sweet smile.

I flattened my lips and nodded before guiding him out the door of the building.

"How do you feel?" I asked.

I can't believe how quickly this poisoning has impacted people so far. One minute they were fine, the next, they were sick. Am I next? Are we going to make it out before too many of us are sick?

"A little like death, but otherwise I'm dandy," Zane let out an airy chuckle.

It was exceedingly difficult to help Zane walk in the sand as his legs continually gave out on him as we walked, causing his feet to dip into the sand and drag every few steps.

From the front of the group, Yulie kept glancing back at Zane and I, as we struggled to keep in sight of the group as they speed-walked through the ruins. She threw Brenur a concerned look as he kept pace with the group, carrying

Cameron effortlessly. Then, she jogged toward the back of the group, joining Zane and me.

"Let me help you," she offered, sliding Zane's other arm around her shoulders.

"What about you and the baby?" I asked.

"If I'm going to get sick, I'm going to get sick. There's nothing I can really do to prevent it. It's better for everyone if we get out of here quickly. Not like you aren't doing a great job or anything, but we aren't going to get out of the ruins anytime soon if you try to move Zane by yourself."

I nodded in appreciation.

Zane began to giggle uncontrollably. Yulie and I exchanged concerned glances.

"Guys," Zane managed to speak through the laughter. "I look like a drunk lady's man. Getting dragged around by two pretty ladies because I can't stand up."

He snorted.

I rolled my eyes with a subtle amused grin and Yulie chuckled.

An hour had passed walking through the ruins, with no end in sight. No one else in the group had fainted, though Eve, Trent, Astraea, and Bexa had all mentioned feeling lightheaded and a little dizzy at times, but the group still pushed onward. Skylar, Persephone, Gwenn, Yulie, Brenur, and I were the only ones without any symptoms thus far.

"I love you," Zane muttered weakly. His eyes looked dull, he only moved his feet occasionally and with a lot of effort, and his mouth hung open slightly as he took deep, labored breaths.

"What?" I asked, feeling my pulse race as I was caught off-guard.

"I love you," he repeated.

I could see Yulie bite her lips to suppress a smile, keeping her eyes forward.

"No, you don't," I said matter-of-factly. "You're sick, so you're not thinking straight."

"Yes, I do. Eos, you've been by my side—literally— through everything. You've stuck with me no matter what stupid decisions I've made, and you've made everything worth it."

I felt my expression soften at his words.

Even if I'm important to him, he's sick. He doesn't actually love me—he's not well. If we get out of here alive and he heals, I'll see if he says it again. If he does, I'll know he means it. If not, I'll know it was only a mixture of him thinking he's not going to make it and maybe hallucinations.

"Okay, Zane," I said calmly.

"'Okay?'" he repeated with a tone of disappointment.

"You mean a lot to me, too, Zane."

"That's it?"

"I—" I stuttered.

Yulie looked at me like I just stole candy from a child.

"*What?*" I mouthed to her.

"She loves you," Yulie reassured him. "She's just not ready to say it yet."

I stared back at Yulie, my mouth gaping open. She smiled.

"I know," Zane chuckled airily. "It's pretty hard to resist my charm."

He threw his head back as if to pretend to flip long hair.

"I don't know," I teased. "It seems like your hair has lost a bit of its form."

Zane's smile faded.

"We haven't been able to shower in a while, in case you haven't noticed. I also don't have any more hair gel."

"Chill," I said. "It was a joke."

Zane nodded. "I know. I'm just saying."

"Your hair really that important to ya'?" Yulie asked.

"It isn't about the hair," Zane laughed, his voice weak and his speech slurred. "Your appearance is sometimes the only thing you have control over. If you look like you've got your life together, sometimes you can convince yourself that you do. The styled hair is a part of that."

"Alright, whatever you say," I snickered.

"I don't feel well at all," Zane said, his face flushed. "I can't see straight. Are we getting close?"

"I don't know," I answered in a hushed voice.

I eyed my bag, bouncing on my hip as I helped maneuver Zane.

"Gwenn!" I called toward the group.

She turned rapidly to face me, her blonde curls bouncing as she turned and walked backwards.

"Can you get my map out of my bag for me?" I asked.

She nodded, trotting to my side and fishing out my map as we walked. She unfolded it and held it in front of me. Using my free hand, I traced my finger from the approximate place we spent last night to where I believed we currently were walking.

"There," I said, pointing to a section on the map. "Or, at least, that general area. But we don't know how far the ruins stretch. That wouldn't be on a New Territory map. The only useful thing it shows at this point is the coast."

"Wait," Yulie started. "We don't have to get out of the ruins necessarily. Not all ruins are toxic. Maybe we've passed the toxic part?"

"We have no way of knowing for sure. At least, not a desirable way of knowing."

"Yeesh," she said, eyeing Zane, who could hardly keep his head up at this point.

From the front of the group, Skylar looked back at us, a hint of concern wrinkling on her face.

"I'm going to scout up ahead," she hollered to the group, taking off sprinting in the direction we were headed.

Yulie and I looked at each other and shrugged. The group maintained the quickest pace it could, but clearly fatigued from carrying Cindee, Bexa and Eve were beginning to slow down to the speed of the tail end of the group.

"Cindee's out now. How goes it with you?" Bexa asked me in a puffy breath.

"Well," I said. "Better than these guys." I motioned with my head to Cindee and Zane.

Bexa snorted.

"Feeling dizzy or anything yet?" I asked her.

"Nah. Just a bit sore and tired."

"That's fair."

"You?"

"Same. Hey, by the way," I started, motioning with my free hand for her to come as close as she could as I whispered to her. "Zane said he loves me. Toxins? Or truth?"

Bexa's face lit up in a gleeful smile.

"Truth! I'm assuming, at least. We can all see it in the way he looks at you and the way he talks to you. That boy adores you!" she answered in a half-whisper. Worried he'd overhear, I peeked at Zane, but he was too out of it to realize anything that was going on.

I shrugged.

I feel like he really does care about me, but how awkward would it be if, when he's better, I say that I love him too, and he looks at me like I'm crazy because he doesn't remember saying it first?

I rolled my shoulders under the weight of Zane's arm pulling down on me, trying to work knots out in my muscles. It was as if he stopped walking altogether.

Wait.

Continuing to walk, I paused the shoulder rolls for a second, my eyes wide.

I love him too?

Letting the expression fade from my face, I proceeded.

"If you need to rest, let me know," I offered to Yulie.

"I'm okay. You?" she asked.

I nodded.

Time passed slowly, and I felt as though the group as a whole was only growing slower. Eventually, we heard the rapid patting of Skylar's feet as she returned, still running.

"We're almost there!" she screamed at us.

I felt a lump form in my throat.

Almost to Fortitude? It's real?

"The edge of the ruins is close. You can't see it from here, but there are actually some trees and such just past the border of the ruins. I promise—we're close," she grinned hopefully through exhausted breaths. "There's a wall of taller buildings obstructing the view beyond the ruins a bit, but there's an alley between them."

Oh, I thought. *She means almost out of the ruins. That's fine. I'll take what I can get.*

"Zane," I called softly, tapping his chest with my free hand. "Did you hear that?"

Nothing.

"Zane?" I stopped walking, and Yulie did the same.

"What's wrong?" she asked.

"He's unresponsive," I answered, my skin going cold at my own words.

Yulie and I lowered Zane's unconscious body to the ground carefully, and I fished a bottle of water out of my bag, unscrewing the lid and shakily holding it to his lips. I tipped it back, just enough to pour a little water which just rolled down the side of Zane's face.

"Please wake up," I began to panic, shaking him. "Please?"

Members of the group began to take note of our absence as they walked, and they turned to watch as I frantically hovered over Zane.

"I love you too," I said to him, my eyes stinging as I stared at him on the sandy pavement. "I love you too!"

No response.

Please wake up.

"Let's get out of here quickly," I instructed. "Somebody grab Zane's feet. Three of us should be able to carry him out a lot quicker. The sooner we get away from whatever chemicals are around here, the better. Somebody please help us with him."

"I'll do it," Skylar offered, wrapping her hands around Zane's ankles.

Yulie, Skylar, and I eased ourselves up, lifting Zane from the ground.

"Everybody keep moving!" I demanded.

The group picked up the pace, speed walking through the remains of the ruins.

"How far until we reach the edge?" I asked Skylar.

"Not very. Walking at this pace? Probably ten minutes," she answered. She had Zane's left ankle in her left hand, the other in her right as she stood between his feet so she could walk facing forward.

"Okay," I nodded, unsatisfied. "And if we run?"

She looked over her shoulder and cocked an eyebrow at me.

"*Go*," I uttered, turning our speed walk into a paced run.

The members of the group began taking the hint, taking off running through the streets of the ruins. Bexa and Eve lagged behind, still trying to carry Cindee in their arms. Seeing them struggling, Gwenn approached the two girls, offering to take Cindee's legs so the other two could hold her under her arms. The three worked together, quickly catching up with the rest of the group.

"I see the edge of the ruins!" Persephone called from the front of the group.

Sure enough, within minutes, the entire group had reached an alleyway between some tall buildings lining the border of the ruins. The alleyway was shadowed by the brick buildings, which looked untouched along their bottom halves, but destroyed at the tops. We formed a line through the alleyway, able to fit easily, despite carrying some of the group members out as teams. On the other side of the alley, there was a scape of low mountains a short distance away. Covering the mountain, there was an abundance of trees and other greenery.

"Let's get to the trees and get everyone in the shade," Skylar advised.

We continued for a couple minutes, running toward the edge of the mountains. When we finally reached it, Yulie, Skylar, and I carefully lowered Zane at the base of a tree, alongside some delicate-looking periwinkle flowers.

"Is he awake yet?" Eve asked.

I tapped Zane's chest and jostled his shoulders again.

I shook my head.

"Cindee's out, too," Bexa said as her, Eve, and Gwenn lowered Cindee beside Zane.

"And Cameron?" asked Astraea.

Brenur nodded, laying Cameron next to Cindee.

"Eve's been really dizzy for a while now, I really think she should lie down, too," Astraea whispered to me.

"Eve," I called.

She was naturally one of the palest people in the group, but now, she looked almost grey.

"You need something?" she asked, stumbling toward me.

"I think you need to sit down," I advised.

She agreed complacently, sitting down in a half-fall and taking out a bottle of water.

"He's breathing and he's got a pulse," Skylar said, her fingers against Zane's neck.

"How do we wake him up?" I asked.

"Prop his feet up," Astraea said. "Do it to the others. Helps with blood flow."

Those of us closest to the sick helped prop their feet up using their backpacks. Then, we sat in silent wait for what felt like forever until Cameron began to stir.

Groaning, he tried to sit up.

"Woah—" Brenur said, holding him steady. "I think you should lay back."

"What happened?" Cameron asked, leaning against the trunk of the tree.

"You passed out. Here—" Brenur handed him a water. "Drink."

Shortly after Cameron awoke, Cindee's eyes fluttered open, and we got her drinking water as well.

I grabbed Zane's hand, rubbing it between my palms anxiously.

Come on…

Just then, I felt one of his fingers twitch.

"Zane?" I asked hopefully, sitting upright.

He grumbled.

"Oh my gosh," I breathed with relief, leaning with my forehead on his chest.

"Water," he sputtered with a dry cough.

"Oh," I said, grabbing for a bottle, sloshing water on my hand as I shakily unscrewed the cap, handing him the bottle.

He thirstily chugged the bottle, water dribbling down his chin.

Bexa squatted behind me, placing a hand on my back. I turned to meet her smile.

"He's gunna' be alright," she reassured me genuinely.

I nodded with a relieved expression.

"Keep them drinking," Astraea advised softly. "Everyone should be, honestly. It could only help."

The sky was growing dark as we all sat under the trees in an unspoken agreement to spend the night where we were. When I decided it was time to sleep, I wiggled closer to Zane, who was resting against a tree trunk.

"How are you feeling?" I asked.

"Much better already," he answered, his usual perk returning to his voice.

"Really? That fast?"

"I mean, I don't feel ready to go on any lengthy runs, and my head hurts, but I feel not half-dead, so that's pretty exciting."

I giggled, leaning my head on his shoulder.

"I'm glad you're okay," I sighed sleepily.

He kissed the top of my head and we sat there silently.

"Are you sleeping?" I asked in a hushed voice, wondering if I could readjust my position without waking him.

No response.

He has no clue I said 'I love you' while he was unconscious earlier.

The corner of my lip turned upwards as I thought about what I could tell him while he sleeps without him having any idea. I've never been one to drone on about feelings, so the thought of telling him when he's awake made me a bit nervous.

"I love you," I said in a whisper, placing my hand on his.

I don't doubt it, but for now I'll stick to saying it while he's unconscious.

"I love you, too, Eos," he whispered back.

CHAPTER TWELVE

The next morning, I woke up to yelling.

"Where's my gun?" I could hear Skylar growling, holding her bag upside down, the contents spilled on the ground at her feet.

When no one answered her, she grew even more enraged.

"One of you rodents *stole* it! Fess up! Was it you?" She glared at Persephone.

"Why would I take your gun?" she spat back.

"I didn't ask you that. I asked *if* you stole my gun," Skylar answered with an eerie coolness.

"*No,*" Persephone responded with a tone of subtle mockery.

"Dump out your bags!" Skylar demanded of everyone.

"Sky," Cindee started. "I think you're being a bit irrational. No one stole your gun. Did you leave it in one of the ruins one night or something?"

"Don't call me irrational. Empty your bag," she paused between each word, gritting her teeth.

Stunned, Cindee unzipped her backpack and dumped the contents to the ground, revealing nothing but a couple of water bottles, some medical supplies, and food.

Skylar grumbled impatiently, glaring at each individual in the group as they followed Cindee's lead, pouring their bags out onto the ground. When Zane followed suit, the gun tumbled out of his backpack and onto the ground. Everyone stared in silent horror as Zane looked down at the gun, confusion growing on his face.

Skylar stared at Zane, her expression melting from somber disappointment to pure rage. She stormed over to him, scooping up the gun and slamming Zane back against a wide tree trunk, pinning him with her arm.

"Don't ever touch my gun, *ever*," she hissed in his face.

Directing her attention to the rest of the group and raising her voice, but still pinning Zane, she continued to speak.

"You all need my protection a hell of a lot more than I need you!" she said. "If you think this crap's going to fly with me, you are *sorely* mistaken. I don't care how close or far we are from Fortitude, I can leave at any point and leave you all without backup."

"We haven't needed your protection yet," Persephone dared to speak.

Skylar let her arms slowly fall to her sides before she turned on her heel to face Persephone.

"What was that?" Skylar asked in mocking sweetness

as she tilted her head and pointed the barrel of the gun at Persephone's leg.

"You don't need to do this," Cindee spoke up. "I don't know why Zane had your gun, but I'm sure we can talk this all out and keep going while we have the day ahead of us. We don't have much water left, so we need to make use of every minute."

"I wasn't asking you, kid," Skylar retorted, still staring unblinkingly at Persephone. "You've got a point though. But I'm not going anywhere with any of you until I figure out why he thought it was okay to steal my gun."

Skylar turned to face Zane again as she waited for an answer.

"I don't know why it was in my bag," he answered honestly, the usual glimmer in his eyes gone as he stared at the gun, defeated and confused. "I know you have no reason to believe me, but I didn't take it."

Skylar scoffed.

"Typical thief. Pathetic."

I felt my heart racing as my stomach sunk with guilt seeing Zane's depressed gaze.

"He didn't steal your gun, Skylar," I spoke up. "I took it and hid it in his bag."

"Excuse me?" she asked, turning and meeting my eyes with disgust.

"I was bored," I lied.

"You were bor—" she scoffed, trailing off.

"Every day felt the same, and I was bored, so I thought it would be a funny joke. I didn't know you'd get so upset."

Fortitude

Lies. More lies.

"You see, what's funny is... I'm not even surprised. Or disappointed. I'd expect this kind of childish behavior from *you*."

She tucked her gun in the back of her pants and repacked her bag. Without another word, she started to walk off.

"Where are you going?" Cindee called to her.

"Fortitude. If you're coming with, get moving," she answered without stopping.

Everyone rapidly shoved their belongings back into their bags and trotted to catch up, leaving Zane and I behind. Zane simply stood there, his stuff still on the ground at his feet as he looked up from it, meeting my eyes. He felt betrayed, beyond a doubt. His gaze seemed sunken, his arms limp at his sides, and his posture slumped. He paused for a moment before taking his stuff and leaving to be with the group as they hiked through the rocky terrain along the side of the low mountain.

Why do I have to ruin everything?

"Zane!" I called, running to catch up to him and the group. "Wait, please!"

I walked alongside him, but he wouldn't even look at me.

"I'm sorry," I said. "Really. I didn't realize she was going to get that mad."

His brow furrowed as he focused on not acknowledging me.

I lowered my voice as I continued.

"I didn't do it because I was bored," I admitted in a gruff whisper.

He glared angrily at me.

"I did it because I was jealous and stupid."

His face contorted into a look of confusion and disbelief.

"She was right to call me childish," I said ashamedly. "You and her were spending a lot of time together, and she was flirting with you, and you seemed to like it, and I didn't want to lose you. I know we didn't used to get along... at all. But then you started to mean a lot to me, and I couldn't stand the thought of her just waltzing in and taking that from me. I should've handled it differently—"

"That's putting it lightly," Zane scoffed. "You should have told me how you felt and you could've avoided this whole thing."

"I'm not very good at the whole expressing feelings thing," I admitted.

"You don't say."

"Look, I'm sorry. I don't know how or if I can make it up to you. I just... you needed to know why I did it, and that it isn't that I'm a terrible person who does mean stuff out of boredom—"

"No," he interrupted. "You just do it because you're selfish."

"*Selfish*?" I repeated.

"Yup."

"So, I'm selfish for not wanting to lose you? After everything we've been through?"

"No," he answered. "You're selfish for the way you handled it. I understand how you could've felt threatened, and I don't blame you, but you didn't need to do that. You could've just told me."

"I'm sorry. I can't change what I did though."

"I'm well aware," he answered, picking up his speed to keep up with the group.

I let myself fall behind the group a short distance, knowing that nobody wanted anything to do with me, not even Bexa, who knew that I had been messing with Skylar and Zane, but didn't know the extent of my latest ruse.

As we walked, I dug through my bag for something. When I felt the coolness of the metal stroke against my fingers at the bottom of the bag, I fished it out.

My ring from Fabian.

I'm no better than you, I thought, remembering how my childhood friend, Fabian, had betrayed Zane and me in Fallmont when we went in search of the Skeleton Key. The sapphire and copper ring glimmered in the sunlight as I tilted it in my palm. Ashamed, I let the ring tumble from my hand, landing in the rocks and sand with a gentle *pat.*

If this is how I lose Zane, I have nothing left. I wish I could just wake up in my bed back in Rockhallow, as if all of this was just some bizarre dream. I wish I was never exiled to Avid… that I never found out about the Skeleton Key… that I never escaped and went to all of the exile towns… that I never ended up killing an official… that I never met Paren… that I never had to see Lamb die… that I never saw Fabian again… that I didn't come across this group of exiles in the ruins… that I wasn't kidnapped by a psychopath doctor and tortured… that I never told Zane I loved him… that I never met Zane at all.

175

The day went on as we trekked through the low mountain range, taking occasional breaks to rest and eat. Every time the group stopped, everyone grouped off, leaving me standing alone along the edge of the group, looking awkwardly for somebody willing to speak to me. Each time, without fail, I ended up sitting away from the group, alone. During one of our stops, I decided to dig out the burlap "L" that Zane had cut from Lamb's backpack after she passed away—one for both of us as something to remember her by. I stroked the rough burlap between my fingers as I halfheartedly munched on a pack of crackers. I didn't have much of an appetite, but I was beginning to feel weak.

Without notifying me, the group stood and continued travelling again. With a disheartened sigh, I tucked away the fabric scrap and followed behind as before.

I wonder what Lamb would think of all of this.

As I kept busy with my thoughts, I felt a burning sensation on the scar on my stomach, and a lump formed in my throat. Taking a deep breath, I pushed away the sensation and tried to refocus myself on our destination. At this point, the sun was setting. We were near the top of one of the many mini mountains we had been hiking over throughout the range.

"Stop here for the night?" Skylar asked the group, careful not to make eye contact with me as she addressed them.

Everyone agreed, finding places within the group to drop their bags and get comfortable.

"I'll take first watch," Skylar volunteered.

"I'll join," Cameron offered.

Fortitude

I saw Zane talking to Cindee as the two of them, Gwenn, and Eve all sprawled out near each other. Realizing I wasn't welcome without even having to ask, I set up my makeshift bed at the crest of the mountain, keeping everyone in sight but allowing myself to have some distance from their hateful eyes. I lie there looking at some ruins in the distance, wide awake with my blanket spread out over my legs. When the sky was dark, something on the other side of the mountain caught my eye.

A purple light.

That must be the purple light Skylar was talking about.

I felt a chill ripple over my skin and I started yelling before I could even process what was happening.

"Guys!" I screamed, standing to my feet to get a better look at the source of the light. "*I found it!*"

There was confused chatter from the group as they began to approach me.

"What are you talking about?" Yulie asked groggily. Once she stepped up beside me and could see the purple light, the squinty creases on her face softened and her mouth hung open in shock. "Is that—?"

I nodded with uncontained excitement.

"What's Crazy harping on about?" Skylar called up from the rest of the group.

"Fortitude," Yulie replied breathlessly, keeping her eyes on the purple light as if it would disappear if she looked away for even a moment.

At this point, everyone was clustering at the top of the mountain with me, each one of their faces lighting up with amazement as they realized our search was not in vain.

"It's real," Skylar breathed, sounding ever so slightly choked up. "I didn't think I would ever find it."

"What are we waiting for?" Cindee asked, bouncing with anticipation. "Let's go!"

"It's dark out," Trent grumbled.

"We can see it from here—it can't be that hard to just follow a bright purple light. There's enough moonlight to see a little way in front of you. Just watch your step," Cindee argued. "I don't know about you guys, but I've done enough of this walking every day stuff. I'm ready to get to Fortitude!"

I could hear the sound of crumbling rocks beneath her feet as she took off running in what looked like a controlled fall down the mountainside.

"Keep your momentum!" she shouted back at us all with a giggle. "I almost fell."

Everyone laughed at how eager Cindee was, but we knew we all felt same way. We were ready to finally reach Fortitude after what felt like forever trekking through desert and ruins. After everything we had been through, we were *finally* almost there.

We all sprinted after Cindee, who was already halfway down the mountainside, still giggling wildly as she ran. When we reached the bottom of the short mountain, I could feel my feet hit soft sand, sinking with every forceful kick off of the ground as I bolted toward that bright violet glow.

The closer we got to the source of the light, the larger it grew until it seemed to tower over us. The light was coming from a single skyscraper within expansive ruins that grew closer and closer to us. The ruins themselves looked similar to Fallmont in structure, but significantly larger, and the city itself was vastly more expansive. The buildings had clearly sustained some level of damage to them from the war, but what looked like ruins from the distance actually concealed a city just beyond the blackened buildings on the outskirts. When we reached the entrance of the city, I could see a paved road leading into it. On the right side of the road was a grimy green sign with white letters spelling out "LOS ANGELES" in large letters. A thin line of red paint crossed out the white letters, and "FORTITUDE" was spelled out above it in matching paint.

Once we reached the side of the paved road, we slowed to a walk. I could hear everybody panting and wheezing around me as we tried to catch our breath. There was nobody at the entrance, and there was no gate prohibiting us from entering. We simply walked into the city, swallowed by the blackened outskirt buildings. Each of us kept our gazes fixed upon the towering skyscraper emitting the purple haze, which stood erect in the middle of the city. There were tall streetlamps lighting the road into the city, but it wasn't until we passed through the damaged outer layer of buildings that we saw Fortitude itself.

In front of us was a lively courtyard with colorful light displays across many of the windows on surrounding structures. In the middle of the courtyard was the purple-lit building, framed by two additional skyscrapers—one on the left, one on the right. Bordering the pavement of the courtyard were shops, restaurants, and numerous other skyscrapers. Some of the buildings had open clothing displays and flashy signs advertising various styles of apparel. A man with a hunched back scurried past us, poking at pieces of litter on the ground with a stick, collecting the trash in a large black bag. I could hear the buzz of the lights flooding from every direction, and I could smell something fried in the air. There were probably close to a hundred people scattered throughout the courtyard around the purple-lit building. Everyone had smiles on their faces and seemed to be having a great time as they talked with friends on the street. The group of us clustered together, lost in the lights around us as we stared up at the center skyscraper.

"Club Belladonna," came a smooth voice behind us.

I turned and met the eyes of the speaker. The voice came from a tall man with ebony skin, a shaved head, and deep brown eyes that reflected the violet light. He was wearing a pressed and fitted suit, and his teeth were stunningly straight and pearlescent as he smiled warmly at us.

"Sorry?" I asked, confused.

He motioned with his head to the center skyscraper, emitting bright purple light from its windows.

"That's Club Belladonna."

I must have revealed that I was still perplexed, as he let out a deep chuckle.

"I forgot… they don't have clubs in the cities or the exile towns. How long have you guys been out there?"

Everyone began to babble amongst themselves trying to determine how long we've actually been wandering. Nobody seemed to agree, since everyone had escaped their exile towns at different times.

"It depends on who you're asking," Cindee answered the man.

He chuckled as we continued to stare up at the dazzling purple skyscraper.

"I'm sorry, beautiful," the man started, concentrating on me. "I didn't catch your name."

"Eos," I answered.

He grabbed my hand, bowing his head slightly, lifting my hand and softly kissing the top of it.

"Legend."

I could feel my cheeks grow warm as I followed his eyes.

"I can show you around, if you'd like," Legend offered.

I nodded awkwardly.

"Sure," I answered.

He took my hand and placed it in the crook of his arm as he escorted me toward Club Belladonna.

"Eos!" Cindee shouted after me as I let Legend guide me away from the group. "Where are you going?"

I paused and turned to meet her concerned gaze. I shook my head subtly after my eyes fixated on Zane's expression. His eyes were turned down as if looking at the floor under his feet, pretending I wasn't even there.

As I began to turn back away, I caught a glimpse of Cindee's expression of rejection as she looked to the other group members, hoping someone else would speak up to stop me.

"The entrance is on the other side," Legend said as he guided me around the massive building.

"How many people live in Fortitude?" I asked.

"A couple thousand. Give or take."

"A couple *thousand?* How?"

Legend chuckled.

"Fortitude has been around for almost as long as the exile towns. It didn't take people long to start running away from the towns, which used to be easier when the New Territory first started exiling people. After a while, the officials started realizing things and increased security, but not tremendously. When exiles started disappearing without explanation, that was simply less mouths to feed, and the escaped exiles never seemed to cause them any problems because all they wanted was freedom. It's a little misleading, too. We aren't all criminals. Most of the people were exiled, but there are also people here who simply didn't agree with the way the cities were being governed and decided to run away. Over the years, a lot of the people here started families and made Fortitude their home. We aren't much different than the cities, really."

I allowed him to guide me as I took in my surroundings in silent awe.

"Right this way," he turned around the corner of the club, revealing a simple brick wall at the base of the skyscraper with a steel door situated in the middle. There was a muted rhythmic thumping sound coming from behind the door. Legend pulled on the handle and the door swung open. The thumping turned into music as an expansive room full of a few hundred people was revealed. Inside, there was a sort of electronic song playing loudly throughout the room, shaking the floor beneath my feet.

Devices hung from the ceiling, projecting purple lights around the room. The devices spun and changed direction with the beat of the music, moving the lights around the mass of people in front of me. The people themselves seemed to move as one solid mass, following along with the music as they danced. I stood there staring, taking it all in.

The longer I stared, the more I observed. One woman in a horrifyingly skimpy green dress danced, her backside grinding up against a man behind her who was holding up a glass of some kind of drink, liquid sloshing out of his glass as the lady danced.

Wait… the woman is holding a drink, too. How is she dancing and holding that at the same time?

I looked around some more.

Most of these people have drinks. Is it alcohol? How do they have alcohol here?

"You still with me?" Legend shouted over the music, pulling me from my trance.

I nodded, my gaze bouncing between him and the dancers.

My arm still in his, he guided me straight toward the mass of people.

"Where are we going?" I asked.

"What?" he asked, cupping a hand around his ear. "You're going to have to speak up!"

"Where are we going?" I repeated, louder than before.

"I'm just showing you around," he said, parting a way through the mass of dancers.

"I've never heard music like this," I observed, Legend leading me through the crowd.

"It's called trance music… technically. It's a bit of a mixture of things," he said with a deep laugh.

On the other side of the dancing crowd was a bar. The counter was a reflective metal and the barstools had cushy black seats. It was much fancier than the simple bar back in Rockhallow.

It feels like ages since I tried to rob that bar. I would've never guessed I'd be where I am now just because I tried to steal some rum.

"Sit," Legend said with the same warm grin, motioning to the only available barstool. "What do you like to drink?"

Feeling ironic, I told him I enjoyed rum.

The seat cushion sunk as I sat. Legend leaned casually against the counter beside me, motioning with a quick, two-fingered flick and a nod at a bartender.

Behind the counter, there were a couple girls who could barely be older than me, and there was a guy. He looked to be in his mid-twenties. He was muscular, with a flirtatious grin and messy blonde hair. The male bartender approached Legend with a crystal glass with about an inch of caramel-colored rum. When the bartender tried to walk away to take another order, Legend stopped him.

"Don't be rude," Legend chuckled to the bartender. "You can say 'hello,' friend! She's my guest. She's a lovely girl—she won't bite!"

"Hey," the bartender said with a half-smile and a non-committal nod.

I flattened my lips and nodded back.

"Oh my—" Legend let out a bellowing laugh, throwing his head back. "You two need to loosen up! For heaven's sake, Tophian, you're a bartender! Where are your people skills?"

Tophian let out an exasperated sigh as he smiled.

"Sorry, man, it's just been a crazy night. You know how it is. I'm covering Deb's shifts this week, so I haven't had an evening off all week," Tophian answered.

I swirled the rum around in my glass as he spoke, hesitant to drink.

I've never actually tried rum before. Tried to steal it? Yes. Tried to drink it? No.

"Something wrong with your drink?" Tophian asked.

"What? Oh! No," I giggled. "It's fine."

"You're a bad liar. She's a bad liar, Legend," Tophian teased. "Definitely not from Equivox."

I shrugged playfully. "Got me."

"This could be fun!" Legend said. "Let's make it a game. Let's figure out where she's from!"

I felt my lips stretch into a wide smile at the thought of them trying to guess.

"Okay," I agreed. "Let's see what you've got!"

"Wait, wait, wait!" Tophian stopped us. "Let's make this more interesting. For every wrong guess Legend makes, he has to take a shot—"

"Woah!" Legend interrupted. "She might not be an exile—she might be a city girl. That means *nine* possible guesses! You're either really confident in my guessing abilities, or you want to get me completely plastered!"

"Maybe I'll let you guess on that, too," Tophian joked.

"What happens when he gets it right?" I asked. "*If* he gets it right before he's passed out, at least."

"When and if he gets it right, you have to drink your rum," Tophian proposed, his eyebrows rose enthusiastically.

"Deal."

Legend laughed excitedly, rubbing his hands together.

"Okay, let's see what I've got!" he said, eyeing me. "You're either from Bellicose, Avid, Equivox—which I ruled out! Clamorite, or Delaisse. Or you're a city girl. You could be from Fallmont or Eastmeade, or maybe one of the smaller towns… Rockhallow or Nortown."

He continued to think out loud as Tophian and I listened eagerly.

"You're too quiet to be from Clamorite," Legend mused.

I shrugged with a sly grin.

"I'm not going to help you rule things out. You have to make guesses about where I *am* from."

"Fair, fair," he said. "That crazy cool hair of yours seems pretty artsy. I know some people in the cities have artsy hair, but it's really common in Delaisse. I'm going to guess Delaisse."

I made a honking sound, signaling with two thumbs down.

"Huh!" he exclaimed, his eyes wide and lips turned downward in a look of surprise.

"Bottoms up!" Tophian said, pouring Legend a shot.

Legend tipped back the shot with a grimace and an exuberant howl.

"I bet you're from Fallmont! You're a city girl, aren't you?" he guessed.

"You're terrible at this!" I laughed.

Tophian handed Legend another shot.

"Really, man? You already had a shot ready?"

"I guess that just gave you a hint on how confident he is in your guessing skills, huh?" I smirked.

Legend scoffed, tossing the drink back into his open mouth, slamming the empty glass back on the table.

"She's sassy. I like it! She's gotta' be from Avid or Bellicose. Thieves and aggressors are always confident like that. You don't look too aggressive to me, but I see a competitive streak in you, and I've been surprised by a lot of exiles from Bellicose before who don't look like the type. Is it Bellicose?"

"Is that your next guess?" I asked smugly.

"Yes—no! Yes! Agh! Okay, I'm sticking with yes!"

I held out a double thumbs-down again, sticking my tongue out at him playfully.

"Is it Avid? Really? A thief?" Legend laughed in surprise, tossing back another shot.

"Yup," I admitted, looking down at my glass of rum.

"I have to ask," Tophian started. "I'm always curious what thieves steal when they get caught. Sometimes it says a lot about them. What'd you steal?"

I chuckled airily, staring into my glass.

"Rum."

Both of the boys burst out laughing as I tipped back my glass, swallowing the rum. I choked as my throat began to burn.

"Blegh," I managed, fanning my open mouth dramatically.

"It's been fun!" Legend said to Tophian. "I should probably show my friend here where she'll be staying. Get some rest tonight—stop taking shifts for Deb! I'll see you around."

Legend held out a hand to me.

"Shall we?" he offered.

I placed my hand in his and stood from the cozy barstool.

"Hey—" Tophian called to us.

I turned back around to face him, cocking an eyebrow.

"I didn't catch your name," he said.

"Eos."

"Welcome to Fortitude, Eos."

CHAPTER THIRTEEN

Legend escorted me out of Club Belladonna, leading us toward a shorter, plain building across from the club. The building had a lit awning above the front door, and plain, uniform windows around all the walls.

"What is this place?" I asked.

"It used to be a hotel," he answered.

Upon seeing the confusion on my face, he continued.

"Hotels were where people used to stay when they would travel to other cities and such. They were buildings full of private rooms with their own bathrooms. People would pay to rent a room for however long, and they could stay there."

Sounds similar to Avid, but nice enough for private bathrooms. This might not be too bad.

"What about my friends?" I asked.

Are they wandering around confused right now? Did they find their way into Club Belladonna? Or did somebody else pick them up along the way to show them around?

"They're fine. I'm sure they're just exploring. I'll go

look around for them though, after I show you to your room. If you'd like."

I nodded.

"Why did you only offer to show me around?"

"You stood out to me," he answered simply, approaching the door of the hotel.

"What?"

"I don't mean your looks. I mean, yes, but no. All the women in your group are beautiful ladies. I just meant that you're the one who looked the most lost."

"Great. I'm the most pathetic," I sighed as we stopped outside the front door.

He laughed.

"Not like that. I just mean that your eyes show me that you've been through more than any of them have. It isn't a matter of being 'pathetic.' It's a matter of being tough for too long. It starts to show. The way you were holding yourself… the way you looked up at the lights with a greater look of relief than anyone else in your group… I could tell you needed a little fun. I may have noticed how you looked when you got here, but I also noticed how happy you looked at the bar. You loosened up. You smiled. When was the last time you did that?"

I looked back at him in silence, feeling a sense of relaxation creep over me.

"You're safe here. Come on, I'll show you your room," he grabbed the large brass handle of the glass door, pulling it open for me.

I stepped inside, looking around at the wide room. There was a green marble countertop on my left with a young boy standing proudly behind it. On the right, there was a modest buffet of pastries and fruits on a table against the far wall. The room itself was full of short, mahogany tables and stiff, velvety, scarlet-colored armchairs.

"Sir," Legend said, greeting the young boy at the counter as I moseyed curiously toward the buffet.

Their conversation grew muffled as I found myself browsing the food in front of me, spotting a curious looking machine with two gridded metal plates.

"Alright, Eos, I got you a key to a room," Legend said, walking toward me, twirling a key ring around his index finger.

"You okay?" he asked, noticing me observing the contraption.

"It's a waffle-maker," he said with a chuckle. "I'd offer you a waffle, but they only prepare the batter for breakfast. Do you want something else instead for now?"

"Um," I looked around, spotting a blueberry muffin and picking it up.

"I'll show you to your room. It's on the second floor. There are some nicer hotels here, I promise, but we also have a lot of residents, and naturally, the fancier places have no vacancy."

"That's fine," I said, taking the key from him and following him to a staircase just past the marble counter.

The second floor was one long hallway with cream walls and a gaudy patterned carpet. Every wall was lined with identical doors, each with its own number plate affixed in the center.

"210," he said, stopping at one of the doors. "This is you. I talked to the bellboy and made sure I could reserve the rooms in this hall for you and your friends. I'll go look for them, unless you need anything else."

"I'm not sure how to ask this without seeming creepy, but where do you live?" I asked.

He grinned. "If you need me, look for the big hotel directly across from the entrance to Belladonna. You'll know which one it is—it's the most excessive-looking building in the area. I'm in room 801. You're welcome to come over at any time."

"Okay, one more question," I started.

"Go on."

"What do I have to do?"

"I'm sorry?" Legend asked, a clueless look on his face.

"Do I get assigned some kind of task? Do I scavenge for supplies? I'm assuming people don't just live lives of leisure here. How does Fortitude stay standing? How do you all get supplies?"

"Whoa, sweetheart, slow down," Legend chuckled. "We get our food, medical supplies, even our alcohol from connections some of the people here have with people inside the cities. Family and friends, ya' know? It's a process, but we actually get a lot of supplies. When it comes to clothes, we get new things here and there, but a lot of it is a sort of trade system. We have stores where you can pick out as much as you want, within reason, and you bring stuff back when you're tired of it. Of course, try not to be a slob with your clothes—someone else is going to want them when you trade them in. As for work—the residents here typically apply for different jobs. There's no overall leader, but we've developed a system where different people head different things. There's a family in charge of Club Belladonna, there are people in charge of each of the hotels and restaurants, and so on. Everyone is expected to pull their own weight, but no one really checks to make sure you're working. It's sort of like an honor system. You'd be surprised how cooperative a community with a large population of criminals can be when they're motivated by gratitude rather than law. If you decide to stick around and want a job, let me know."

"I'll keep that in mind," I said. "I think I'm going to wash up and get some sleep. Thanks for everything."

Legend nodded, his eyes seeming to sparkle before he turned and walked off, leaving me at the doorway. The hotel key he left me was a plain, dull gold color. I unlocked my door, testing out the light switch as I entered. The lights worked, illuminating the room in a soft glow. Inside the room, there was a wooden table with two chairs against it. There was a tall brass lamp in the far corner next to a window, which was covered by thick red curtains, and there was a large bed done up with clean linens and thick pillows. I smiled to myself, setting my bag on the floor.

I stepped further into the room, spotting another door on the wall. When I opened it, it revealed a simple bathroom with all of the amenities, as well as some basic toiletry items. I cupped a hand over my smile.

I don't remember the last time I was able to actually shower.

I eagerly peeled my grimy clothes off and hopped into the shower. Within minutes, the bathroom was completely steamed up, and I smelled like eucalyptus as I lathered my hair. The suds in my hair turned brown the more I scrubbed.

This shower is long overdue.

When it came time to wash my body, my eyes locked on the scar across my abdomen. I gritted my teeth, my eyes beginning to burn as I blinked back tears. I stood there, frozen as I remembered the rush of cold fear when Asa had me helplessly laying there as he cut into me. My chest suddenly felt heavy, and before I knew it, I was crying.

I don't know what I did to deserve everything that's happened to me. I was greedy, I stole, but I don't deserve what I've been through. Nobody deserves to go through being tested on by a psychopath, having to watch their friend die, and witnessing their boyfriend being tortured.

I fell to my knees in the shower, my chest heaving as I tried to block out the sobs. Eventually, I gave in, letting it wash over me like the water spraying over my back. After a while, I collected myself enough to rinse off.

When I finished my shower, I put on my spare outfit from my bag and brushed my teeth. The hot shower helped me realize just how sore my legs were from walking for so long. Sleepy and sore, I pulled back the clean white comforter on the bed, curling up underneath. As soon as I shut my eyes to try to sleep, there was a knock at my door. My eyes shot open at the sound, but I closed them again, deciding to ignore the knocking.

Whoever it is can wait. I'm tired, and I'm comfy.

~

The next morning, I woke up feeling like I actually got rest. Feeling lazy, I stretched with an exaggerated groan, going limp again.

I don't have to go anywhere. Just because I found out Fortitude is real doesn't mean I have to leave right away to release the other exiles. I need to scope the place out for a while first, right?

I turned to face the window. The room was still dark, but I could tell the sun was up. The curtains blocked all of the sunlight, yet a tiny sliver of light poked out between the curtains. Lethargically, I moseyed to the window and pulled open the curtains.

Big mistake, I thought as my face scrunched up, my eyes blinking back the light.

As my eyes adjusted to the harsh light, I was able to make out my view. Across from my window was a street. Along the side of the street was a sidewalk lined with storefronts. Directly across from me was what appeared to be a small café. There were little metal tables and chairs outside the café, with people sitting, munching on pastries and chatting with smiles on their faces.

Ooh… That reminds me! There's breakfast downstairs!

I opened my door, ready to run downstairs to snag some food to bring back up to my room when I almost tripped over the large pink gift bag sitting right in front of my doorstep. I bent down curiously, spotting a little white card hanging off of the handles.

"From: Legend. Happy first day of freedom. I hope to see you at Belladonna tonight."

I set the note aside, riffling through the crinkly tissue paper, reaching for the contents of the gift bag. My fingers graced a silky fabric. I pulled the fabric out of the bag, holding the gift up in observation. It was a simple black dress made out of a thin, smooth fabric. It looked rather short, and I've never been one for dressing up. I brought the bag and its contents into my room and set them on my bed. Looking out the window again, I tried to observe what the people all along the street were wearing. None of them were in dresses, so I assumed Legend wanted me to wear the dress to the club, if I decided to go. Leaving the dress on the bed, I went downstairs for breakfast.

When I reached the lobby, most of my group was already down there, sitting at the mahogany tables with plates of food covering the tables' surfaces. Trent and Persephone shared a table, Brenur was busy getting food from the counter, and Gwenn, Eve, Bexa, Astraea, and Yulie crowded around one of the seats at a table, blocking me from seeing whoever was sitting in that chair. As I drew closer, I noticed the blonde hair of Cindee as she sat, face in her palms, sobbing. I felt a lump form in my throat at the sight, and I decided to approach Bexa first.

"What happened?" I asked in a hushed voice.

"Do you remember Braylin?" she replied in a whisper.

"Cindee's brother?"

Bexa nodded.

"What about him?"

"Cindee was looking at the breakfast options and just bust out crying. The only thing we've been able to get out of her is his name. I'm not really sure what the deal is, but I guess something had to have triggered a memory. The poor thing has been like this for about ten minutes now. You missed the worst of it."

I looked at the breakfast counter, spotting the waffle-maker.

I remember Braylin telling me his favorite food is waffles, and I remember him telling me that his and Cindee's mom used to make them fresh waffles. I'd bet anything that the waffle-maker is what set her off.

Fortitude

I gently nudged my way through the wall of girls surrounding Cindee, and I squatted beside her.

"Hey," I started softly.

She didn't look up, but rather kept her face in her hands as her body shook with every sob.

"I think the waffle-maker is a sign," I said.

Cindee stopped sobbing. She sniffed and, uncovering her face, turned to face me with red, swollen eyes and tearstained cheeks.

"What?" she asked, squinting at me.

"Braylin liked waffles. He told me about how your mom used to make them for you guys, and how she would cover them in syrup. I think the waffle-maker is a sign that Braylin is safe," I said genuinely.

She wiped her nose with the back of her hand with a loud, wet sniff.

"The officials snatched him up and we have no idea where they took him or if he's safe! What if I never see him again?"

"You will. After we get established here, maybe we can go looking for him," I suggested.

I still hadn't told the group about the Skeleton Key and my plans to use it to free exiles, but I felt like now was still not the time.

"Do you want to split a waffle with me?" I offered. "I've never had one before."

Still blinking back tears, Cindee scoffed. "You've never had a waffle? Seriously? Did you live under a rock?"

I laughed at her, and she joined me, sniffling between weak giggles.

"I'll be right back," I said, walking over to the waffle-maker. Beside it were little cups and a large tub with a spout. I stared at it for a moment, somewhat confused.

"Cindee," I called, turning to face her. "Are there any special steps on how to make a waffle?"

She burst out in shaky giggles, getting up from her chair and joining me.

"Here," she said, filling a cup with the batter from the tub. "It's easy."

I watched her pour the batter into the metal waffle-maker, closing the two halves of it and twisting the metal waffle mold upside down using a handle. The machine beeped once, and a little digital timer began to count down. When the time ran up, the machine beeped a few times, and Cindee flipped the mold back over and opened it, revealing a fully baked waffle, which she pried out of the machine and onto a plate with a fork. Then, she brought it over to a different tub, this one containing a thick, brown liquid. *Syrup*. She spooned the syrup out over the waffle, being careful to fill every square of the waffle with the sugary goo.

I grabbed a handful of forks and knives, following Cindee back to the table. I handed Eve, Gwenn, Astraea, Bexa, Yulie, and Cindee each a fork and knife, keeping one for myself.

"For Braylin," I said with a smile, cutting into the steaming waffle.

"For Braylin," the girls repeated, slicing off pieces of the waffle.

The syrup oozed across the plate as I brought a large piece of sticky waffle to my mouth. It was sweet and crisp when I bit into it, and I felt some of the syrup stick on my lips as I chewed.

"This is really good," I mumbled excitedly, my mouth full.

The girls all laughed in agreement as we polished off the waffle in a matter of a minute.

Hearing other voices approaching, I looked toward the stairs, spotting Skylar and Zane.

Why are they coming downstairs at the same time? Did they share a room?

I felt my heart sink in my chest as Zane made brief eye contact with me before looking back at Skylar as they continued their conversation on their way into the lobby.

I nibbled on the inside of my cheek as I gawked at them. Zane walked right past me, acknowledging me solely with a disappointed sadness in his eyes, and the two of them began to serve themselves breakfast.

Well that settles that. I'm going to Club Belladonna with Legend tonight.

CHAPTER FOURTEEN

I decided I wasn't hungry anymore, so I hurried back to my room, locking myself inside.

It's like everything we went through together never happened.

I paced across my room, my heart pounding behind my ribcage.

What does he see in her?

My breathing quickened.

Forget him.

I stormed out of my room, locking the door behind me before I left, exiting the hotel and making my way toward some of the shops. Club Belladonna was lifeless without its purple glow. I assumed it must be closed during the day. Walking down the street, I noticed a quirky looking shop about a block away from my hotel. The outside was an obnoxiously ostentatious green, with magenta lettering spelling out *Totty's Trends*. Unsure of what to expect in any of the shops, I decided to check it out. I pulled open the plain glass door, jumping when I heard an echoing ring. There were a few other people in the shop, and they all turned to stare at me as I noticed the metal bell situated above the door.

I remember some of the shops back in Rockhallow had bells to alert the employees when a customer entered. Why did I jump? Has it really been that long since I've been in a normal city?

I pulled my shoulders back and adjusted my hair, trying to play it cool. Everybody went about their business as I began to take in my surroundings. The store was a kind of boutique, with narrow aisles of clothes hung up on long metal racks. In the back corner of the store, there was a sign pointing to a changing room, which appeared to be empty. I began to peruse the rows of shirts, picking out a few that I liked, as well as some new pants. Draping the clothes over my arm, I walked over to the changing room. I tapped gently on the door. It wasn't locked, so I pushed my way inside with my armful of clothes, dropping them on the bench inside the changing room. I tried on the different outfits, setting aside a couple that I liked. When I stepped out of the changing room, I bumped into a petite lady standing with her arms crossed in front of me.

"Sorry," I said, excusing myself as I stumbled out of the changing room with the clothes.

"You're supposed to ask an associate before you use the changing room," she said, using a hand to toss her blonde bob.

"Sorry," I repeated. "I've never been here before."

"It's a pretty common rule."

"I'm new to Fortitude. I just got here yesterday."

"Oh!" she chirped. "My mistake. So, this is your first shopping trip?"

I nodded.

"Has anybody explained anything to you about the exchange program?"

"Sort of?" I said. "I know that I can trade clothes for other clothes whenever, and to keep them in good shape, but I don't know what to do if I only have a couple outfits to begin with, and I doubt anyone would want them— they're really gross."

"Hmm," she hummed pensively. "Wait here."

She hurried away, disappearing behind a doorway partially concealed by the checkout counter. A few moments later, she appeared again, a subtle smile on her face as she returned.

"I wanted to check with my manager before I made any promises. She says you can select as many outfits as you'd like—no strings attached. But just this time. Of course, you can bring them back and exchange them at any time. You can exchange clothes through any other stores as well. Fortitude has some outside connections that provide shops with gently used but discarded clothes from the cities and exile towns. We clean them up and offer them in exchange for other clothes—that way no one person hordes all of the clothes."

"Really?" My eyes widened and my face grew warm. "Thank you so much."

I spent hours carefully picking through the clothes and trying them on until I could make up my mind. I carried my bundle of clothes to the counter as the petite blonde folded all of the clothes and placed them into a jumbo, bright green paper bag, tucking the hangers into the bag as well.

"I really appreciate this," I said genuinely.

Handing the bag over to me with smile, she said, "Of course! Good luck with everything. See you again sometime!"

I left the store and could immediately tell I was hungry. On my way back to my hotel to drop off my bag, I caught a whiff of something sweet and my stomach immediately began to grumble.

Maybe I should get lunch, first.

I remembered the café from my window and decided to go in search of it. It wasn't hard to find once I neared my hotel.

I remember going to restaurants in Rockhallow with my parents, but I don't know how it works here. Do I wait to be seated? Do I just walk away when I'm done eating? Legend didn't say anything about any kind of currency.

"You lost?" I heard a familiar voice from behind me.

I turned, spotting Tophian ambling toward me with a wide grin.

"You lost?" he repeated.

"Umm," I hesitated. "Not lost, per say. More like confused."

"Okay," he said, staring back at me for a moment. "Go on?"

"I don't know how to order food here," I admitted.

He laughed sweetly.

"It's not hard to order food. You just tell them what you want. If you're too scared to talk or something, you can just point to the thing on the menu," his eyes squinted as he laughed.

"No," I let out a slightly amused sigh. "Not like that. I just mean… Do I seat myself? What happens when I'm done eating?"

"I know what you meant. I'm just giving you a hard time. I haven't had lunch yet; do you mind if I just join you?"

"Please," I said, grateful that I could learn by observation.

Tophian strutted into the café, holding the door open for me. A cloud of scents washed over me as I entered. It smelled like fresh bread and cinnamon and coffee. There was a long glass display counter with baked goods behind it, there were little metal tables scattered throughout the café, and the walls were plastered in tacky pale blue floral wallpaper. Tophian led me over to an empty table and pulled out a chair for me. I thanked him and sat down, leaning across the table as I spoke.

"So, you just seat yourself?"

"It depends on the restaurant. This place is one that you seat yourself. You just kinda' play it how you see it. If it looks like a nicer place, you should probably wait to be seated. It's just like in the cities."

"In the cities? Where were you from?" I asked. "Rockhallow never had any nice restaurants. We had a few places kind of like this, as well as a few where you had to wait to be seated, but they weren't 'nice' by any means."

"I've never been to Rockhallow. I know a girl from there though. She works in one of the other restaurants as a chef," he said, thumbing through a tall menu.

He rested his elbows on the little table as he browsed the food options, and the table wiggled with every page turn.

Fortitude

"As for where I'm from… do you mean pre-exile or post?" he continued.

"You're an exile?" I asked, remembering that Legend said some of the people in Fortitude were never exiled.

"Yup. Pre-exile, I'm from Fallmont. Post, I'm from Bellicose."

"Huh," I said, trying not to judge as I pondered what he might have done to be exiled.

"It's killing you, isn't it?"

"What?"

"You're literally squirming in your seat," he chuckled. "You want to know why I was arrested."

"Maybe a little."

"That's unfortunate," he teased, refocusing on the menu. "Did you decide what you want to eat?"

"Not yet," I said, picking up a menu.

The menu had a list of sandwiches and soups. After skimming over it all, I decided that I wanted everything. Nothing on the menu sounded bad, but I settled for the chicken salad sandwich.

"You order at the counter here," he instructed, motioning to the glass counter.

"Ah, okay," I said, nodding my head as I looked at the counter.

"I'll take the beef stew and a croissant with a water."

I sat there for a minute, looking from Tophian to the counter, back to Tophian.

"What?"

"You just order with any of the people behind the counter. They'll bring it out to us when it's ready."

"You want me to order for you?" I asked.

"Yup."

"Lazy," I laughed.

"Nah. Call it a teaching moment."

"I know how to order food at a counter!"

"Oh really? I don't believe you! I guess you gotta' prove it!" he said, lounging back in his chair with a smug grin.

I walked over to the counter with feigned confidence and joined the cluster of people giving their orders. When I was able to make my way to the front, I placed mine and Tophian's orders.

Now what?

I scurried back to the table and timidly asked Tophian what to do next.

"Now, you sit. They'll bring it to us."

At the table, Tophian told me about how he arrived in Fortitude about two years ago, when he was 23.

"A bunch of us left all at once, and I got pretty close to the people in my group on the way here," he said. "I mean, that's bound to happen when you travel with people for days on end through the desert. I still talk to some of them sometimes, but for the most part, we all went our own ways within Fortitude."

"Do you still see them sometimes?" I asked.

"Naturally. I mean, Fortitude is pretty big for what it is, but in the grand scheme of things—Fortitude isn't some endless city. I see them all the time—some more than others. What about you? Did you come with anyone?"

"Yeah," I said quietly. "Our group has had thirteen different people in it, not including myself. We lost one on the way, but we gained another."

I felt my teeth grind as I thought about Skylar.

"You lost one? I'm so sorry to hear that," Tophian said, his voice growing somber.

"I mean, he was taken by officials. We don't know what happened to him."

"He's probably in Ironwood."

"You think so?"

He nodded.

"Why's that?"

"There are a few people here who know friends and family who didn't make it here because they were arrested by officials. Apparently, most of them were sent off to Ironwood. I guess they just assume that, if they escaped one exile town, they can escape them all. Personally, I don't see how anyone could. It's exhausting enough trying to escape one. Heck, it's exhausting waiting for the right moment—the right conditions—to escape one… let alone multiple."

Little does he know.

"They claim that there's no way they can go back to the prison system, but I think they just don't want to try. I think we've had this exile town system way too long, and now the city leaders are just comfortable. I also think they just like being able to justify keeping us out of the cities forever to protect their precious little status quo," he said, aggravated.

"Not all criminals are monsters," I added. "I've met some amazing people who were exiled for things that shouldn't have even counted as crimes."

"Exactly! That's what I'm saying! They want to keep everyone out who doesn't perfectly fit their ideals. They see everything as a threat."

"What I don't get is how the city leaders haven't noticed how many supplies are disappearing. There are more people here than even some of the cities!"

"Well, we have insiders who fudge the ration reports and people who get us shipments of various supplies, but Fortitude has been around for a pretty long time itself, so we have our own food and supply productions, too. If you're interested in a job in that area, let me know. I have a couple friends from that group I told you I was with, and they work in production."

"Thanks, but I'm good. I'm still surveying the options for now."

I also don't know when I'll be leaving again to release other criminals. Should I release them in small groups over time so the officials don't notice? Or would they even notice or care?

"Eos?" Tophian called, snapping his fingers in front of me, pulling me from my thoughts.

"Hm?"

"I asked you if the rest of your group was from Avid," he said.

Apparently, I missed that question.

"Oh. No," I said. "Out of the fourteen total of us, four of us were from Avid. One was from Bellicose, three from Delaisse, two from Equivox, and four from Clamorite."

"Wow! All five towns, huh?" he huffed. "That's impressive. How exactly did you all end up together?"

"I'm not sure exactly how. I was one of the last people to join the group."

"Where are they all now?" he asked. "If you don't mind me asking."

I shrugged. "I don't really care."

"Ouch. Spent too much time with them out there or something?"

"Or something," I groaned, just as a teen boy with bad acne and greasy hair set our drinks on the table before scurrying off to grab our plates.

The food looked amazing. I hadn't had great food since I lived in Rockhallow. The meals in Avid were decent, but we were limited based on what rations we were sent, and ever since I ran away from Avid, I've been living on stolen rations and cans found in ruins. The plate the waiter set down had a thick sandwich made of fresh bread and a heavy layer of chicken salad, a pickle spear, and some french-fries piled up on the side.

I stared down at my plate, speechless.

"Dig in!" Tophian said, ripping off a piece of his croissant and dipping it into his beef stew.

Tentatively and still gawking, I picked up my sandwich, feeling the weight of it in both my hands.

"Something wrong?" he asked.

"This is amazing," I breathed.

"You haven't even tried it yet," he chuckled.

I bit into the sandwich and a medley of flavors filled my mouth.

"Oh my gosh," I mumbled in excitement, my mouth full.

Tophian smiled pleasantly as he continued eating and watching me as I enjoyed my meal. Before I knew it, I had polished off the entire plate full of food.

"Room for dessert?" Tophian asked.

"Dessert?" I asked, my eyes wide as I looked back down at my empty plate, feeling sleepy and content, but incredibly full. "I'm not sure I can eat another bite, but dessert sounds really, really good."

"How about this," he said. "Do you like chocolate?"

I nodded.

He walked over to the counter without another word and returned a minute later with a small paper bag.

"What's this?" I asked as he handed it to me.

"A chocolate croissant. They're my favorite. Save it for later."

"Thank you," I smiled gratefully.

"Of course. Ready to go? Do you just plan on heading back to your room, or do you have more places you plan on shopping?" he eyed my green shopping bag.

"I think I'm going to go rest in my room for a while."

We stood, and Tophian grabbed my bag for me, leading me out the door.

"Are you working tonight?" I asked.

"Not tonight. Finally."

"Are you planning on going to Belladonna at all? Like, for fun?"

"Nah. Not really my scene, despite the fact that I work there. Or maybe it's *because* I work there. It loses its novelty when it's your job."

"That makes sense."

"Why were you asking? Do you plan on going again tonight?"

"I think so," I said, feeling a twinge of guilt when I thought about Zane.

No. You know what? Who cares what he thinks? He isn't even speaking to me right now. I don't have to tell him I'm going, and if he finds out, he finds out. I don't care. I'm not going to spend the night in my room with only my self-pity to keep me company.

"I mean, yes. I'm going. Legend invited me," I corrected myself confidently.

"Oh cool," he replied. "Legend's a fun guy—he makes sure the people around him are having a good time."

We were at the door of my hotel, and Tophian opened the door for me, handing me my bag.

"I enjoyed lunch!" he said. "Let me know if you're ever looking for someone to eat with. I'm usually out and about."

"Thanks," I said, stepping inside.

"Have fun tonight!" he said before the door shut. I

turned back and gave him an unconvincing smile through the glass door before making my way to my room.

When I reached the top of the stairs, I could see another pink bag sitting in the hall in front of my door. Curiously, I approached it, picking it up and unlocking my door. I brought the bag inside, putting my shopping bag on my bed before digging the gift out of the pink bag. Retracting my hand, I pulled out a pair of strappy black heels and a small comb.

I put the heels and comb next to the dress and dumped the tissue paper out of the bag so I could fold up the gift bag and tuck it in the small closet in my room. When I dumped out the tissue paper, I heard a rattle come from the bag. Lifting up some of the tissue paper, I saw a thin, elegant silver necklace.

Wow.

I admired the necklace for a minute before placing it on the bathroom sink.

I really hope the dress and the shoes are my size, or I'm going to feel really bad about not wearing Legend's gift tonight. Tophian and I spent a lot of time talking at lunch, so it's already early evening. Is it too early to get dressed?

Eager and inquisitive, I began to strip out of my old outfit and into the dress. It was a bit snug, but comfortably so. The fabric was stretchy and felt silky against my skin as it hugged my waist and hips. Then, I slid my feet into the heels, strapping them up around my ankles. My feet were blistered from all of the walking recently, but I ignored the nagging pain as I wobbled, trying to steady myself and walk to the full mirror behind the bathroom door.

I haven't worn heels in at least a year. The last time I wore heels was to my great aunt's funeral in Rockhallow. Tonight's going to be interesting.

I traced my fingertips along the wall for balance as I slowly stepped toward the bed, grabbing the comb and brushing out my snarled hair before easing toward the bathroom, closing the door behind me to get a better look in the mirror.

Dang.

I barely recognized the girl in the mirror. My hair, finally clean and brushed, lay in soft black and platinum sheets against my shoulders and falling as far as my chest. The dress was short; coming up past mid-thigh, and the neckline plunged in a deep V shape. I stared at myself in the mirror, unsure of whether I liked what I saw or not.

I should probably get used to wearing heels again before I go to Belladonna.

I stumbled out of the bathroom, deciding to pace around my room until I felt comfortable enough to be in public in heels again. Needless to say, it took a while. Eventually, I figured I was as good as I was going to get, so I flopped backward on my bed with a dramatic sigh.

What time does Club Belladonna even open?

My room was growing dark as the sun began to set. Keeping the curtains open, I flipped the light switch by the door and the light flickered on. I sat back down, picking up the paper bag from the café and taking out the chocolate croissant.

Come to mama.

I munched on the croissant, still feeling full from lunch, but knowing that I should probably eat some kind of dinner.

I may as well head to the lobby and see if I can find out when Belladonna opens.

Knowing I'd have to descend stairs in heels, I mustered up some confidence before leaving my room, locking the door behind me and taking nothing but my room key, which I tucked into the top of my dress. Luckily, nobody was behind me on the stairs, so nobody saw me shakily step my way to the bottom. Once I was in the lobby, however, I heard a voice from across the room.

"*Damn,* E," Bexa said, her jaw dropping. "Going somewhere?"

I suppressed a smug grin.

"Seriously," she continued. "What's the dress for?"

"Wouldn't you like to know?" I smirked.

"Yes, I would. That's why I'm asking!"

"None of your business," I said neutrally.

"E, come on. I'm not mad at you about Skylar's gun and all that drama. What's done is done. It was a crappy thing to do, but I've done far worse. I'm not judging."

I stared back at her with my arms crossed.

"Okay, fine," I caved. "I'm going to Club Belladonna with Legend."

"What?" she asked.

"Club Belladonna is the purple glowing skyscraper, and Legend is that guy who I left with last night."

"And you're going out with him?"

"Yup."

"What does Zane think of that?"

"I don't care."

Bexa let out a disapproving sigh.

"What?" I asked.

"Just give him time. Don't go screwing things up. He's going to forgive you—he just needs time to cool down."

"I saw him and Skylar come down to breakfast together—I think they spent the night together," I revealed.

"Ah," Bexa frowned. "I'm sorry, Eos. Maybe they didn't? Maybe it was just a coincidence of timing?"

I shrugged.

"Either way, I'm going."

"*Yowza!*" I heard a male voice from behind me.

I turned to face Cameron, who was in lounge pants, holding a book.

"You clean up nice," he smirked, falling back into a chair and propping his feet on the table as he opened his book.

"Thanks."

He gave me one last look before burying his nose in the tattered paperback in his hands.

"You might want to get going before Zane comes back and finds out," Bexa advised.

"I don't care what he thinks. And wait—'gets back?' Where'd he go?"

"I'm telling you—don't mess things up between you two. It'll get better."

"Where'd he go, Bex?"

"I don't know. Why does it matter? He was by himself—don't worry about it."

"You're right. I'm going to head out. You're welcome to join if you w—"

"No thanks," Bexa swiftly interrupted.

"I didn't figure," I smiled as I left to walk to Club Belladonna.

The air was a bit chilly, and I could feel goose bumps on my legs as I carefully made my way to the door of Belladonna. The city looked entirely different at night in comparison to during the day. During the day, the streets were full of people chatting with friends, carrying shopping bags or rushing from building to building. Now that the sky was dark, the buildings illuminated in colorful hues, the streets were mostly empty except for a few drunken stragglers and some small clusters of people roaming about, and the only sounds were the rhythmic thumping of Club Belladonna mixed with the occasional rush of wind.

My hand wrapped around the metal handle of the club's door, I took a deep breath, and I pulled the door open. The booming music seemed to flow outward, like a popped cork. Hands clenched, the back of my neck began to sweat as I nervously wedged my way through the crowd, taking a seat at the bar. The two female bartenders from last night were there again, but this time a third female bartender was with them. She was a stocky woman with long, curly chestnut hair and a thin scar on her cheek. She approached me and asked what I wanted to drink.

"Something strong," I answered.

"You waiting on a date?"

"Not exactly. I don't know what it is."

"Sounds complicated. Need to talk?" she asked as she poured me a shot and set it in front of me.

"I'm good, thanks," I smiled weakly.

"Alright. If you need me, holler. My name's Deb."

I nodded before tossing back the shot.

"You're getting drunk before you even see me? Ouch!" I heard Legend speak up from behind me.

Startled, I jumped and choked on the alcohol in my throat.

Patting my back gently, Legend chuckled as he sat beside me.

"How does the dress fit?" he asked, his eyes trained on mine.

"It's shorter than I'm used to, but it fits well."

"Short isn't bad, but if you don't like it, you don't have to ever wear it again. My feelings won't be hurt," he said, letting his eyes wander for a second.

"Okay. They might be a little hurt. But I won't hold that against you."

I felt my face grow warm as I smiled.

"Do you want to dance?" he asked politely.

"I don't really dance," I admitted. "You wouldn't want to see me if I tried."

"I'm sure you're a fine dancer!"

"I haven't really danced since I was little."

"Really? Huh. Any reason?"

"Rockhallow never really had any occasions that people danced at. Weddings were usually the only time people danced, and I was only ever invited to one, and it was when I was maybe ten years old. I didn't even really dance much at the wedding. Other than that, the only time I really danced was at a dance my school had for the little girls and their dads, but they only did that once when I was young."

"You've never danced with anyone aside from your dad?" Legend asked, bewildered.

"Not really."

"Come on," Legend clamped his hand around mine. "No excuses!"

"No, really, I'm okay!"

Ignoring me, he tugged on my hand until I stood from my stool, uneasy on my heels.

"Wait!" I said, steadying myself. "I'm not good in these shoes."

"I've got you. I won't let you fall—I promise," Legend offered his arm.

"If I do, you're coming with me," I threatened playfully.

"Sounds fair!"

I took hold of his arm, using him as a counterweight as I walked. He led me straight into the middle of the crowd. With him by my side, we slid easily through the mass of dancers until he was satisfied with where we were.

When he stopped, I released his arm and stood, facing him.

"Now what?" I asked, looking around me. We were completely crowded in place.

"Just do as the crowd does. Follow the rhythm of the song. You hear the beat?" he asked, clapping his hands to the beat in demonstration.

"They look like they're bouncing or something though," I observed. "Is that all I have to do?"

"Just do as the crowd does," he repeated, catching the movements of the people around us and bouncing in place. He stared back at me in wait.

I hesitated for a moment, studying his timing before I joined, bouncing carefully in my heels.

"There you go! Easy—see? Now add some flair to it! It can be simple," he instructed, throwing his fist in the air in a punching motion with each jump. "You don't have to know how to dance."

I've done things far more terrifying than this. I can do this.

I imitated his arm movement, but it just felt awkward.

"This is stupid," I said, feeling discouraged and embarrassed. "I look like an idiot."

"No, you just need to get your own move. I know you're from Avid, but you don't have to steal my dance moves!" He laughed wildly at his own joke.

Just do something. Anything.

I took my fist down and instead held my hands above my head as if about to snap my fingers, alternating which hand was higher.

Legend let out an excited call as I gained confidence, following the bob of the mass. Suddenly, the song began to change tempo as it transitioned into another song, leaving me dancing to the speed of the original song for a moment until I caught on.

"You're getting the hang of it," he encouraged me.

"Is this all you guys do?" I asked after a while. *This all feels rather repetitive.*

"Why? Are you bored?" Legend's smile faded.

"No—it's just… I was just wondering," I lied.

"I think you just need to loosen up a bit," he said, dancing with more enthusiasm than before.

I smiled halfheartedly, my legs growing sore from bouncing in heels.

"Come with me," Legend said, pausing and offering his arm to me again.

This time, he guided me out of the herd of people and toward an elevator tucked away in the corner of the club. The elevator had stainless steel walls, dim fluorescent lights, a simple royal blue carpet, and circular metal buttons numbered one through thirty. Legend inserted a key into a keyhole below the buttons and pressed his finger into the one marked with a bold "30." A blue ring illuminated around the button, and I could feel the elevator shift.

"What's on floor thirty?" I asked.

"It's a surprise," Legend put a finger to his lips in a hushing gesture.

I watched the screen above the elevator door as red lights displayed which floor number we were passing.

2…3…4…5…6…7…

"What about the rest of the floors?" I persisted.

"Mostly hotel rooms. Some are game rooms, private bars, things like that."

8...9...10...11...12...13...

"What exile town are you from?" I asked, trying to make conversation.

Legend simply put his finger to his lips again.

I sighed.

14...15...16...17...18...19...

I picked my foot up, rolling it to stretch my sore ankles with a crack.

20...21...22...23...24...25...

"I don't like surprises," I stated matter-of-factly.

Legend shrugged with a sly grin.

26...27...28...29...

"You're not secretly a psycho killer, are you? I've had my fair share of those. Please don't take me to the penthouse to kill me," I half-joked.

30.

CHAPTER FIFTEEN

The elevator dinged, pausing for a moment before the metal doors slid open, revealing an expansive lounge room with dark, tawny lights, plush velvet sofas, a tall refrigerator, and windowed walls on every side.

Woah.

"What is this place?" I asked, stepping out of the elevator, gaping at one of the window-walls.

"This is the Belladonna Penthouse Lounge," Legend answered, his arms spread out wide in display.

"Fancy," I breathed, approaching a window-wall and staring out at all of the buildings and people below. I could even see a bit of the mountains beyond the limits of Fortitude.

"Do you want anything to drink?" Legend offered, opening a fridge full of canned drinks.

"I'm fine, thanks," I said, crossing my arms casually as I turned back to admire the view.

"I wish my room had this kind of view," I chuckled.

"It's beautiful, isn't it?" he asked, popping the tab on

a can of soda before joining me at my side. "So, you want to know how I wound up here?"

"Mm?" I mumbled, staring out the window, not wanting to seem overly curious.

"I'm from Fallmont originally. So was Tophian, but Fallmont is a big city—we didn't know each other until Fortitude. When I was 22, I started a business in my city. At 20, I developed a more gas efficient car that would simply use parts of retired trucks used by officials, as well as scraps from outdated machinery. We got the old parts for free from the trash collector. Our idea could cut the gas usage of the cities by nearly half, and we were confident it would work. However, it was difficult to find and convince investors. Plus, the city wouldn't let just anyone have the retired trucks—one would need a *lot* of money to buy one off the city. My brother and I set out to raise funds for a truck. We put every dollar we made aside. We did yard work, housework, errands, even babysitting. After a year, we hadn't even scraped the surface of the cost. We were too optimistic at first, but after that first year, we decided to improvise. My brother and I were always naturally gifted at technology, and one day I came up with an idea to meet our financial needs within four months. We used the money we saved to buy a computer and some simple software. As soon as we set everything up, we began to develop a scheme in which we were able to access the bank accounts of over 6,000 people in Fallmont. After that, we slowly funneled the necessary funds from their accounts into a private account I held. We did it slowly... a few dollars per hit... not enough for it to be detected. In three and a half months, we had enough for one of the retired trucks. We bought the truck, did the mechanical work to upgrade it to be more gas efficient, and a few months later, we had more investors than we knew what to do with. We bought out one of the buildings in Fallmont and dedicated it to the collection of parts, upgrading of trucks, and managing of funds of the company. When there was a mechanical issue with one of trucks that resulted in the engine catching on fire, we lost a lot of our investors."

He paused, and out of my peripheral vision, I saw him take a long swig of his soda.

"When we lost investors, we couldn't afford to complete further research to resolve the engine problem, so we resorted back to our original method of funding our operations. Unfortunately, this time we were in a bit of a time crunch to solve the problem before more of the trucks experienced issues, so we took money out of the accounts significantly faster than we did the first time. Then, somebody caught onto us and reported it to the bank only hours before I went to make a withdrawal. Officials were waiting for me at the bank and took me directly into holding until a trial. During the trial, they were conflicted over whether to exile me to Avid, Equivox, or Delaisse."

"Delaisse?" I asked, turning to face him.

He grew silent, refusing to make eye contact for a moment before reaching into his pocket, pulling out a small metal tin. He opened it, revealing a handful of disk-shaped red pills.

"I don't understand," I said, looking back up at Legend.

"It's called Sanguine."

"What is it for?"

"They're for making you happy, they're for giving you a fun time, they're for making you forget, they're for whatever you need them to be for. The word 'Sanguine' even means 'happy and optimistic.' There are some people here who have been through some serious stuff, and Sanguine can take it all away, even if it's only for a little while."

"I still don't understand," I pondered aloud.

"I knew a guy in Fallmont who made and sold Sanguine under the table. It's an illegal drug—it isn't medicinal or anything. He made some good money selling it, and there was a time while my brother and I were initially raising money for the truck when I tried my hand at selling it. I was pretty good at it, and I learned how to make it myself, though it was cheaper and easier for me to work for the guy who introduced me to it. Things went well until he started demanding every cent of the money I made, rather than the agreed upon cut of cash. I stopped working with him, but I had a couple customers that were insistent upon buying from me. I suppose they grew to trust me and saw me as their dealer, so I made enough just to sell to those select few. When I was arrested, I was found in possession of Sanguine, adding to the complication of my exile. Since I wasn't seen as too much of a threat outside of the cities, they decided against filling a cell in Ironwood. Instead, they held a two-day trial to determine which exile town would be most appropriate for my crimes. In the end, they decided that Equivox best encompassed my crimes: I deceived the bank as well as 6,000 citizens of Fallmont, I made and sold drugs to unwitting people, and I made it worse on myself when I tried to convince the court that I was being framed. Needless to say, they had proof against me and didn't appreciate me blatantly lying, which swayed them in their decision of Equivox. I spent hardly a week in Equivox before my brother picked me up and drove me to Fortitude."

"Hold up," I stopped him. "What do you mean 'drove you to Fortitude?'"

"My brother had one of the trucks we were using for research, so he simply told the gatekeepers that he filled the gas tank and needed to drain it as a part of the development of the next mechanical update. They didn't give him any problems and simply let him go with a trunk full of food and jugs of gas—'to get back when it runs out,' he said. He would tell them he needed to test how far the truck could go before running out of gas, but he needed the additional gas to get back to Fallmont. Instead, he drove straight to Equivox, picked me up, and we drove to Fortitude. He said one of his old school buddies told him about how he heard about a group from Clamorite who escaped and made it to Fortitude. He asked about Fortitude, got whatever information he could, and he was on his way to take me there."

"Is he in Fortitude now, too?" I asked.

"No," Legend answered flatly. "He said it wasn't for him, so he turned around and headed back the way we came."

"Do you know if he made it back or if he got caught?"

"He made it back. And then back here. And then back to the city. And back again."

"What?"

"My brother chauffeurs escaped exiles to Fortitude every month. He does it for me, and a little for them, all under the guise of 'mechanical testing.' Last time I saw him, he told me the business is going really well, and through these monthly trips, he's learned so many other ways to improve travel for the officials."

"That's incredible," I said softly.

Incredibly useful, really. When I begin to free exiles, I really should see about teaming up with his brother to make transportation a heck of a lot easier. He only picks up exiles that have already escaped, but what if he made more trips and transported the ones that I freed?

"You've been through a lot," he blurted. "I can tell. I don't know what you've been through, and I won't force you to talk about it, but I'd be lying if I said I wasn't curious."

I inhaled deeply, contemplating whether I should open up to Legend or not.

It's like climbing the tree in Avid to reach the wall surrounding the town—I just have to jump.

I sat down on the plush couch, which sunk under my weight.

"It's a long story—get comfortable."

I proceeded to fill Legend in on the details of my arrest, my experiences in Avid, and everything up until now—everything except the Skeleton Key. When I mentioned the other exile towns, I merely stated that I had been searching for more supplies, but that I had been aimlessly wandering for a while until I came across a map. It was a lie, but it didn't change the important details of what I had been through. I skipped over my plans to free other exiles, and instead, I told him about Lamb's death, Zane's torture, Asa's hospital, the campers, the chemical sickness in the ruins, and how I lost the trust of my group. When I had finally finished my story, Legend let out an exasperated sigh.

"Damn, Eos. I didn't realize how bad it was."

"What's done is done. I have to live with everything that happened."

"What if I told you that you don't have to?"

"Pardon?"

Legend pulled the metal tin back out of his pocket. The pills rattled noisily within as he opened it, holding it out to me.

I stared at the pills, speechless.

Take one, was the first thought in my mind.

Why am I not more conflicted about this? Drugs are bad— right? They're what lowlifes do for a good time. But Legend said these pills could help… What if they relieve some of my pain? I know he said they aren't medicinal—at least, not in theory. Is it so wrong to want to take pain relievers if they're for emotional pain?

My eyes shifted from the pillbox to Legend, and back again before I tentatively reached for a single pill, thoughts firing in my mind at a million words a minute. I turned the tiny red pill over in my palm.

Even if it gets rid of my pain, my guilt, and my anger for an hour, it's worth it. Unless it's really dangerous. Even then, it's still tempting.

"Does it have any side effects?" I asked, my eyes trained on the pill in my hand.

"Nothing severe. You'll likely feel a little dizzy, a bit jittery maybe. The worst that could happen is that you faint, but out of all the people I've given Sanguine to, only two have ever fainted, and they woke up shortly after. A couple have gotten ill, but not seriously."

"How many people have you given Sanguine to?"

"Almost everybody dancing downstairs has taken Sanguine before."

"That many?"

"Yes ma'am."

Wow. Honestly, I'm sick of having to feel everything that I've been through. I've been through it all anyways—what's the worst that can happen?

I stared at the pill, imagining any potential risks involved but determining that even the potential benefits far outweighed the cost to me.

I reached for Legend's soda can, taking a sip as I popped the scarlet pill into my mouth and swallowed.

CHAPTER SIXTEEN

Legend and I sat there in silence for a while. He watched me, concerned, but I continued to stare at my empty palm.

"How long does it take until it works?"

"Not very long. Fifteen minutes, maybe."

"How will I know if it's working?"

"You'll know."

Minutes crept by slowly.

"I don't think it's working."

"It's been two minutes, Eos," Legend stifled a laugh.

"Why is time going so slow?" I whined.

"You're nervous, so you're thinking too hard about time. That makes it go by even slower. You need to get your mind off of it. Tell me something about yourself—something happy."

"Okay," I pondered. "You remember me telling you about going to that dance with my dad when I was little?"

"Yeah?"

"Well, we were dancing, and I was having a lot of fun. I was really close to my dad back when I lived in Rockhallow. Now, keep in mind, I was really young. But anyways, I was having a lot of fun, and I didn't want to stop dancing, even though I had like three cups of lemonade. Needless to say, I was so determined to dance the entire length of the school dance that I ended up peeing in my dress. I was wearing a pretty frilly dress that my mom bought me, so nobody else noticed until I got home and my mom was helping me get ready for bed."

"You peed yourself the only other time you've been dancing?" Legend asked, biting his lip, his eyes beginning to water.

"Yup," I admitted.

Legend burst out in snort-filled laughter, nearly doubling over on the sofa.

"I was five!" I defended as I snickered.

"Well, think about it this way… You danced today, and so far, you haven't peed yourself. Hopefully the Sanguine doesn't mess with your bladder control."

"Hold up—" I said, my eyes bulging. "You didn't tell me that was one of the side effects!"

Legend flattened his lips, subtly tilted his head, and shrugged lazily.

I gaped at him, my mouth hanging open for a moment.

"I'm joking," Legend admitted with a smirk. "I had you going there for a minute, though!"

"You're a terrible person, Legend," I said with a lighthearted scoff.

"You're not the first person to tell me that, but you might be the first who didn't mean it."

My eyes met his and I exchanged an apologetic gaze before my vision began to grow fuzzy. It was subtle at first. I fixated on his face, and at first it just appeared to be blurry, but the longer I stared, the more it seemed every cell on his face was moving independently of the others until his whole face seemed to faintly buzz.

"I think it's working," I said, still staring unblinkingly at Legend's buzzing face.

"I think so too," he said.

"Why?"

"Well," he muttered plainly. "You've been staring at me for a few minutes now with this incredibly ridiculous and baffled look on your face."

I squished my eyes shut, holding them for a second before opening them. The cells on his face still seemed to buzz ever so slightly.

"Are you ready to go back downstairs and dance for a while?" he asked.

"What?"

"Trust me. It's going to be even cooler than before. The Sanguine is still going to take a bit to take full effect, but you need to try dancing while happy like this."

I accepted his offer and let him help me into the elevator. When it reached floor one, it let out the same quiet ding and the doors slid apart. What originally was a simple room with purple lights and dancing people became a full sensory moment. The beats and sounds of the music felt amplified, and I felt as though it was coursing through my veins with a rhythmic thumping. The lights seemed to swallow me up in shimmering violet particles, and the mass of dancers moved before me in a synchronized wave. Without another word, Legend led me back into the middle of the crowd and he began to dance. My chest began to feel warm. The coziness crept from my torso and along my limbs until I felt an uncontrollable smile begin to form.

"This is what it's like to feel happy, Eos," Legend said, seeing my smile as I started to dance to the beat of the music, no longer caring what I looked like or who was watching.

The music filled my head, and I moved as one with the other dancers. Legend put his hand on my waist, spinning me so my back was to him in one swift motion before putting his other hand on the other side of my waist, using his hands to move my hips in a side-to-side grind. Even though his grip was firm, it felt like a tickle, causing me to shutter. He danced closer and closer to me until he was pressed up behind me, his hands still on my waist.

A few songs later, the sensation of every particle around me moving independently of the others grew stronger, and the particles seemed to move faster. Legend spun me back around to face him, a wide smile on his face.

"I want to show you something," he said, guiding me back toward the elevator.

Just as we were about to step into the elevator, I heard a familiar voice shouting my name over the sound of the music.

I saw Skylar walking briskly toward us, but Legend pulled me the rest of the way into the elevator, causing me to stumble over my heels. He pressed the button marked "7" and a button marked "close doors" as quickly as he could, but just before the large metal doors slid completely shut, an arm jutted into the elevator, stopping the doors and forcing them to open again.

"Can we help you?" Legend asked with a tone of blunt irritation.

"Okay, Mr. Suave Guy… I initially just wanted to ask Eos a question, but what you just did there was hardcore sketchy, so now I think I'm going to take her back to her room, and you're going to leave her alone. M'kay?" She spoke in faux peppiness before snatching my wrist and tugging me out of the elevator and through the club, leaving Legend in the elevator with a befuddled expression etched across his entire face.

"What were you thinking?" Skylar lectured me as she pulled me through the crowd and toward the door of Club Belladonna.

"Uhh," I hesitated, trying to steady myself as she forced me out, my vision altered and my whole body still feeling tingling warmth.

"I knew you were stupid, but I didn't realize you were a total idiot," she grumbled, opening the door for me.

The night air was crisp, with an initial rush of wind, sending my hair fluttering around my head. I continued stumbling after her awkwardly as she pulled me in the direction of the hotel.

"Take the damn shoes off, girl," Skylar said, dropping my wrist.

She stood, hovering over me as I squatted down and pulled off my heels.

"Wait a second," she said as I began to stand again.

She grabbed my jaw and steered my face so I was eye-level with her. "Are you high right now?"

I stared back at her, watching her face as it seemed to vibrate against the shimmering lights of the skyscrapers on the street.

"What did you take?" she demanded.

"I—"

She glared at me angrily.

"It's called Sanguine," I answered.

"Did that guy give it to you?"

I nodded.

"Ugh," she growled, pulling me along again until we reached the entrance of our hotel, where she yanked me by my wrist up the stairs, past my room, where she took out a key and unlocked a door.

"In," she said, holding the door open.

"This isn't my room," I observed, stating the obvious.

"I'm well aware. It's my room."

"Why are we in your room?"

"I'm not leaving you alone tonight. Someone needs to keep an eye on you until the drugs run their course to make sure you're safe."

"I'll be fine," I said. "I feel good!"

"Of course you feel good. Drugs aren't supposed to make you feel bad. If you don't remember though, I'm from Delaisse, and I've seen my fair share of cases where someone took drugs and things didn't go in their favor. So, needless to say, you're staying in here tonight."

Without another word, I flopped backward on her bed with an exaggerated huff. Skylar took a seat in a crimson armchair in the corner of the room, her arms crossed and her face crinkled in concentration as she seemed to search for what to say next.

Eventually, I fell asleep without acknowledging her obvious anger. When I woke up, it wasn't morning. Skylar's curtains were still pulled back, revealing a dark sky and a bright city, and her room lights were on. My head was pounding. I sat up, only to be met by Skylar's continued stare of disapproval.

"Why are you still staring at me?" I asked, massaging my temples.

"Because I've been watching to make sure you're not going to die on me or something. Plus, you're sleeping in my bed, and I can't sleep sitting up like this."

"I can switch," I offered, standing up and almost falling over as my sense of balance faded and my vision went blurry.

"Just stay there. It's fine."

I continued to throw occasional glances her way to see if she was still watching me as I sat there, holding my head in my palms.

It feels like someone is stomping on my brain. This sucks.

The longer I sat there in silence, the more I drew into my own mind.

I'm in Skylar's bed. I wonder if Zane spent the night at her place, or if she spent the night at his. Has he been in this bed, too?

"What's wrong with you now?" Skylar grumbled.

"What?" I looked up at her.

"You look like you just caught a whiff of rotten cheese. Are you going to be sick or something? If you are—go to the bathroom. I don't need you puking on my bed."

"No, I'm not going to be sick. My stomach is fine."

"What's your problem then?"

I sat there, not wanting to speak for a minute. Then, I slowly raised my gaze to meet her eyes.

"You slept with Zane, didn't you?"

"What?" Skylar's face contorted into one of pure confusion.

"You two slept together," I stated.

"Where did you get *that* from?"

"You two walked down to breakfast together."

"That's seriously the only 'evidence' you have?"

"It's enough."

"No, Eos, it's not. Zane and I didn't sleep together. I went knocking on his door that morning so I'd have someone to eat breakfast with. In case you haven't noticed, he's the only one in the group who actually seems to genuinely see me as a friend—"

"—You like him—"

"—*As a friend*. Don't interrupt me. Look… Zane is funny, he's sweet, he's attractive, and he *really* cares about people, but I have no business with him as anything more than a friend. He's taken, and I respect that. It isn't my place to come between that. Zane deserves better than you, Eos, but he's a great person and he deserves to be happy. I can tell you make him happy. That's all I want for him. He's the closest thing to a best friend that I have right now. He took me into the group with open arms despite our past encounter, and he made me feel like I belonged. I had been wandering alone through ruins and desert for longer than you can imagine, so understandably, I was grateful for how openly he took me in."

"So, there's nothing going on between you two?" I asked, still suspicious.

"Nothing. He's just my friend."

"How do I know I can believe that?"

"You're welcome to ask him yourself, but I don't think he'd appreciate the lack of trust you have for him. I'm not going to tell him about any of this. If you want to sabotage your relationship more than you already appear to be trying to, be my guest."

"I'm not trying to sabotage the relationship!" I retorted.

"Really? So, dancing up on some hot guy in a suit, taking whatever drugs he hands you, and leaving with him is you *not* sabotaging your relationship?"

"You saw me dancing with him?"

"Yep. I came in while you two were dancing, and as soon as he saw me making a beeline for you, he started pulling you to the elevator."

"Why would he do that?"

"You tell me. He seemed like the sleazy sort, and I have no idea why you picked him to hang out with."

"He's nice. He showed me around the first night, got us all our rooms, and he gave me this outfit. He's sweet."

"He's sketchy as hell."

"Fine, so he's a little sketchy. But Zane wants nothing to do with me after I hid your gun in his things, and I don't blame him."

"It was a crappy thing to do, and I don't blame him either, but he still cares about you. He just feels betrayed. Everything could go back to normal between you two if you just made it up to him."

"How can I do that though? Simply saying sorry isn't going to magically make everything okay."

"Well, not hanging out with sketchy guys would be a good start."

"Crap. Does he know about Legend?"

"He only knows that you walked away with him the other day."

I breathed a sigh of relief.

"I still don't know how to make it up to him though," I muttered.

"Maybe just try talking to him. Hear him out and see if some old-fashioned communication helps," Skylar said, her words laced with condescension.

I nodded in reluctant agreement.

"I'm going to go talk to him now," I said, attempting to stand. "Which room is his?"

"You're not going anywhere right now. Like I said— you and I aren't friends, but you're just going to make things worse if you try to talk to him when you're like this. Lay back down. You can talk to him in the morning over breakfast."

"Okay," I agreed, my headache getting worse. "Fine."

I lay back down.

"Are you sure you don't want the bed instead? You should get some sleep, too," I offered.

"I'll live."

Without another word, I dozed off again. This time, when I awoke, the lights in the room were off, the curtains were closed, and it was entirely dark. I woke up to an echoing thud from the ceiling above the bed. Sitting upright swiftly, I listened for more noises. Just as I began to let my guard down, there was another sound from upstairs—this time it was a crashing sound, followed by another thump. I tried to look to Skylar in her chair despite the darkness of the room. I could see a figure there—she was still in the chair.

If she were awake, she probably would have said something about the noise.

I let my bare feet drop off the edge of the bed as I sat up. This time, my head was feeling better. It was still pounding, but the pain was dulled, and my balance had improved substantially. I tiptoed to the door, slinking out and shutting it carefully behind me. The hall lights were bright and disorienting at first as I stood there, blinking rapidly. When my vision had adjusted, I quietly made my way for the stairs to the next floor. At the top of the stairs, I visualized where Skylar's room was located on the second floor in order to figure out which door on the third was the room making all the noise. I approached the door, consciously light on my feet. The door itself was left cracked open, so I gingerly pushed it open with a cautious finger, craning my neck to get a better look into the dark room. Identical to the other rooms, this room had a large window on the far wall. The curtains were pulled open, allowing enough light from the other buildings, especially

Club Belladonna, to illuminate the interior of the hotel room in a muted purple. I caught a glimpse of the figures inside the room and immediately covered my mouth, throwing myself out of view from the doorway. Inside was a man squatting beside another man, who was on his back on the floor. The squatting man clearly had a knife in hand, and the man on the floor was presumably dead.

Taking a deep breath and holding it, I peeked once more into the room. This time, I was able to make out blood dripping from the knife in the one man's hand as he stood, the droplets of blood appearing deep violet from the light as they dripped from his blade. Just then, I was yanked backward by my hair, and someone's hand shot over my mouth.

"My room, *now*," Skylar hissed.

She pushed me toward the stairs, following behind me as we ran to her room, keeping our weight on our toes to prevent as much noise as possible.

When we reached her room, she shut the door behind her, locked it, and flicked on the light.

"What—" I managed.

"I saw it too. I don't know who they were or what exactly happened, but I figured we didn't want to be around him long enough to find out," she said, breathing heavily, her hands on her knees and her hair draped in front of her face.

"Should we warn the others? What if their doors aren't locked? We don't know what that guy wanted with the other one. What if he comes after someone else?"

"Okay," she said, closing her eyes in thought before continuing. "We're in room 204. I'll take 201 to 205, you can take 206 to 211. Brenur and Yulie are sharing a room, and so are Trent and Persephone, so we only have eleven rooms. Just tell them to lock their doors. Be careful. Wherever you spend the night—lock the door. I'll see you in the morning."

She got up and speed-walked to room 201.

In the morning? Wherever I spend the night? I guess she means I'm good to sleep in my own room now, hence why she assigned me rooms 206 through 211… because I'm room 210.

I knocked on the door of 206, but there was no answer. I knocked again and a groggy Bexa pulled open the door from the other side.

"Eos? Is everything okay?" she asked, her hair out of its bun for the first time since I had met her. It was wavy and a bit frizzy, and it came down to nearly her waist.

"Lock your door and keep it locked until the morning. Some guy upstairs killed someone. Skylar and I are warning everyone to lock their doors," I said, trying to keep my voice even and calm.

"Seriously?" Bexa asked, her mouth gaping. "I thought I got away from that kind of stuff when I left Bellicose. Thanks for the warning! Are you going to be okay?"

"Yeah. I just have to let a few people know. Be safe, okay?"

"You too," she said, closing her door. A second later, I heard the heavy *thunk* of her deadbolt.

I proceeded to warn the inhabitants of rooms 207 and 208—Cameron and Astraea. At room 209, I knocked multiple times with no response. Just then, Skylar quickly approached me from down the hall.

"Cindee is spending the night at Gwenn's. She's

normally in room 209. She's safe," Skylar informed me before reentering her room and bolting the door.

I nodded, skipping room 210 and going straight for room 211.

Knock, knock, knock.

"Coming," I heard Zane call from inside.

My veins turned to ice at the sound of his voice.

Crap. What do I say? Do I just give him the same warning as the others? Do I try to talk to him?

Before I could decide what to do, Zane opened the door. His hair looked devoid of its usual gelled styling, and he was in shorts and a grey t-shirt. I clearly woke him up.

"Uh," I hesitated.

His serious eyes scanned me over in the black silk dress without a word.

"I need to talk to you," I said boldly.

Zane stepped aside, beckoning me into his room with his arm.

He shut the door behind me and turned on the lights.

"Lock it," I advised.

"What?" Zane asked, taken aback.

"Skylar and I saw a man upstairs. He killed someone, and we've been warning the group about it."

"Is everyone okay? Shouldn't we leave?" Zane began to panic.

"Everyone's fine. Everyone locked their doors. We don't know what the guy's motive was, so hopefully he has no business with us."

"Did he see you and Skylar?"

"No," I said confidently.

"Good," he breathed, sitting on the edge of the bed. "What did you need to talk to me about?"

"Everything I did. I want to come clean about everything, and then I'll hear you out. If you decide you never want to talk to me again, that's fine," I babbled nervously, sitting beside him, a puzzled and intrigued look on his face. "I cut Skylar's shoelaces, I made it look like a mouse got into her granola bar, I made her drink a lot of laxatives by pouring them in her water, I hid her gun in your things, and then I went dancing with another guy tonight because I thought you and Skylar slept together but she told me you didn't, and I'm so sorry for everything."

I began to sniffle, letting my face fall forward into my hands, which were palms-up on my knees. He sat beside me silently for a moment before placing a hand on my back, rolling it in gentle circles.

"I forgive you," he said. "I've given it some thought, and if some guy had wanted to join our group like that and you were that eager to let him in, and if you became buddy-buddy with him like Skylar and I did, I'd probably do worse than what you did. Heck, Luka and I really messed with you when you first came to Avid. I got what was coming to me, hey?"

I giggled weakly, wiping my nose with the back of a hand.

Zane stood, returning with a couple of tissues from the bathroom. I nodded in gratitude, taking them and blowing my nose obnoxiously.

"So, the laxatives," Zane said with a light chuckle.

"The water bottle she shared with me?"

"Yeah," I mumbled guiltily. "I never meant for you to drink it."

"That was brutal," he said with a huff. "I don't think my colon has ever been as pristine as it was after that. I'm just grateful it was while we were in some ruins with bathrooms, however non-functioning they may have been. A toilet that doesn't flush is better than having to do that in the middle of open desert!"

I laughed feebly, and my laughter turned into sobs. I felt terrible. I never meant to hurt him or cause this much trouble.

"Eos," he said delicately, dropping to his knees in front of me as I sat at the edge of the bed crying. "It's okay. It was funny after the fact. I'm not mad at you! I promise! I love you!"

"Why?" I managed.

"Why what?"

"Why do you love me? I'm a terrible person. I'm greedy, I'm petty, I'm irrational," I whimpered before blowing my nose again.

"You're not a terrible person. You've saved me before—you're selfless. You helped lead an entire group of good people to their freedom—you're important. You handle emergencies with grace and wit… most of the time," he chuckled. "You're entirely rational."

I looked up from my lap, meeting his eyes. Even if you put Zane's eyes in a crowd of a million other eyes, I could pick his out almost instantly. I stared into his eyes for a moment while neither of us spoke.

"You've been put into situations no one should ever

have to go through. You're entitled to a few mistakes. I think people would be concerned if you went through everything you went through and *didn't* act out somehow. You're the strongest person I know, E."

"I bet Bexa could beat me in an arm-wrestling match," I joked.

"Bexa could beat *anyone* in an arm-wrestling match," Zane smiled.

Still kneeling in front of me, Zane took my hand and kissed the top of it, squeezing my fingertips.

"Do you want to spend the night here?" he asked. "I think I'd feel better knowing you're here anyways, considering there's apparently a psycho in the building."

"Yes, please."

"I have some sweatpants and a t-shirt you can wear to bed, if you want. Might be more comfortable than that dress, though I quite like it on you," he smirked.

"The fact that you're even insinuating that I'm attractive when I have this much snot smeared on my face… that's love right there."

Zane chuckled, fetching his sweatpants and shirt from the closet.

"I haven't even had a chance to wear them yet," he said, handing them to me.

In the bathroom, I caught a glimpse of myself in the mirror. My eyes were puffy and undeniably bloodshot, and my hair had turned into a tangled mess. The dress had begun to ride up, showing more of my thigh than I would have wanted, had I noticed before. I slid Zane's clothes on. The pants were too long and drug beneath my feet as I shuffled sleepily to his bed. Zane was already lying in bed, but when I opened the bathroom door, the lights were off and he wolf-whistled at me from the bed with a goofy grin.

"C'mere," he said, pulling back the blanket for me.

I crawled in, letting him cover me with the plain white comforter. Exhausted, I snuggled up against him and he draped his arm across the top of my pillow, allowing me to nuzzle up even closer to the side of his chest. He was warm, and things finally felt right again.

I don't ever want to leave.

CHAPTER SEVENTEEN

The morning came too quickly.

When I woke up, I was in bed alone. The curtains were drawn back, letting the warm sunlight fill the room, and there at the foot of the bed was Zane, holding a tray with a plate and a glass on it.

"I brought you breakfast," Zane said with a sweet smile, showing me the tray.

There was a glass of juice and a plate with a giant waffle on it.

"What's that on the waffle?" I asked, staring in suspicion at it.

"Chocolate pudding," he answered, his smile wide.

"On a waffle?" I questioned. "And for breakfast?"

"I don't see why not!" He sat on the bed with me, placing the tray on my lap carefully.

I took the fork and knife from the tray, carving off a hunk of the chocolate pudding waffle, turning it over on my fork as I looked at it.

Just try it.

I stuffed the forkful into my mouth and chewed.

Well, it's the thought that counts.

"So?" he asked excitedly. "How is it?"

"It's..."

"Not good?"

"It's edible," I smiled apologetically.

Zane laughed.

"That's fine. It was just an idea. I can go get you a normal waffle, if you want."

"This is fine," I said, cutting off another piece and offering it to him.

"So, because you don't like it, you want me to suffer too?" he teased.

I nodded enthusiastically.

He bit off the chunk of pudding waffle and moaned overdramatically.

"It's *so good!*" he said in a muffled, full-mouth voice.

I raised an eyebrow at him with a smirk.

"Okay, well it's not amazing. But it's really not that bad!" he defended.

We finished off the rest of the waffle together, talking about the shops and restaurants we visited the previous day. After we finished, I returned to my room to get ready. Sporting a flowy metallic top and simple black jeans, I made my way to the hotel lobby to speak to the bellboy about what Skylar and I saw last night. I didn't feel safe wandering around last night with a murderer in the building, but I felt better about being out this morning now that it was daylight.

A different young boy than my first night was standing at the counter in the lobby, this one's face was covered in acne scars, his curly brown hair sitting in a lifeless lump on top of his head, and his nametag labeled "Corbin" was crooked.

"Hi, Corbin," I greeted him, reading his nametag.

"Good morning, ma'am. Can I help you?"

"I wanted to report something I saw in the hotel last night," I started, lowering my voice.

"Of course," the boy said, taking out a notepad and a pen. "I can submit any complaints to my manager."

"Well, this is a little more complicated than a complaint," I said awkwardly. "There's a man on the third floor who was killed."

"Again?" the boy huffed, setting down the notepad.

"Wh—" I stopped. "What do you mean 'again?'"

"Ma'am, this is a city full of criminals. Sometimes people are killed. It happens. And it's a hassle to clean. Do you happen to know the room number?"

"I—"

"No worries. I'll find it. Third floor?" he asked, rummaging through a supply closet behind him and pulling out a small machine.

"Don't you want to do something about the killer?" I asked, bewildered.

"There's nothing I can do about him or her," the boy responded politely.

"You can report him or arr—"

"Arrest him? Where would we put him? We don't have our own exile towns… We are sort of against the concept. We also don't have a prison. Fortitude holds a belief system of ultimate freedom and the quest for personal happiness. The most I can do is report it to the manager, but the most she can do is investigate and request that the guest finds a new living arrangement. Based on how he sounds, I don't foresee him taking that very well, but my manager is tough," he chuckled. "Would you like me to inform her?"

"Please," I huffed impatiently.

"Yes, ma'am." Grabbing the notepad and pen, he scribbled a note before walking up the stairs with his machine.

I growled in frustration, storming away.

I feel obligated to handle the situation somehow, but the only way to take care of the killer is to kill him myself, and I'd rather not step into that territory again. We just have to make sure we keep our doors locked at night… Maybe I should see about moving us to a different hotel. Legend might have some suggestions for my predicament. Hopefully he isn't mad at me for Skylar pulling me away. He wouldn't blame me for that, would he?

I left the hotel alone, making my way in the direction of Club Belladonna, remembering how Legend said his hotel was the most excessive hotel in the area and was located right across from the entrance to Club Belladonna. When I reached the doors of the club, I turned around with my back to the door, scanning the city for an excessive-looking building. When Legend called it excessive, he wasn't lying. I had never noticed his hotel until I was looking for it—it was blocked in part by a large, plain skyscraper between his hotel and the club, but I could see his peeking out behind it. It was an ostentatious skyscraper with mirrored windows on all sides and light-up signs covering large chunks of its surface advertising things such as sodas, boutiques, and restaurants. Once at the front of the hotel, I passed beneath an awning before the door. The bottom of the awning was completely covered in lightbulbs, which flickered different colors that were visible even in the brightness of the day. The doors spun in a bizarre rotating fashion, but once inside, I could understand why Legend would pick such a strange hotel. The inside had a grandiose cream marble staircase, a classic black piano in the center of the wide-open marble floor, a crystal chandelier suspended above it, and a sleek black bar counter at the far end of the lobby.

Fancy.

"What are you doing here?" chimed a cheerful voice to my left.

"Tophian! Hi!" I greeted him with a brief side hug. "I'm looking for Legend's room."

"There's an elevator at the top of the stairs. He's in room 801. Just coming for a visit?"

"Something like that. There was an incident at my hotel last night and I don't really know what the protocol is in Fortitude for stuff like that."

"An incident?" Tophian pried, his smile fading.

"A man was killed in my hotel, and the kid at the front desk said that's normal. That's anything but normal! Killing people is bad. Dying is bad. The way that kid seemed unaffected by it all—bad."

"Yikes."

"Is there anything I can do? Is there someone who

can look into the murder or anything? I don't want something to happen to one of my friends."

"Not really, unfortunately. I hate to break it to you, but your bellboy was right. Murder is fairly commonplace anywhere in Fortitude. You're also right though—it's bad. There's nothing anyone can do though. Criminals come to Fortitude to be free, and the moment we start restricting that is the moment we become just like the corrupt cities."

"Isn't letting people get away with literal murder a bit corrupt itself?"

"Definitely. I'm not saying I agree with it, but when you run away to a city comprised of criminals, you're bound to come across ones with truly bad intentions."

I let my shoulders slump in defeat.

"But hey, look, maybe Legend can give you some advice or something. I don't know. If nothing else, being friends with Legend has a lot of perks. He's incredibly connected in Fortitude, so I'm sure if you asked, he could work something out for you. You're already here, so you may as well talk to him."

I nodded, saying goodbye to Tophian before heading upstairs.

The elevator was similar to the one in Club Belladonna, but instead of 30 floors, this one had 16. I tapped the button marked with an 8 and watched the doors slide shut. Once on the eighth floor, the elevator dinged and the doors opened. The hallway paired well with the elegance of the lobby—the floors were polished black tiles and the walls were pristine white with a few portraits of important-looking people placed carefully on the walls. I turned left and walked the length of the hall until I reached the end—room 801.

I rapped on the door a few times and stood stiff, waiting. A minute later, the doorknob turned and Legend opened it, greeting me with a wide smile.

"Eos," he said taking my hand and kissing it. "Come in!"

"Whoa," I breathed upon seeing the interior of Legend's hotel room.

It was hardly a "room."

Legend's door opened up to a spacious kitchen with a high ceiling. Connected to his kitchen was a dining room complete with a long table, set as if for a large family. Beyond the dining room was a modern looking living room with plush couches similar to that of the lounge in Belladonna. There were multiple doors connected to the living room that I assumed led to a bathroom, a bedroom, and perhaps another bedroom.

"Do you like it?" Legend asked, opening his fridge and taking out a pitcher of water with lemon slices floating in it. "Water?"

"Sure," I answered as he poured us both glasses.

"Did you just come to visit?" he asked, handing me the glass and pulling out a chair at the dining room table for me.

"Not exactly," I admitted before telling him about the incident at my hotel.

"Ah, yes," he said, sipping on his water. "I hate to tell you this, but Tophian and the bellboy know what they're talking about. Murder and every other crime out there eventually come up here. Murder is one of the less common crimes around here, but it definitely isn't rare, especially when we get the occasional bloodthirsty

Bellicose. Most of them were arrested for foolish reasons and aren't genuine threats to the people around them, but naturally there are some that are truly aggressive for no reason."

"Is there anything you can do about it?" I asked, feeling hope fading.

Legend sighed.

"Not really," he answered. "I made sure you and your friends were in the nicest hotel here with vacancy. I can move you all to another one, but it won't be as nice or as safe as the one you're in now. We mostly just have outer edge hotels with vacancies, and the farther out you go from the center, the more riffraff you'll find. However, if you want me to move *you* to a nicer hotel, I can. There are a couple vacant rooms in some of the nicer hotels, but not enough to keep your friend group together. Some would have to stay in your current hotel. If that's something you'd be interested in though, it can be arranged."

"I can't leave them there with some psycho living near them," I answered without hesitation. "Believe me, I'd love an even nicer place. I'm grateful for where we're at, I just want my friends to be safe."

"Understandable. Just know that there's really nothing more I can do. Sorry, sweetheart."

"It's fine," I said, disappointed.

"So, I have to ask," he said after a couple seconds of silence. "What was your friend's deal last night?"

"We aren't exactly friends," I said.

Even if she isn't a boyfriend-stealing tramp, I still don't really like or trust her. I'm grateful that she respects Zane though.

"As for her 'deal,' I don't know. I think she sees it as

255

me being unfaithful to my boyfriend, who also happens to be her best friend."

"Boyfriend?" Legend asked, his grin melting.

"Yeah. One of the guys in the group I came here with. The one with brown hair. Average height. Kind of skinny. His name's Zane."

"I see," Legend's voice faded. "And you? Do you think you were being unfaithful?"

"I'm not sure. I was mad at him when I first got here. It's a long story. I kind of wanted to rebel in a way, you know? I figured he'd never forgive me for the thing that caused a bunch of drama between us in the first place, so I wasn't really afraid of messing things up any more than they already were."

"And now?"

"Now everything is better. We worked out our issues," I nodded continually to myself as I spoke.

"I take it you don't want to go back to Club Belladonna with me tonight?" Legend asked, his voice warm and inviting, yet tainted with a hint of disappointment.

"Probably not. I'm sorry, Legend," I said genuinely. "I had a lot of fun though—thank you. Sanguine was fun too, but I think I need to stay away from it. I need to learn how to cope with my past, not stuff it in the back of my mind."

"Can I give you something?" Legend asked, beginning to rise from his chair beside me.

I nodded and he disappeared into one of the connected rooms, appearing a moment later with a new dress. This one was slightly longer than the black one, and it was a shimmery robin's egg blue. In his other hand, behind his back, he revealed a set of matching flats. With a contagious smile, he handed the shoes and the dress to me.

"Thank you," I said, taking them graciously. "How are you getting so many things for me without trading in all of your own clothes?"

"I have connections," he chuckled warmly.

"Well tell your connections I said thank you," I said, holding the dress and shoes before me, admiring the way the light reflected off of them.

"I know you didn't like how short the last dress was, and you weren't too comfortable walking in heels, so I figured this outfit was a good fit for you."

"Yes, thank you," I said, folding the dress and draping it over my arm. "I should probably get going, but it's been really nice visiting."

"Alright," Legend said, escorting me to the door. "If you're ever bored, feel free to visit again. I loved having you here! Or if you ever feel like rebelling again, let me know."

Legend winked subtly with a sly grin before shutting the door after me.

Back at my hotel, I hung the dress up in my closet before walking to Zane's room. I tapped gently on the door to get his attention. He answered with a book in hand and a sweet smile on his face.

"How has your morning been?" he asked, letting me inside.

"Good," I said. "I saw some friends and visited with them for a while. You?"

"It's been pretty uneventful. Cameron gave me this book and told me I should read it. I guess he finished the whole thing in a day and figured I'd like it," he said, flashing me the cover before folding the corner of his current page and setting the book down. "Have you had lunch yet?"

I shook my head.

"Eos, would you like to go on our first official date?" Zane smiled toothily.

"I'd love to," I said with a giggle.

"There's a little café next to the hotel that has really good food. How does that sound?" he asked, putting his shoes on.

"If it's the same one I'm thinking of, it's the one I tried yesterday."

"Is that a bad thing?"

"Not at all, actually."

Zane held out his hand when he reached me at the door.

I stared back at him, confused on what he wanted.

"Take my hand," he laughed. "I'm trying to hold your hand."

"Oh," I blushed, taking his hand and walking with him. Before leaving the hotel, he locked his door behind him.

"If there's a murderer in our building, it wouldn't surprise me if there's a thief," he stated. "Oh, *wait.*"

~

At the restaurant, Zane and I ordered our food at the

counter together and found an empty table.

"I've been meaning to ask something," Zane started. "Just a quick matter of business and then I promise I won't be so serious on our date."

"Okay, shoot," I said, crossing my legs.

"When do you want to go back to the New Territory with the Key? You still want to free the other exiles, right?"

"Yes," I said, internally dreading the trek back to the New Territory, and then back to Fortitude. "How about we leave in a week? Give us a bit more time to get to know the place and rest up before we make that trip back."

"Sounds like a plan. Who all do we invite to come with us?"

"I think it should be just you and me," I answered plainly.

"Really? Just us?"

I nodded.

"Why's that?" he asked.

"It's always been us. I also don't want to put anyone else at risk, and we don't need everyone in the world knowing about the Key."

"You still don't trust them with the Key?"

"I do, but I think it's just best to keep as few people involved as possible," I said.

"Alright. Me and you. One week. It's a date!"

"I think this date is going to be better than that one," I sighed.

"No doubt," Zane snickered. "That hike sucked. Big time. But it's the right thing to do."

"It is. By the way," I sidetracked. "I made a friend here who has a brother who owns a truck. He drives between the New Territory and Fortitude every month. I could talk to him about joining his brother, which could make the trip a lot easier. I can't believe I almost forgot his brother has a truck!"

"That would be amazing! Imagine how much faster and easier that would be," Zane babbled excitedly. "We could at least get a ride back to the towns from your friend's brother. I doubt we could get a ride back to Fortitude because we will probably have a lot of people with us, and they'll need us to guide them."

"I know, but it will cut the travel time there drastically," I stated.

Just then, our food was delivered to our table and we began to eat as we continued talking about less serious things than helping exiled criminals escape.

"Have you been to the club yet?" I asked Zane.

"Nah," he scoffed. "Not really my thing."

"I didn't think I'd like it either, but I had fun. So, you're saying you wouldn't go with me if I asked?" I grinned cheekily.

"I'd rather not, but if you asked, I would," he sighed in a woe-is-me fashion.

"We don't have to go," I said. "I was only curious. I wouldn't be heartbroken if we never went to the club together."

"How about, instead of going to the club tonight, we go on a walk around Fortitude after dark tonight? The city is really pretty at night, and you and I haven't had a whole lot of time one-on-one since we joined up with everyone else."

"I think that sounds amazing," I said, taking an unflatteringly large bite of my sandwich, a glob of tomato squishing out the back and landing on my plate with a *plop*.

Zane laughed, snacking on his fries as he watched me in amusement.

"Wear something pretty tonight," I teased with a cheesy wink and a grin.

"You have lettuce in your teeth," Zane said, almost choking on his soda while laughing.

~

After lunch, we made our way back to the hotel, where Zane went back to reading his book and I decided to take a nap beside him to pass the time. As I slowly drifted off, Zane held his book open with one hand and softly stroked my hair with the other until I was asleep.

Hours later, I woke up from my lengthy nap to Zane gently nudging me.

"E, do you want to get ready for our walk soon? It's getting dark out and the lights are starting to really show," Zane asked sweetly.

"Sure," I groaned as I stretched and sprawled across the bed.

Lethargically, I pushed myself into a sitting position, taking a moment before standing to my feet and ambling to my room. When inside, I pulled the dress off its hanger, put my hair in a messy bun so I could shower without getting my hair sopping wet, and I changed in the bathroom, pairing the dress with the same necklace as the previous night. This dress felt much more comfortable—I didn't feel concerned about bending over and flashing everybody. The bright, sparkly blue contrasted with my streaked hair, and the fit of the dress flattered my shape in a more subtle and natural way than the black silk dress. Not only that, but I could actually walk in these shoes.

As I was combing out my hair, there was a knock at the door.

I set the brush down and answered the door. When I opened it, there was Zane, wearing a simple black suit and a smile. His hair was in its usual gelled style as he stood proud, a hand behind his back.

"Well, *hel-lo*, gorgeous!" He whistled, looking me up and down.

My face grew warm as I smiled uncontrollably.

"You look nice, Zane!" I said, shutting and locking my door behind me.

When I turned back to face him after locking my door, he was holding out a single red rose.

"My lady," he said with a goofy smile.

"Thank you," I said, taking the rose and kissing him on the cheek.

"Shall we?" he asked, offering his arm.

"Who knew you could be such a gentleman?" I teased.

"I've always been a gentleman; I don't know what you're insinuating!" he said sarcastically, leading me downstairs and out of the hotel.

"Yeah, sure! Remember when Luka stole my towel and my clothes in Avid and you just gawked at me and

made fun of me?" I reminded him, a tone of jest in
my voice.

"Hey! Not fair! If I was naked and ran into you, you'd
stare at me too, don't even lie!" He laughed.

"Touché."

Outside, it was fairly warm in comparison to the
previous night. There was a soft breeze that smelled faintly
of tangy saltwater mingled with the intoxicating aroma of
fried food.

"What about that time you stole the Skeleton Key
papers and ran off to find the Key without me?"

"Hmm," he pondered aloud. "Okay. You got me.
That was a jerk move. I was terrible to you in Avid. I
didn't used to be a jerk, and I'd like to think I haven't
really been one since Avid. I changed in Avid and became
someone I didn't like. I was cynical, rude, selfish, and
everything else I hate."

"You're better than that now," I reassured him.

He turned to me with a smile as we walked.

"I have to ask," I said. "I want to pick your brain a
bit, if you don't mind."

"Go on," he replied.

"Is this somewhere you'd want to spend the rest of
your life?"

"Meaning?"

"I guess I just mean that, after we help free as many
exiles as we can, do you plan on living in Fortitude
indefinitely? I mean… I know there will always be more
exiles over time, and we could save them, too. But as far as
'home,' would you stay here?"

"I'd like to think so. You?"

"Me too," I said. "Maybe eventually we can move out of the murderer's hotel and into a nicer one, when and if rooms open up."

"That'd be preferable," Zane chuckled. "You know, when I was younger, I never imagined growing up and living with a murderer as a neighbor."

"I can't say that's something I dreamed up either," I laughed.

"I'm glad we can make light of it, but I really do feel bad for that guy you said he killed last night. I wonder if the murderer was provoked or if he just did it for no reason. You said you didn't really see what either of them looked like?"

I shook my head.

"I'd feel a lot better if you continued staying in my room at night, if you don't mind. I just like knowing you're safe," he said, his eyes began to look sad.

"I think that's a great idea," I said.

It isn't that I'm scared necessarily. I feel like I've been through enough that I could protect myself, but I'm not going to turn down an offer to stay in his room again.

We continued wandering through the city's streets, admiring the lights in and on each of the buildings, pointing out the ones we thought were the most pretty or the most ridiculous. When it started to get really late, we turned around and made our way back to the hotel.

At the hotel, Zane decided to stay downstairs and have a snack before bed, but I went straight upstairs to start getting ready for bed. As I climbed the stairs, I heard panicked chatter and someone was crying. I ran the rest of the way up the stairs, spotting a cluster of my friends crowding around one of the doorways. I joined them, standing on tiptoes to see over them and into the room.

"What happened?" I asked Cameron, who was at the back of the group.

"I think someone got hurt," he said. "I just got out here and haven't been able to figure out."

I felt my heart sink, so I wormed my way through the group at the door until I was beside Bexa.

"Who got hurt?" I asked.

She looked at me solemnly before speaking.

"Someone attacked Yulie while Brenur was away. She's bleeding pretty bad, but we don't know if there's even a hospital here."

CHAPTER EIGHTEEN

I felt my skin go instantly cold as I stood there, trying to process the situation.

"Let me through," I demanded, pushing my way into the room.

Yulie was lying on the floor, clutching a bloody towel to her abdomen. Letting out pained wails, she writhed on the floor while Brenur leaned over her, frozen.

"When did this happen?" I asked him, trying to stay calm.

"I—" he stuttered, tears forming in his eyes.

"We need to get her some kind of medical attention. I know someone who would know where to go. Keep pressure on her wound and I'll be back as soon as I can," I said, turning on my heels and darting through the human barricade.

When I sprinted through the lobby, I heard Zane shout something after me, but I didn't stop. The air felt cold against my bare legs as I ran, and my feet pattered rapidly in the blue flats as they hit the pavement. I reached the door to Legend's hotel and barreled through the revolving doors and up the marble stairs, nearly tripping on the slick floor.

Once I reached the door to room 801, I began furiously pounding on it with my white-knuckled fist.

"Legend! Open up! Please!" I cried, panting between every word. "It's an emergency!"

The door opened and Legend stood there, staring back at me with eerie calmness.

"You okay?" he asked, watching me as I tried to catch my breath.

"My friend. She's been stabbed. She's pregnant. Is there anyone here we can take her to for medical help?"

"Of course! Fortunately, she lives in this hotel as well. Fifth floor. I'll go with you," Legend offered, leading me to the elevator with a quick step.

On the fifth floor, he directed me to one of the rooms, where he knocked at the door, calling for a woman named Holly. When the door finally opened after what felt like ages waiting, there stood a tiny redheaded woman with tight curls in her hair, a pink nightgown, and noticeably chapped lips.

"Legend!" she chirped upon recognizing his face. "How are you, old friend? I haven't seen you in a while. Why the late night visit? Who's your friend?"

"This is Eos. A friend of hers has been stabbed… a pregnant woman. Are you up for a house call?"

"Of course!" She ran inside and returned with a large duffle bag before shutting her door.

"Aren't you going to grab shoes?" Legend asked, staring at her pale bare feet.

"Not necessary," she said, speed walking to the elevator. "If someone has been stabbed, especially a pregnant woman, every second counts. Come on—I don't know where I'm going!"

We followed after her into the elevator, and from there I led the way, rushing back to the hotel. When we reached the second floor, I shouted to everyone at the door to move out of the way for the doctor.

Holly made her way through the crowd and into the room with Legend following her. Before I could get a view of what was going on, everyone clustered around the door again, forcing me to hang back in wait.

This is too much like what happened to Lamb. What if we didn't get to her in time? We didn't have a professional for Lamb, but is there really that much Holly can do for Yulie? I can't handle another friend dying like this.

The more I thought about Lamb, the more the scar across my belly began to burn. I felt my heart racing as I began to hyperventilate.

I need to leave.

Clutching my stomach, I raced downstairs to the buffet, where I poured myself a cup of water. I took a seat, chugged the water, and sat there with my face in my arms on the table as if I could block out everything around me.

"E?" I heard Zane call. "Are you okay?"

I heard his footsteps as he approached me, followed by the sound of the chair beside me scraping against the floor as he sat down.

"I heard what happened," he started, his voice deep and uneven, refusing to break down. "Is it just me, or does it feel like we've been through this before and it didn't end well?"

I could tell he was treading lightly, trying not to mention Lamb's name, as if it was simply her name that triggered me.

"It isn't just you," I said, muffled by my arms, my head still down.

"Maybe this time will be different. You found a doctor who can help her! All we can do now is wait."

We sat there, my face buried in my arms and Zane's hand placed tenderly on my back until we heard a bunch of people storming down the stairs. I peeked up, spotting Brenur, Cameron, Skylar, and Bexa all carefully rushing Yulie out of the hotel, with Holly and Legend leading them. Cindee, Eve, Astraea, and Gwenn all trailed behind, their paces slowing to a trot as the group left the hotel in an obvious panic.

"Where are they taking her?" Zane asked the girls who stuck behind.

"Dr. Connors said Yulie needs to be brought into her clinic on the other side of the courtyard. I guess it's really bad," Gwenn said, her sentence growing more incoherent with every word as her speech turned to blubbering sobs.

"She's going to be okay, Gwenn," Cindee said, wiping tears from her own eyes and throwing her arms around Gwenn.

Eve joined the hug, wrapping her arms tight around Gwenn and Cindee, while Astraea stood beside them, petrified and speechless.

"You too," Eve said, grabbing Astraea and pulling her into the hug.

"Are you going to be okay?" Zane asked, lowering his face and resting his cheek on the tabletop beside my head.

"What are we going to do?" I asked softly so the girls wouldn't hear.

"We're just going to have to wait and see if she's okay," he answered.

"I don't mean about that, Zane. What are we going to do to protect everyone? Are we really going to bring a bunch of criminals here and hope that they all get along? That they'll be safe? That they themselves aren't crazy?"

"There's no guarantee on any of that. We have to have faith. Saving them is the right thing to do."

"Is it?" I began to doubt. "Maybe not all exiles deserve their freedom. I know a lot exiles that are amazing people, but there are clearly some that don't need to be anywhere near innocent people."

"You do realize that the dangerous ones are going to be in exile towns with the good people, too, right? There's nothing we can do to distinguish, and even if there was, I don't think it'd be as easy as choosing all except them to free."

"I don't think there's an easy solution, but I think there's a solution," I started to ponder, my voice trailing off.

"What is it?"

"The prison system."

Zane chuckled for a moment, stopping abruptly when he realized I was serious. "The cities did away with the prison system except for Ironwood, and they've only sent a couple people there a year. How do you expect *us* to start a prison system?"

"I don't."

"I don't think I understand what you're getting at."

"We need to talk to Raine Velora and convince her to reinstate the prison system."

Zane's face contorted into one of both amusement and extreme concern.

"E, you're just upset. You're in shock. That idea won't work. You know that."

"It could, though!" I said, sitting up. "Think about it. It has been so long since the war—there are plenty of people to start up another prison. It could start with one. Every exile could have a retrial to determine whether they are put in prison or released back into the cities!"

"Back into the cities?" Zane huffed. "Think about what you're saying, Eos. Raine would never go for that."

"What have I got to lose if I tried speaking to her? I could go to her peacefully. Even if I'm caught on the way, I'll be brought to her ultimately anyways through a trial, and I could tell her then. There's no reason not to reinstate the prison system! Instead of life sentences to exile towns, people could be sentenced to prison for different amounts of time depending on the crime. That would allow the people who aren't completely terrible to once again be with their families *and* they can be contributive members of society. There's no reason not to try!"

I was standing at this point, my voice growing squeaky and defensive. Eve, Gwenn, Cindee, and Astraea were staring at me as if I had two heads.

"Please, sit down. Let's talk about this," Zane said, trying to calm me.

"Legend's brother lives in Fallmont. He drives

between Fortitude and Fallmont all the time! I could see about staying hidden in his car and he could deliver me straight to Raine's doorstep. Then I just have to get into the city hall like we did before."

"Do you really think she's going to listen to an exile who has escaped her precious exile towns numerous times? Not to mention, you threw acid on her officials. I don't think she's your number one fan."

"What have I got to lose from trying?" I asked.

"Oh, I don't know!" Zane mocked, his face growing red in anger. "Your freedom? Oh! Your *life?* Hell, Eos, this has to be the stupidest idea you've had to date!"

"So, we're just going to sit around and let people attack our friends? Are we still going to help the exiles to Fortitude so they can have their freedom, then sit around and watch people attack each other? Or worse?"

Zane stood, arms crossed, sucking his teeth for a minute before he spoke.

"I'm coming with you," he said matter-of-factly.

"Wait, what?" I asked, his change in heart catching me off guard. "Why'd you change your mind?"

"I didn't. I just don't want you going alone. I don't agree with you, and I think this idea is reckless and ill-thought, but when has anything we've done been safe or logical? We escaped not one but *five* exile towns… some of them more than once. We've broken into and out of multiple cities. All for a key. I think our reasoning now is a heck of a lot more selfless than it was when we first went after the Key. I may not agree with the method, but I agree with the heart behind the mission. You're doing this to protect the people you've grown to love, and some people you've never even met. So, I'm going to go to protect the person I've grown to love."

Zane uncrossed his arms to wrap them around me.

"How are you so optimistic after everything?" he asked.

"Honestly, I'm not sure I believe everything I'm saying. I just know that I thought everything here was going to be perfect, and it wasn't. Terrible things even happen here. But I'm sick of feeling sorry for myself and my situation—I have no right to complain about it if I'm not willing to risk everything I have to change it."

"When do we leave?" Zane asked, still holding me in his arms. I could feel his heart racing anxiously.

"As soon as we can. The next time I see Legend, I'll ask him when his brother is visiting next to see if he can give us a ride when he goes back to Fallmont."

"And until then?"

"We just try to stay safe and keep everyone else safe," I lowered my voice into a whisper. "Don't let anyone else join us. The more people we have, the harder it's going to be to get in without a lot of attention. Plus, if I bring in a big group of other exiles to speak to Raine, I feel like she's just going to see it as me rubbing it in her face that a lot of people have escaped the towns. I'm sure she's not oblivious to it, but I want to keep the peace as much as possible."

"I think you're right about that," Zane agreed. "What do we do until Legend is back and we can ask him about his brother?"

"I guess we just wait. I really think we need to distract those four before they all have panic attacks," I said, glancing over Zane's shoulder at Gwenn, Eve, Cindee, and Astraea.

"We should take them somewhere. Shopping? Dessert date? Dancing? What's even open this late at night?"

"Let's take them to Club Belladonna. We don't have to dance. We don't even have to stay there very long. Let's just get them a bit tipsy and relaxed." I smirked at the thought of the four of them drunk.

"Can you imagine Astraea drunk?" Zane whispered with a muffled chuckle. "She's so quiet, but I bet if you get a couple drinks in her, she won't shut up."

"I'll take you on that bet," I said with a confident grin.

"Hey, girls," Zane said, dropping his arms and approaching the four. "How would you feel about going to the club for a while to try to get our minds off everything?"

"Shouldn't we see if we can visit Yulie?" Eve asked.

"I don't think the doctors want people visiting her tonight. Let's give it a day so they can do everything they have to do," Gwenn advised.

"So, does that mean you want to go to the club?" Zane repeated. "Honestly, there's nothing we can do right now, so it's best to not think about things for a while."

Eve and Astraea looked appalled by the notion of fun during such a time, but Cindee immediately started smiling and jumping.

"That's *exactly* what we need!" Cindee chimed.

"Do we need to wear anything special?" Gwenn asked, eyeing my shimmery blue dress.

"Anything you've got is fine," I said. "Some people dress up, some don't. Your outfit is cute anyways—you'll be fine."

"Lead the way!" said Cindee.

The six of us left the hotel and made our way to the door of Club Belladonna. Even Astraea and Eve had an air of gratitude about them when we stepped foot into the club. It was as if they forgot everything else they had been through the moment they were enveloped by the sensory experience of the dance floor.

"This is incredible," breathed Astraea beside me.

"This way," I led them toward the bar, where Tophian greeted me with a warm smile and a shot of rum.

"Rum?" I asked with a giggle. "Is that necessary?"

"Yes ma'am! Drink up!" He let out a bellowing laugh.

I rolled my eyes playfully and drank the shot with an involuntary grimace.

"This is Zane," I introduced. "Gwenn, Cindee, Astraea, and Eve."

"Welcome to Club Belladonna," Tophian said, nodding to each of my friends. "I'm Tophian."

"Weird name," I heard Astraea mutter to Eve as the four of them sat in the barstools.

"As if you have room to talk, Trae," Eve retorted mockingly.

"A shot of something strong for each of the girls, please," I asked.

"Sure thing," Tophian said, pouring a bunch of shots.

He leaned over the counter, beckoning me closer with a finger.

"How drunk do you want them?" he whispered to me.

"Plastered."

"Will do," Tophian grinned, pouring extra shots and distributing them, three to each of the girls.

Without hesitation, Gwenn tossed back each of the three shots.

"Slow down, girl!" Cindee stared in shock at Gwenn. "I can't keep up!"

She downed her shots with a little gasp after each.

Eve and Astraea were a bit more reluctant, but upon watching their best friends down their shots, the two of them followed.

After a while at the club, everybody was talking and making jokes, and Cindee tried to stand, deciding that she wanted to dance. She had barely gotten off of her barstool when she stumbled and nearly fell to the floor before Zane caught her, helping her back into her seat.

"I think you should just stay there for a while," he said, steadying her on the stool.

"I think Zane's right," Gwenn said, her movements loose and uncoordinated. "You know what else I think? I think *you're* cute."

She turned to Tophian, a dead stare on her face.

"Me?" Tophian chuckled as he polished an empty glass.

"Uh-huh!"

"Well, thank you!" He smiled, setting the glass down and picking up another.

"Dance with me!" She giggled, pointing a finger floppily at Tophian.

"I would, believe me, but I'm working right now. And I don't think it's a good idea for you to stand, either. Are you free tomorrow night? I don't have work, if you'd like to come back and dance with me," he offered.

"Did Tophian just ask Gwenn out?" I asked Zane, quiet enough where the music would prevent Gwenn and Tophian from hearing me.

"I think so," Zane smiled. "Good for them!"

It's because of the good people like them that we go through what we go through.

"Do you want to dance?" Zane asked after we watched drunken Gwenn flirt with Tophian for a while.

"What?" I asked, caught off-guard.

Zane held out his hand, a sincere smile stretched across his lips. I took his hand and let him lead me to the dance floor.

"Do you know how to dance?" I asked, watching him.

My hand still in his, he twirled it over my head, spinning me and pulling me in close before dipping me.

"Not in the way these people dance," he grinned smugly, holding me in a dip before kissing me and pulling me back up.

"When did you learn how to dance?" I asked, stunned.

"Long time ago. My mom made me learn. She told my brother and I that we'd never find girlfriends if we didn't know how to dance," he chuckled, guiding me around the dance floor with swift steps, spins, and dips.

"They're so cute!" I heard one woman coo as she danced with a group nearby, watching Zane and I.

As the song ended, Zane dropped me into one last dip, and few people around us began to applaud. Some of the women smiled and fanned themselves with open hands.

"Keep him!" one woman said, grabbing and squeezing my hand as Zane and I made our way back to the bar.

I smiled at her with a nod, trotting to catch up with Zane.

Back at the bar, Gwenn was still flirting with Tophian, who was now leaning over the counter, clearly enthralled by their conversation. The other three girls giggled and chatted amongst themselves, unaware of their surroundings.

"I think it's time we head back to the hotel," Zane suggested to the girls.

"Aww, come on! Don't be a party pooper!" Eve crowed, another drink sloshing around in her hand.

"Yeah! Zane poops at parties!" Astraea burst out in uncontrollable giggles.

I stared at Zane, stifling a laugh myself.

"Yeah, Zane," I teased. "Don't poop at the party."

"Oh, shut up." He grinned before offering to help Eve and Astraea stand.

"It was nice meeting you," Tophian said to Gwenn.

"Before I leave," Gwenn started. "I have to tell you a secret."

"What's that?" Tophian asked, leaning closer to Gwenn as she sat forward with her hand out, as if ready to cup his ear and whisper to him.

Instead, she slid her hand onto his cheek and planted a kiss on his lips.

"Yay, Gwenn!" Cindee cheered, clapping enthusiastically, almost falling off her stool.

"Let's go," I urged Cindee, helping her out of her stool. "Gwenn?"

"I'm coming, I'm coming," she grumbled before throwing a flirtatious smile and wave to Tophian.

Zane and I served as leaning posts the entire walk back to the hotel. Every few steps, one of the girls would inevitably lose her footing, grabbing onto us and sending us nearly falling to the ground with them.

At the hotel, Zane and I helped the girls into their respective rooms, taking their keys and locking the doors behind us as we left. Before returning to our rooms, we slid their keys under each of their doors.

"Staying at my place again?" Zane asked, a hopeful spark on his face.

I nodded sleepily.

Just as Zane was unlocking his door for us, I heard Legend come up the stairs, calling my name.

"There you are," he said upon spotting me, calling me over to him. "I've been looking for you."

"How's Yulie?" I asked before he could say another word.

"Dr. Connors thinks she's going to be okay," he said, his expression looking grave.

"Why don't you look happy?" I asked, walking over to him. "Something's wrong."

"Dr. Connors doesn't have a ton of experience with babies, so she had me go get one of her coworkers who does. Her coworker had a look at your friend, and she isn't feeling overly optimistic about the baby," Legend apologized.

"What's the word?" Zane called, still standing at his doorway.

I turned to him, my eyes stinging.

"Yulie is fine, but they don't think the baby is going to make it," I muttered, trying to keep my voice steady.

Zane stood staring, his gaze moving from me to Legend, back to me as he silently processed.

"There's *some* hope—they're doing everything they can to save the baby," Legend continued.

"Thank you for the update," I said, my face solemn.

Legend nodded.

"Do you need anything?"

"I don't think so. Just keep me posted if you hear anything. Please," I asked.

"Will do," he said, turning to retreat down the stairs.

"Wait!" I called after him, remembering something.

"Mm?"

"When is the next time your brother comes to Fortitude?"

"He's already here. He's spending the night in my guest room. Why?"

"He's already here?" I asked, my mouth open in shock.

"Yes? Is that a problem?"

"Quite the opposite," I said. "Legend, I need a favor."

CHAPTER NINETEEN

I explained to Legend how Zane and I needed to catch a ride with his brother back to Fallmont. Initially, I didn't plan to tell him our reasoning, but as I saw the suspicion on Legend's face grow, I decided to confide in him.

"You're insane," he said, resting one of his hands on top of his head as he puffed out his cheeks in an exasperated exhale. "There's no way you're convincing her."

"We have to try," I pleaded. "Things aren't working the way they are."

"Yes, they are," Legend argued. "They're just fine. If people want their freedom bad enough, they'll escape just like you did, just like I did, just like nearly everyone here did. Things back in the New Territory suck, but there's a way out. Why would you subject people to time in prison? That's worse than anything!"

"Only the dangerous people would really spend much time in prison!" I retorted. "It would be safer for everyone, and it would let people like my friends go back home after serving a sentence. I've lost a close friend because of the exile town system that might have lived if things were different. Now, I can't change the way things were, but I can change the way things *will* be! I'm going to Fallmont with or without your brother's help, but if he's willing to drive us, it'd save us a lot of time, energy, and resources."

"I'll let you talk to him," Legend submitted. "I don't want any part of this, but if you can convince him—more power to you."

"When is he leaving again?" I asked.

"Soon. Probably tomorrow or the day after. He never stays long—it would arouse too much suspicion back in the city."

"Can I meet with him tomorrow?"

Legend nodded.

"I'll be by after breakfast."

Without another word, Legend turned away and left the hotel.

"Sleep?" I asked, looking over at Zane.

"Yes, please," he said, opening his door for me and locking it behind us.

"Are you sure you want to do this, E?" he asked as we got ready for bed.

"Do what?"

"Go to Fallmont… All that?"

I nodded confidently, my face melting into a serious expression.

"Are you sure you want to come with me?" I asked.

He nodded back.

"You really don't have to," I said, picking up Zane's sweatpants and t-shirt. "I can do this. And if I can't, I don't want you to end up in more trouble with me."

"I'd rather be sent to Ironwood for life with you than be stuck here wondering what happened to you and never being able to see you again if something goes wrong."

"I love you," I said, putting the change of clothes down on the bathroom counter.

"I love you too," he hugged me, his hands pressed flat against my back as he held me tight.

For the rest of the night, we didn't say a word about Fallmont. We speculated about whether Gwenn and Tophian would actually go on a date the next day, whether the girls would wake up with terrible hangovers, and whether Persephone and Trent would ever try to hang out with the group again.

The next morning, I woke up in bed alone and decided to go back to my room to get ready. I stripped off the clothes I had borrowed for the night and stepped into the scalding shower.

This might be the last hot shower I ever have. If this doesn't go well in Fallmont, I could spend the rest of my life in Ironwood. That's where Raine Velora wanted to send me after the first time she caught me. I can only imagine how persistent she's going to be about sending me off this time. I need to make sure she hears me out. I'm not going to let up easy—I'm not risking my freedom without at least planting a seed in Raine's head.

I stayed in the shower, simply enjoying the warmth of it and the eucalyptus scent of the hotel soap. After eventually drying off, I finished getting ready and went downstairs for breakfast. In the lobby, I grabbed an apple and a cup of oatmeal, sitting at an empty table. There were a few other people downstairs, but nobody I recognized. Thankfully, none of them looked like the murderer on the third floor.

While I munched on my apple, Bexa came downstairs, made a waffle, and joined me at my table.

"I heard you're going to Fallmont," she bluntly stated.

"What?" I asked, surprised. "Who told you?"

"I want to come with you."

"Nope."

"Why not?"

"I don't need more people coming with—it'll just make Raine mad that there are more escaped exiles. She already knows I escaped. I'm not about to risk exposing everyone else."

"What about Zane? And I can keep my mouth shut about everyone else. Let me come with!"

"Is Zane the one who told you?"

"No. Eve did. Let me come with."

"No! I don't need more people with—it'll make things more complicated."

"You don't trust me?"

"Bex! Seriously?"

"What?" she growled.

"Honestly," I said, lowering my voice. "I don't even want Zane going. I don't want anyone else to have to lose anything. The reason I'm even willing to try this is to help people like you, like Zane, like Gwenn, and Eve, and Astraea, and Cindee, and Yulie, and Brenur, and everybody else. I don't want anyone to get hurt or get locked up for life. Why let multiple people end up in prison when only one might have to?"

"Are you sure about this?"

"No," I answered honestly. "I'm not. But things aren't going to get better for anyone unless somebody is willing to step up and sacrifice something. Quite honestly, I've been through so much—I can handle it. Even if I end up locked away for the rest of my life, I'll be at peace if I know that I was successful at least in planting the idea in Raine's mind of restarting the prison system. I'll know that there's a chance that my friends can be free, can be reunited with their families, and can be safe."

Bexa nodded in understanding.

"How will we know that it worked? We're all the way over here in Fortitude, and I doubt news of the New Territory will travel to here."

"You know that guy I brought here the other day with the doctor?" I asked.

"The tall, dark one?"

"Yes. His name is Legend, and long story short, he has a brother who lives in Fallmont and he drives to Fortitude once a month. I'll make sure Legend finds out from his brother what happened, and he can relay the news back to you all."

With a nod, Bexa wished me luck and gave me a prolonged hug before making her way back upstairs.

I guess it's about time I meet Legend's brother.

I left my hotel and walked toward Legend's. I wanted to walk leisurely and enjoy this freedom—just in case—but the harder I tried to clear my mind and mosey to Legend's, the quicker and more purposeful my steps became until I eventually reached his door.

I knocked a few times and waited until Legend opened the door, greeting me with his usual warm smile.

"Come in," he beckoned.

I entered his suite and took a seat in the dining room.

"Zaire will be out in a minute. He's had a lazy morning." Legend chuckled. "You want anything to drink?"

I shook my head.

"Actually," I jutted. "A water would be nice."

My throat felt dry and scratchy the more I thought about having to confront Raine Velora. My first encounter with her was less than ideal—after her officials captured us, she proceeded to have them torture Zane in front of me to gain insight on the Skeleton Key. Despite the fact that there are four cities in the New Territory, each with their own leaders, Raine Velora possessed more power than any of the others. As the leader of Fallmont, the largest city in the New Territory, Raine's word was law.

Legend poured me some water and went over to one of the other doors, knocking on it and calling for his brother.

"Be patient, brother!" I heard a man's voice tease.

A moment later, Zaire opened the door and joined Legend and me. He was clearly related to Legend, with a similar smile, eyes, and even voice, but he was shorter, with thicker arms and a rounder face. He had thick freckles speckled solely on his nose, but instead of wearing a suit like Legend, he was wearing a button-up and dress pants.

"Zaire, this is Eos," Legend said motioning to me. "She's from Avid."

"Hi," I said awkwardly, standing from my seat and shaking his hand.

"Legend told me you're looking for a favor," Zaire smiled pleasantly.

"Yes," I started. "My boyfriend and I need a ride to Fallmont."

Zaire burst out in laughter that died out slowly as he met my serious gaze.

"Oh," he said, his smile fading. "You aren't joking. Why would you want to go to Fallmont? If you're an exile, officials would arrest you on the spot, and they'd take me with for bringing you."

I began to explain my plan to him in full, watching his posture as I spoke. He crossed his arms and cocked an eyebrow as I finished by telling him my reasoning.

"Look," he said. "You sound like a sweet girl. You have good intentions—I can tell. Please understand that I can't bring you to Fallmont. It's too risky. My life is good—I've got more freedom than the average citizen. I don't want to throw that all away. I really want to help—I do. But driving two run-away exiles straight to the center of the biggest city in the New Territory?"

"I know, I get that. Please think about it though. You wouldn't have to be seen with us. We could hide in the trunk or the backseat. Cover us with something so we aren't visible. We're going to Fallmont whether or not we have a ride, but you could save us a lot of trouble. We walked the entire way from there to here already, and a lot happened to us on the way that we'd rather avoid completely on our way back, if possible."

"If I do it... *if...* I'm not dropping you off on Raine's doorstep. That's like me locking the handcuffs on myself. I could let you out somewhere inconspicuous in Fallmont and give you directions, but after that, you're on your own. You've never met me, I've never seen you in my life."

"That's fair."

"Look, I've spent a long time building our company up. I've got money, I've got connections, I've got freedom, I've got everything I could want. Do you realize what you're asking me to put on the line?"

"Yes. But you know what you're missing?"

Zaire rubbed the bridge of his nose, staring intently at me.

"Your brother. I know this won't magically bring him home, but think about all the other families broken up forever by the exile town system. If you help me do this, you could help bring families back together."

There was silence for a moment before Zaire spoke up.

"I'm leaving in about an hour. My truck is at the edge of the road leading into Fortitude. Make sure you and your boyfriend are ready to go in an hour. Meet me there."

"Thank you so much," I said, shaking his hand once again, giving him a grateful, yet somber look.

I left Legend's place, returning to my hotel to share the news with Zane, who met my words with extreme relief.

"I'm just glad we don't have to walk all that way," he sighed, the tension on his face melting. "He's a life saver. Probably literally. Who knows what we would end up going through on the way back, especially with just the two of us."

"Have you told Skylar yet that we're going to Fallmont?"

"Not yet. Why?"

"I just figured you'd tell her first, since she's your best friend," I couldn't help hiding the hint of bitterness in my voice.

"E," Zane started, his voice soft and apologetic. "She's not my best friend. You are."

I smiled and squeezed his hand.

"I mean, she's a close second or whatever. Sometimes you're tied and I wait for you girls to duke it out and fight for my affection." Zane poked me impishly.

"You're a jerk," I teased.

"And you're not wrong." He laughed. "I guess I should go tell her though. I'll meet you in the lobby when it's about time to head to the truck."

I nodded, watching him walk off to Skylar's room and knock on her door.

I guess I should say goodbye to some of my friends, too.

I decided to knock on Bexa's door first, wanting to see her again one more time before leaving. I didn't anticipate leaving so soon.

There was no answer at her door.

What if I never see her again? What if this morning at breakfast was my last time seeing her?

I began to feel a familiar lump form in my throat as I stood at her door, pathetic and growing depressed.

Fortitude

I can't think like that. If I tell myself that this isn't going to work, or that I'm going to end up in Ironwood the rest of my life, I'm going to accept defeat, and I can't let that happen. Even if things don't work in my favor—I need them to work in the favor of everyone who has been exiled for life despite being wonderful people.

Next, I tapped on Cindee's door. Before she answered, Brenur came out of his door and went to lock it, a book in his hand.

"Hey, Brenur," I called him out of his focused trance.

"Oh," he said upon noticing me. "What's up?"

I filled him in on Zane and my plans and he seemed mildly unphased, a focused look continually residing on his face.

"Is everything okay?" I asked him. "Is Yulie getting better?"

"She is, thanks. Dr. Connors and her friend seem to think the baby's chances have increased. Yulie is on bedrest for the rest of her pregnancy though, and she's already stir crazy. I came back to get her something to read," he said, holding up the book.

"That's great news about the baby though! I have faith that things will be okay," I said, mustering up an encouraging smile, despite all of my own concerns running through my mind.

"Thanks, E. Be careful out there, okay?" He hugged me and hurried out of the hotel with the book.

Just as we finished exchanging our goodbyes, Cindee opened the door, her eyes red and teary, and snot smeared under her nose.

"Cindee," I gasped. "What's wrong?"

She tried to speak but burst out in high-pitched sobs, throwing her forehead against my shoulder in defeat.

"Is it about Braylin?" I guessed.

She shook her head, continuing to cry.

"What is it?"

"Y-you're l-l-leaving," she sniffled. "A-and Zane."

"It's okay, Cindee!" I hugged her. "We'll be fine. This is for a good cause. Everything will work out—I promise."

"I'm never going to see you guys again!" she wailed, running the back of her hand under her nose with a loud snort.

"You don't know that," I said.

I don't want to get her hopes up and tell her that she will see us again, but I don't want to freak her out more and tell her I'm already anticipating being moved to Ironwood.

"Please be careful," she said. "They took my brother and I don't want them to take you too."

"I promise I'll be careful."

She nodded, her sobs dying off into whimpers.

I said goodbye to her and proceeded to visit Gwenn, Eve, Astraea, and Cameron, filling them in on varying levels of details of the mission Zane and I were going to embark on. After finally saying goodbye to each of them, I checked Bexa's door one more time with no response.

I guess it's about time to go.

I returned to my room, packing my bag with whatever clothes, leftover food, and other essentials I needed, triple-checking that I had the Skeleton Key, which I tucked in my pocket. I slipped my old jacket on and gave my room a final look-over before leaving, dropping the room key in my bag after locking up.

Maybe we'll be lucky.

In the lobby, Zane was chatting with Persephone and Trent, who were eating croissants together at one of the tables.

"Ready to go?" I asked, approaching him at the table.

"As ready as I can be, I suppose," he said, forcing a tone of optimism.

"Good luck, you two," Persephone said with an unconvincing half-smile.

I gave her a simple nod as Zane and I grabbed hands, both of us carrying nothing but our bags as we pushed through the hotel door, throwing a final glance back at the lobby.

It's not too late to turn back.

We walked slowly, as if savoring every step through the lively streets. The further out from the city courtyard we walked, the quieter it became, the more dilapidated the buildings were, and the faster my heart pounded inside my chest.

It's still not too late to turn back.

I kept peering backwards over my shoulder at the city behind me. Once we reached the green Los Angeles sign crossed out in vivid red paint, I could see Zaire's truck. The truck looked identical to the trucks the officials drove—just like the truck Zane and I drove when we brought Lamb back to her family after her death.

I rubbed at my aching scar with my free hand as we

approached Zaire, who was filling the gas tank from a bright red jug.

"I'll be ready as soon as the tank's full," he stated, finishing off the jug and tossing it into the truck.

He closed the back of the truck and turned to us.

"Alright. Ready?"

I looked at Zane and back at Zaire.

"I guess so."

"Hop in."

Zaire opened the door to the backseat.

"I'd prefer if you both stayed in the back. Easier to hide if the need arises," he shrugged. "Sorry."

Zane motioned to the seat with his hands for me to enter first.

I hopped in and slid across the seat to the far end. Zane followed after, shutting the door behind him. Zaire climbed into the front seat and started the truck. Without any further words, he began to pull away from Fortitude, taking us into the desert.

Okay, now it's too late to turn back.

Rather than driving toward the small mountain range we had trekked through before spotting Fortitude, Zaire steered the truck parallel to it, taking us along a road that circumnavigated the mountain.

"About how long of a drive is it back to Fallmont?" Zane asked.

"We'll be there by about dinnertime."

"Wait… what?" I asked, stunned.

Fortitude

"We'll be there by dinnertime," Zaire repeated.

"I know, I heard that. How does it only take part of a day?"

"I don't know. I mean, this truck reaches a pretty good speed."

"It took us *days* to get to Fortitude," I breathed.

"Fun fact," Zaire started. "The average walking speed is three miles per hour. I'm currently driving 60 miles per hour. That's 20 times faster than you walked. Now, I can't drive that fast through some of the ruins because I have to be careful, and I have to slow down a bit when we get near Fallmont, but overall, we're travelling a lot faster than you guys walked. Even if you were speed-walking, it still doesn't compare."

I stared out the window in awe. The mountain looked like a blur beside us as we passed it.

"Do you know what you're going to say to Raine?" Zane asked casually, as if we were on our way to an old friend's house to catch up.

"Not exactly," I began to worry. "I guess I'll just think it out on the way there."

I can hardly think straight—there's no way I'm going to be able to do this. But now I don't have a choice. What was I thinking? We can still turn back.

I opened my mouth to ask Zaire to turn back and drop us off at the entrance of Fortitude again, but no sound came from my mouth.

Why do I feel so conflicted? This is for the greater good. The good of the many versus the good of the one… or two… right?

Zaire drove onwards, and the silence grew so

deafening that he eventually pulled a disc out of the dashboard of the truck, sliding it into a slot. A second later, some slow acoustic music began to play from the truck speakers. It was oddly soothing to watch the blurs of color zip by as I tried to focus on nothing but the music and the moment I was in right then.

Things will work themselves out. I'll tell Raine that the population can handle the prison system, that she doesn't have to sentence everyone who messes up to a lifetime away from their loved ones, and that people can eventually go home after serving their time and they can become productive members of society again. There are so many reasons why it would benefit the cities—I just need to be sure to mention them.

"How did Skylar react when you told her we were leaving?" I asked Zane, keeping my voice low, knowing that Zaire could hear but not wanting to draw attention to our personal conversation.

"She didn't really say much," Zane admitted. "She seemed a bit angry, in a way. She told me we were being stupid and were going to get ourselves locked up for no reason."

"Do *you* think it will be for no reason?" I asked.

Zane paused, his eyes fixated on mine as he pursed his lips together in thought.

"No," he answered.

"You don't believe that."

"I do."

"Why?"

"Because I have faith in you. I believe that you want this enough, and so do I. We're willing to fight for it—to fight for our friends, for the people who have been pulled from their homes, for everybody who has suffered because of the exile town system."

I stared at him, waiting for him to say more.

"Do I think we will magically change Raine's mind and she will release us and reinstate the prison system immediately? Definitely not. I'm just being realistic. I know that *you* know that too. Do I think that we're going to be the start of a chain reaction? Yes. But fires can't start without a spark, Eos, and I honestly believe we are that spark."

I reached for his hand and squeezed it. His hand was warm and sticky, as if he had been sweating.

~

A few hours later, while we were moving down the street of some ruins, Zaire stopped the car, putting it in park and opening his door.

"I've gotta' take a leak," he said, hopping out. "I'll be right back."

"Everything is going to work out, one way or another," Zane said, scooting toward me and wrapping his arms around me.

I took a moment to breathe in his scent and enjoy the simple feeling of his arms around me.

"I don't want to go to Ironwood," I whimpered, attempting and failing to hold back my fear.

"I know, E. Me neither." He chuckled nervously. "No matter what though, even if we end up in Ironwood, I won't let anything bad happen to you. You won't be alone. If nothing else, take comfort in knowing that."

I nodded weakly, leaning my face up to kiss him. His lips locked onto mine as he hugged me closer.

"My innocent eyes!" Zaire teased as he jumped back in the truck, shutting his door and resuming the drive through the ruins.

"How much farther?" I asked, unable to gauge our location.

"A few more hours. It's just past lunchtime. I've got some peanut butter sandwiches in the glove box, if you two are hungry. I forgot to mention that earlier. I keep them for when I pick up strays on my way to Fortitude."

"I'll take one," Zane said eagerly, reaching up and taking a wrapped sandwich that Zaire handed backward.

"You?" Zaire asked me, keeping his eyes on the road.

"Sure."

Zane devoured his sandwich ravenously, but I sat there, continuing to stare out my window as I nibbled at the corner of the bread.

I'm not at all hungry.

Sometime after Zane finished his sandwich, I was still working on mine when he fell asleep, slumped over in his seat. He breathed softly in his sleep, his mouth cracked open the tiniest bit.

"I see the way you look at him," Zaire began to speak to me in a mumbled whisper. "We don't have to wake him. If he's still sleeping when we get there, I can let you out, and we can just be careful not to wake him."

"And leave him behind?" I asked in hushed astonishment.

"If that's what you want. You both are heading into

something you can't back out of once you're there, and even if it ends well overall, it won't end well for you two."

"How will you get him back out? You only go to Fortitude once a month," I reminded him.

"I can tell the officials at the gate that I think I found something during my trip that could improve some function or another of the truck, and that I needed some parts from the shop in order to test it. They'll let me back out no problem. You just have to get him to move from his sitting position to one where he's lying down so I can cover him before I leave so there's no chance of him being seen."

I met his gaze in his rearview mirror and I nodded in agreement.

Zane will never forgive me if I go without him. But I don't need his forgiveness. I'm doing this so people can have a chance to get their freedom back, and the last thing I want is for Zane to lose his because of me. I need Zaire to take him back to Fortitude.

CHAPTER TWENTY

The following few hours seemed to drag on forever. Every ruin we passed through, Zaire slowed the truck so he wouldn't get it stuck in the rubble in the rougher streets. Suddenly, in the distance, I saw a thick cluster of trees and other greenery.

That must be Equivox. We're getting close.

I began to remember some of the issues we came across on the way to Fortitude, such as my run-in with Asa.

I'm so grateful that Zaire is driving us to Fallmont so we could avoid coming across more crazies like Asa. I'm also grateful that Zane saved me from Asa and prevented him from being a problem for any other unfortunate "patients" like myself.

The clump of trees against the sandscape seemed to transform into an emerald smudge as we cruised onwards.

Maybe I deserve this. I've broken so many laws. I killed an official. I caused the death of a guy in Bellicose. One of my best friends died because of me. It's probably in everybody's best interest if I'm locked up, but I don't want to be...

Fortitude

The internal debate seemed to continue to sway in a million different directions the closer to Fallmont we were.

I need this to work. It's worth it if I can convince Raine, even a little bit, that the prison system is better for everyone, I reminded myself.

"That's Fallmont," Zaire pointed to a grey splotch in the distance. "I know it still looks far, but we'll be there in less than ten minutes."

I felt my heart sink. I took a look at Zane, who had begun to slump sideways in his seat as he continued to sleep.

He's exhausted. I wish we were back in his hotel room… I don't know what to do. I don't want to go without him, but I don't want to cost him his freedom if I can handle this myself.

"Last call—are you sure you want to do this? I can drop you two off in some ruins, pick up some more gas, and then come pick you up to drive you back tomorrow, if that's what you decide," Zaire asked.

I stared at the grey splotch, which was beginning to reveal individual skyscrapers the closer we were. Frozen, I stared at Fallmont with my mouth slightly agape.

"I—"

Zaire began to slow the truck to a steady cruise, his eyes glancing at me in the rearview mirror.

"Just keep going. Please don't let me overthink it. I have to do this."

Zaire nodded, speeding the truck back up.

"My brother told me a bit about you. From what he knows and from what he shared with me, plus what I can

301

see now… you're tough, Eos." He let out a huffy exhale. "I admire it."

I let the corners of my lips twitch into a feeble smile, not saying a word as the city before us grew larger, beginning to stretch the length of the windshield of the car.

"There's a blanket on the floor in the back. See if you can get him down a bit more and cover yourselves with the blanket. It's dark, so it matches the seats, and the windows are tinted a bit so you can't see very clearly from the outside, but I'd rather play it safe. Cover up. Now."

I grabbed the blanket from the floor, gently draping part of it over Zane before wrapping my arms around him and carefully pulling him closer to the seat until we were practically laying in the backseat, albeit rather awkwardly.

Zane grumbled sleepily for a moment, wrapping his arms around me before growing silent, his breathing steadying again.

"Stay under there until I tell you otherwise," Zaire said.

I lay there, my arms still around Zane. His body was warm, especially under the blanket. His hair felt soft against my cheek, and I could feel his soft breath on my neck as he slept. I planted a gentle kiss on his head, light enough to not wake him.

A few minutes later, I could feel the truck come to a complete stop.

"This is as far as I can take you," Zaire said softly. "You can come out now."

I uncovered myself and Zane, feeling a rush of fresh, cool air wash over me as the heat of the blanket dissipated.

Still holding Zane and him holding me, I began to ease myself away from him until he was lying across the seat, independent of me.

Zaire stepped out of the truck, leaving his door open as he walked over to my door and opened it for me.

I slid out, careful not to bump Zane. We were in an alleyway between brick buildings. The sun was still up, but was beginning to set, igniting the sky in a vivid reddish-orange.

"City Hall isn't far from here. If you go that way," Zaire pointed down part of the alley. "Continue for about four blocks, make a left and keep walking until you see it. Until you turn left, it'll be a pretty empty stretch. This part of the city is usually empty, especially this time of day. After you turn at the fourth intersection, you'll want to be more careful. Raine has an office on the third floor of city hall, but obviously there are a ton of officials wandering around the building. Be careful, okay?"

I nodded, a lump in my throat preventing me from speaking.

"Good luck," Zaire said, hesitating uncomfortably for a moment before awkwardly hugging me.

He pushed my door shut, leaving me standing beside the truck as he climbed back into the driver's seat, clicking the door shut behind him. I turned away from the truck, beginning the walk to City Hall when I heard a pounding noise. Turning back to face the truck, which had just started to pull away, I saw Zane pounding furiously on his window, a panicked look on his face.

I stared back, stunned. I could see Zane yelling at Zaire as the car crept down the alley. Just then, Zane's door flew open and he threw himself out, stumbling for a couple steps before regaining his balance. I saw Zaire toss me an apologetic look as he took off down the street, turning and disappearing behind a building.

"Eos! What were you thinking? Why were you leaving me behind?" Zane managed, a broken look in his eyes as he stared at me in disbelief.

"You don't deserve this," I breathed, my voice wavering.

"Neither do you, but I'm not letting you do this alone! I told you that already!"

"I know," I said, my eyes stinging. "I'm doing this for the people out there like you. I don't want you to be behind bars for the rest of your life for something I could have done alone."

"It isn't that I don't believe you could do this alone," Zane said. "It's just that I don't want you to have to. Besides, there's no going back now—we're in this together."

"I guess you didn't really give me much of a choice," I said with a half-hearted, weak giggle.

"Of course not," Zane grinned. "You almost got away with it, but the truck doors woke me up."

I groaned.

"So close," I teased.

"Which way?" Zane asked.

"That way," I pointed. "He said to go four blocks, turn left and keep walking. Apparently Raine has an office on the third floor of City Hall."

"Alright. Let's go," Zane said, motioning with his hands for me to lead the way.

Begrudgingly, I started us down the alleyway, counting every intersection we came across.

"I want you to know," Zane started as we walked. "That even if this doesn't work… Even if we don't change her mind, even a little bit—"

"Stop," I interjected. "I don't need the negativity going into this."

"Hear me out," he said calmly. "If this doesn't work, I need you to know that I'm not going to be mad at you."

"What's that supposed to mean?" I jabbed, glaring at him.

"I just mean that you tend to blame yourself for things, and if we get locked up in Ironwood, you're going to torture yourself every day, thinking that you put me in jail. But you aren't. It's my choice, and my choice alone to join you."

"You're coming with *because* of me."

"Let's just say I'm doing this for all of the Lambs out there who deserve a chance," Zane said. "Okay?"

With a grunt, I trained my eyes on the road in front of us again.

One.

"Do you remember Lisette?" Zane asked. "From Clamorite?"

"Yeah," I replied, visualizing tall Lisette, with her messy blonde bun. I remembered how she told us about rioting when the leader of Rockhallow, Patrick Redelle, prohibited her from moving to another city to marry her fiancé. Then I thought of Flynn, her energetic redheaded friend, who wore one of the keys to the Skeleton Key box around his neck, and who was arrested for simply being *too* free-spirited.

"If we're successful, maybe she will get a second chance, and maybe Lisette can marry her fiancé that she had to leave behind. Maybe she'll be able to relocate to his city."

I smiled to myself.

This, I thought. *This is why I'm risking everything.*

Two.

"If we just plant a seed in Raine's head about the whole prison system thing, how long do you think it'll take until it grows into anything substantial?" Zane asked.

"I don't know."

"Humor me."

"Longer than it should, probably."

"And you wanted *me* to stop being negative?"

Three.

"I have to ask," Zane started.

"Mmm?"

"So, I know you hung out with that Legend guy when you thought I was with Skylar."

"Yes?"

"Did you ever kiss him?"

"What?" I asked, shocked.

"I mean, he was Mr. Tall, Dark, and Handsome. I'm just wondering if you kissed him."

"No!" I defended sharply.

"You didn't?" Zane questioned.

"No, I didn't!"

"Good," Zane said, grabbing my hand and wrapping his fingers between mine.

Four.

"We turn left here," I said, stopping at the intersection.

"Did Zaire say how far to walk this way?" Zane asked.

"No. He just told me to be careful after we turn because this street is going to be busier than the one we were just on. Just try to look like we belong. If you think someone is getting suspicious, squeeze my hand. Be ready to run at any moment if we have to. Running is a last resort though—instead of people *thinking* we're suspicious, they'll *know*. I don't want to run unless we absolutely have to."

Zane agreed as we turned down the next street, holding hands and trying to steady our breathing.

"Maybe if we just look like a normal couple, people won't question it," Zane proposed.

"How would we do that?"

"Dang, E. I mean, I know I never had a chance to take you on many dates, but I didn't figure you were that clueless on how to act couply," Zane snickered.

"Now you're just being mean!" I said with a toothy grin.

"Here," he said, using my hand to pull us closer together. "Try to *not* look like someone just peed in your juice or something. Act a bit flirty or something. Giggle, look into my eyes a lot, lean against me sometimes, try to get some kisses."

"That's not going to convince anyone!" I retorted.

"What have you got to lose if it doesn't?"

"Alright," I said. "We'll try it."

As we continued down the street, we came across a few storefronts with people wandering about with bags in hand, chatting energetically. There was an official patrolling the street, a gun on his hip. I leaned the side of my head into Zane a bit as we walked leisurely, giggling as I told a made-up story about some girl from school that spilled chocolate milk on some other girl whom I claimed to dislike. We made sure we conversed loud enough for passersby to hear and believe we were local students. Every so often, I would turn to look at Zane, waiting for a kiss. We were sickeningly mushy.

As we neared the official, I found it difficult to think straight and keep the act up. I grew unintentionally quiet, my eyes lingering on the man's gun. I squeezed Zane's hand, so he proceeded to rant about a science test he flunked, to which I responded with mock pity.

The official's eyes scanned over us, pausing on me for a second before tossing me a singular nod as he continued in the opposite direction.

I let out my breath, a sense of relief flooding over me.

Don't get too comfortable yet. We aren't even at the difficult part.

In the near distance, I could see the familiar wide shape of Fallmont City Hall. The massive marble columns stood erect at the entrance, towering over us when we neared the front steps.

"We belong here," I whispered to Zane, still holding his hand. "We just have to believe that, and no one will be the wiser."

"Don't you think some of the officials might be the same ones who were here when we escaped? They might recognize us, especially you. It isn't every day you see someone with black and blonde hair like yours."

"That's a good point," I began to think, slowing our pace before we reached the doors. "There's a door to the side of the bank tellers' desks, remember? It leads to the stairs. We need to get to the stairs quickly, without raising too much suspicion."

"How?"

"I'm working on that," I began to ponder. "We have two options... We can continue this cute act and see if it gets us to the stairs. *Or,* we can just book it to the stairs and to the third floor."

"If we run, officials won't hesitate to chase us. As much as I love when armed officials put the fear of God in me by chasing me through a government building, I think I'm going to have to go with option one."

"I agree," I said. "I was just emphasizing how few plans we have."

"Well, I guess it's settled. Ready?"

I squeezed his hand.

"Let's go."

He led us through the front doors of the city hall. Unlike our first time visiting Fallmont, Fabian wasn't behind us this time, pretending to take us in as prisoners. This time, nobody even looked our way.

The stairs were straight ahead, next to the bank tellers' counter, as I remembered. I looked up at the dazzling, humongous chandelier hanging in the middle of the tall ceiling. We were a few yards away from the bank tellers when I felt Zane squeeze my hand abruptly.

I turned to follow his gaze, tracing it to an official whose hand had slowly traced its way to the gun on her waist. The official was staring us down, unblinkingly.

I began to giggle at Zane, making something up about my best friend's brother and his girlfriend, but Zane refused to play along.

"Zane," I whispered through gritted teeth. "What are you doing?"

"She knows," Zane hissed. "Walk faster."

We began to hurry toward the door to the stairs when another official joined at the one's side. The two of them began to approach us, their eyes locking down on us.

"*Run*," Zane whispered urgently, tugging my hand as he bolted toward the door, throwing it open and pushing us both inside.

Our feet smacked rapidly against each step as we scrambled upstairs, hanging onto the metal railing—half to catch our balance, half to pull ourselves up the stairs even faster.

At the top of each flight, there were signs labeling the floor. I could hear the officials tromping up the stairs after us.

"You're under arrest!" yelled the female official after us. "Stop *immediately*!"

I heard a gun go off behind us, but Zane and I continued to dart up the stairs.

"Hold your fire!" a man hollered to another official. "There's an alert out on these two for interrogation!"

Despite the arguing behind us, the officials were gaining on us.

When Zane and I reached the top of the third floor, we flung the door open and stepped into the hallway, which had a simple tiled floor and plain grey walls. There were florescent light fixtures above us, which seemed to flash as we passed beneath each one.

"Look for Raine's office!" I commanded Zane just as four officials burst through the door to the stairs.

We sprinted down the hallway across the slick floor, my shoes squeaking against the tile.

Department of City Health, I read off of a sign at one of the doors.

Secretary of City Funding.

With every sign I passed, I felt hope fading. One of the officials was gaining on us noticeably faster than the others.

"*Here!*" Zane called, skidding on the floor as he stopped at a door, marked *City Leader.*

The door was propped open a few inches by a wooden wedge under the bottom of it.

Zane pushed the door open and we both bolted inside. I kicked the wooden wedge into the hall, slammed the door shut behind me, and twisted the lock and the deadbolt. I kept my fingers gripping the deadbolt tight, in the event that one of the officials had a key to Raine's office. Holding the lock, I turned to face what was an incredibly confused and alarmed-looking Raine Velora.

She sat behind her desk, her raven-black curls without a single hair out of place, her skin as pale as ever, and her navy blue suit pressed without a wrinkle. Her lips had a deep maroon lipstick flawlessly painted on, and her hands were beneath her desk as she sat upright. She stared back at us, narrowing her eyes.

"I know you," she observed in a cool voice as she sat behind her desk, unmoving.

"Yes," I said, staring back at her, my heart thumping inside me, shaking my chest with every hard beat. "You do."

There was a frantic banging on the door as an official called out for Raine.

"It's okay," Raine called out from her desk to the official. "Stand down and wait for further instruction."

The noise at the door stopped; however, I didn't trust the officials not to try to enter, so I kept my fingers clamped down on the deadbolt knob.

"I wouldn't have figured you'd come back for a visit, Miss Dawn. What can I do for you?"

"I need to talk to you about something, but I need you to keep an open mind," I started.

"This should be interesting. Please continue."

"There are a lot of good people in the exile towns," I said.

Raine scoffed.

"Please," I begged desperately. "I'm just asking you to hear me out."

Raine cocked an eyebrow at me, and kept her lips pursed.

"There are a lot of good people in the exile towns. I've met people who were arrested for defending other citizens, people who were arrested for trying to provide for their families," I glanced at Zane, who was exiled after stealing for his family due to their lack of money from paying for treatment for his sick brother.

Zane looked at me, a glimmer of admiration in his eyes as he flashed me a subtle encouraging smile.

"I've been to all of the cities in the New Territory," I admitted. "There are a *lot* of people in the New Territory. The war was many years ago, and the population has had time to recover. It's time to reinstate the prison system."

Raine looked down at her lap before her eyes flickered up to meet mine.

"It won't work," she stated.

"You don't know th—"

"Criminals are all the same. They're greedy. They're violent. They're liars. They're defiant. They're no use to society. Why in the *world* would I want to let them back into the cities to put all of the citizens in danger?"

"They aren't all like that," I refuted. "I met a man in Bellicose who was arrested for starting a brutal bar fight. Do you want to know why he started that fight? A woman was being harassed by another man, and my friend decided to stand up to the guy."

"We have no room in the cities for people who start bar fights to impress pretty girls," Raine said, tilting her head slightly, as if talking to a child.

"Zane," I said, motioning to him as he stood there, beads of sweat resting on his forehead as he watched us nervously. "He was arrested for stealing. Do you want to know why he stole? Because his brother was incredibly ill, and his family spent every dollar they made on his treatment, so Zane had to steal to provide for his family."

I decided to forgo the fact that the moment Zane was actually arrested was for stealing a bracelet—the bracelet he ended up giving me back in Avid. The bracelet that I kept at the bottom of my bag with the linen "L" from Lamb's bag.

"So, instead of getting a job and *actually* providing for his family, he decided to steal from other people? I'm still not following you, Miss Dawn."

I felt my heart begin to race even faster.

I can't tell if I'm panicking because I'm mad, or I'm nervous that this isn't going to work.

"I've got another," I said confidently. "There's a young woman in Clamorite who was arrested because she wanted to move to a different city to marry her fiancé, who was from another city—he was a driver."

"I believe I know the young woman you're talking about. She was from Rockhallow, and Mr. Redelle, her city leader, referred information to me regarding her arrest. She was rioting in the streets and disrupting local businesses. Her defiant and disrespectful actions belong in the exile towns—not in my cities. Miss Dawn, unless you can provide substantial evidence in favor of the prison system, I'm afraid I'm going to have to decline your offer. Unfortunately, you are not only an escaped exile, but an escaped exile who attacked multiple officials in your previous visit to Fallmont. I can't simply release you; I hope you understand that."

"Okay, listen," Zane spoke up, approaching the corner of Raine's desk, resting both of his hands on its surface as he leaned against it. "What if you do just a few

314

retrials for some of the exiles with less serious cases. If the court determines that they can be released back into the cities, perhaps under a sort of probation, you can try it. If it goes well for them, after a while, do more retrials. Then, for anyone arrested from that point on, the courts can give different sentence lengths to criminals based on crime and severity."

"It won't work," Raine reiterated.

"It will! You don't know that it won't unless you try it!" Zane raised his voice, growing impatient and defensive.

"Or, I can avoid the trouble altogether and simply stick with this system because it *actually* works," Raine began to furrow her brows at Zane.

"No, it doesn't! Look at how many towns and cities we've been able to pass between! If dangerous criminals actually wanted to hurt your citizens, they could, and they would. But if you lock up the dangerous ones forever and you only temporarily lock up the ones who aren't, you can start a society of rehabilitation of contributive members of the cities."

"I'm not doing it, and that's *final!*" Raine's voice boomed through the room as she sat, maintaining her proper posture. "Security!"

Almost instantly, there was a jingling at the door as an official began to unlock it. I felt the deadbolt begin to push against my fingers as I stiffened, trying to hold it in place.

"Call them off!" Zane demanded, staring wildly at Raine, who sat there with nothing more than an irritated look in her eyes.

My fingers grew sweaty as I pinched the deadbolt, twisting in the opposite direction of the official behind the door.

"Call them off!" Zane yelled, a vein in his neck beginning to bulge as he leaned in toward Raine, pounding his fists on her desk.

"*Please*," I pleaded, throwing a desperate look at Raine, whose eyes were trained on Zane.

Raine was breathing heavily, though her lips remained sealed. I turned my focus back to the lock as I began to secure the deadbolt using both of my hands.

"Give us a chan—"

Just then, there was a sharp, abrupt crack.

I looked to Raine's desk just in time to see the pistol in Raine's hands, now above the desk as Zane toppled forward, limp.

CHAPTER TWENTY-ONE

My fingers slipped off the deadbolt as I lurched forward, falling to my knees.

It was as if time had slowed and the air around me had turned to lead.

I couldn't breathe.

I couldn't speak.

I couldn't move.

The room fell silent as my entire body quaked with every heartbeat, faster and faster until the only thing I could do was let out a piercing scream. I sat there on my knees, horrifically wailing while staring at Zane, his body draped across Raine's desk. Officials began pouring into the room. I felt one of them grab my hands, forcing my wrists behind my back. There was a soft click as handcuffs were secured to my wrists and two officials pulled me to my feet and proceeded to lead me out of the room. As they tried to turn me toward the door, I kicked wildly, my eyes never leaving Zane. Once on my feet, I was able to notice the pool of thick blood forming on Raine's desk. Raine had set her gun on her desk and was now watching me as I was dragged away, kicking and screaming. As I was being pulled through her office doors, she threw me an apologetic glance before the officials forced me around the corner, where I could no longer see Zane.

The officials steered me down the hall, back toward the door to the stairs. I went limp as they dragged me—one official on each arm, holding me in a way that my feet slid swiftly over the tile floor.

"No," I cried between sobs.

They continued to drag me down another hallway toward a door. An official pulled open the door, letting the two at my sides escort me through.

"No!" I wailed, beginning to kick my legs wildly, causing the officials to lose their footing and stumble, but they wouldn't release their grip on my arms.

I screamed at the top of my lungs again until my throat felt raw and I was gasping for breath. The officials looked more than aggravated as they forced me down the hall with them, squeezing my arm every time that I let out another scream.

This hallway looked familiar. Every door had a card scanner, unlike the hallway of offices.

This is where they kept Zane and me when they were going to transport us to Ironwood. This is where we were when we unlocked the Skeleton Key box and when we threw the acid on the officials, allowing us to escape.

I dug my feet into the floor as best I could, but the officials were stronger than me and lifted me from the ground to the point where only the tips of my shoes made contact.

I screeched at them, trying to throw my legs into them as they walked down the hall in unison. When the same official who unlocked the hallway stopped at a door, the two at my sides halted as well, waiting as he scanned his card. The same official then reached for the bag over my shoulder, opened the door, and the other two tossed me carelessly inside the holding cell. The door slammed shut behind them, leaving me in the room alone.

I scrambled to my feet, pawing helplessly at the doorknob in vain. Pounding on the door in desperation, I eventually sunk to my knees, exhausted and defeated.

He can't be dead.

I began to nibble on my thumbnail before pausing and frantically wiping tears from my eyes and my cheeks. I pulled my hair back, out of my face, holding it there as I stood and began to pace.

What if he's just hurt? Maybe he's not dead?

Hyperventilating, I kept visualizing the moment. There was the crack of the gun before I turned around to see.

Zane fell so quickly. And his body almost seemed to flop onto the desk. Maybe it knocked him unconscious, but maybe they can save him? Maybe it wasn't fatal?

But then there was the blood. It was this dark crimson puddle that grew on Raine's desk like a blossoming red rose.

You can't lose that much blood. He's gone. Face it. He has to be, right?

The tears beginning to flood my eyes again, I ground my teeth together before releasing a bellowing scream that morphed into breathless sobs.

Zane's dead. Raine won't even consider the prison system. I'm going to spend the rest of my life in Ironwood.

I leaned back against a wall weakly, sliding into a sitting position. I slumped forward, my face buried in my arms. Sniffling, I inhaled slowly and shakily, held my breath, and exhaled. Repeating this for a while, I tried to consider my options.

I could—

No. That won't work.

Maybe if they…

That's improbable, if not impossible.

My best shot is to make a run for it when they try to come in to get me.

I looked up from my arms and focused on the doorknob, feeling the Skeleton Key in my pocket.

There's no keyhole. They use keycards. Damn.

I groaned.

Just then, I heard the soft beep of the scanner outside the door and an official opened it.

"Congratulations," she said sarcastically. "You're a priority prisoner. I looked at our checklist for the evening to see if we had any arrests. You didn't just get the red flag next to your name, you got the red flag and 'ASAP' written next to your name. Looks like I'm taking you to Ironwood tonight."

I stood slowly, keeping my face lowered, but my eyes fixated on the official, who had a lazy appearance about her stance as she leaned against the doorframe. Stepping forward carefully, I sucked in a deep breath before barreling at her, full speed.

She stepped to the side just as I was about to reach her, her facial expression never changing. The second my foot crossed the doorway, two other officials snatched my arms, catching and stopping me in place as I nearly fell forward by the abrupt halt. I felt a prick in my arm and turned to see the official from my door pressing the plunger on a syringe. I gave her a disgusted look that began to fade as the hallway around me grew dark.

~

When I woke, I was still handcuffed with my wrists in front of me as I sat in the backseat of a truck between two officials.

Wow. They're really not letting up on security around me this time.

The tears had dried, and I felt the crumbly feeling of crust in the corners of my eyes. Wiping it away groggily, I began to blink rapidly. Things were blurry, and it was almost night.

"Where's Ironwood?" I asked, my mouth dry.

The driver and two officials in the back were silent, looking straight ahead as if I never spoke.

"Please. I'm just asking out of curiosity. I've never seen it, and I'm about to spend the rest of my life there. The least you can do is tell me where it was hiding all this time."

I thought about the Skeleton Key in my pocket.

If I know where it is, I can use the Key, escape, release my first group of exiles, and lead them to Fortitude. I hate the fact that some of them are undoubtedly dangerous, terrible people, but the rest don't deserve the life sentence Raine and the other leaders have placed on them. Since she isn't willing to consider the prison system, I'll just have to take things into my own hands.

One of the officials shifted in his seat uncomfortably before speaking up.

"It isn't in the New Territory. That's why you've never seen it. It's a little closer to the coast, and it's south of the New Territory," he said, still staring straight ahead.

"I didn't know there was anything outside the New Territory," I lied.

"Ironwood is the only thing," the official replied confidently.

Little do you know, I smirked.

"How long have I been out? How far of a drive is it?" I pried.

The officials were quiet.

"So *now* you're going to stop talking? What have you got to lose by talking to me?"

"Our dignity," the official on my other side muttered.

I scoffed.

"Do you even know what I was doing when *your* leader put a bullet in my boyfriend's brain?" I growled, my heart thumping powerfully and my eyes stinging.

Nothing.

The official who first spoke wiggled awkwardly in his seat again.

"I was peacefully approaching Raine to talk to her about possibly reinstating the prison system. Have either of you ever arrested someone you felt bad about arresting? A mother trying to feed her children? A brother trying to protect his sister? Maybe someone who was going through a phase and vandalized a building, even though they probably never would have done it again?"

Silence.

"I risked everything by sneaking into Fallmont. I know that. But I feel so strongly about this issue that I was willing to risk it. The prison system would work in everybody's favor—it would punish people for doing wrong, it would protect citizens, and it would maintain rights for those arrested for petty crimes. Raine wasn't even willing to *consider* the possibility that her methods are no longer right for the New Territory. She got so defensive of her cruel judicial ways that she shot my boyfriend."

"That's not what happened," the driver spoke up. "Raine reported the incident after you were taken into the holding cells. She acted in self-defense because your little boyfriend was demonstrating alarming aggression. Raine didn't feel it was safe to let him proceed with his actions— she was protecting herself and the citizens of the New Territory from an escaped, aggressive exile."

"No. Z—" I stopped. His name was stuck in my throat like a sharp piece of glass.

"No," I started again. "He wasn't going to hurt anybody. He was desperate. We both were."

"Mason," the other official spoke. "Don't listen to her. That's how they get to you, and that's how you end up working gate patrol instead. You can't sympathize with the criminals—they're all liars. Even the ones that aren't sent to Equivox are liars."

Mason slumped his head in brief shame before fixating his eyes on the road ahead of us instead.

Time crept by in painful silence. My leg began to shake nervously, so I closed my eyes and tried to focus on something else, but everything else was too painful. Instead, I picked at a rough patch of skin on my hand with furious concentration.

A few hours later, I could see the front of the prison ahead of us. The closer we drove to it, the more I could make out.

The outside was grey brick, with multiple guard towers surrounding the enormous building. A prickly barbed wire fence walled in the prison. The truck continued moving straight toward the fence, stopping at a small grey booth next to a gate. The driver of the truck rolled down his window and leaned toward the booth with his ID card, handing it to someone standing inside. A few seconds later, the gate creaked open wide enough for the truck to pass, and the driver retrieved his ID card before continuing through the gate.

The driver pulled right up to a massive steel door where four officials were waiting.

One of the officials outside approached the truck, opening one of the doors. The official on that side of me stepped out of the truck and turned back to face me.

"Out."

Without questioning it, I scooted out of the truck, struggling to step out carefully with my hands cuffed.

The other official exited the truck after me and handed some paperwork to one of the Ironwood officials, as well as my bag.

"Was she carrying any weapons?" an Ironwood guard asked.

"Uhh—" Mason stumbled.

"Did you forget to search her?"

"I—"

"Incompetent moron," the Ironwood guard grumbled gruffly. "Raine will be notified in the next report about your carelessness. We've got it handled from here."

The Ironwood guard stood proud, his arms crossed and his lips pursed in wait.

The man who opened the door grabbed me by my cuffs and tugged, leading me to the steel door. I submitted, eyeing all of the officials with their guns at their hips.

The two officials from Fallmont climbed back into the truck without another word, the gate reopened, and the truck drove off, kicking up sand from the road.

"Sir," called one of the guards.

The angry Ironwood guard grunted.

"Would you like me to search her now? Or take her straight t—"

"Just start the process. We have to wait for Patricia— protocol requires a female official to search a female prisoner."

I was pulled into Ironwood by my handcuffs and the thick steel door crashed shut behind me. The inside of the prison was even drearier than the outside. In front of me was a dingy room full of cheap plastic chairs. The official continued to tug me past the room full of chairs and down a short corridor, where I was brought into a small, white room.

Another official entered the room with us. This one was a young woman with a helmet and face guard on. Even behind the thick plastic of the face guard, I could tell she was pretty. Her eyes were silvery blue, and her hair was pulled into a low ponytail of thick black curls. She was holding a stack of stained orange fabric in her arms.

"The prisoner was never searched," said the guard escorting me.

"There's no need at this point," the female said, holding up the pile of orange fabric.

The other guard nodded before exiting the room, closing the door and leaving the female official and me in the room alone. She reached forward and unlocked my handcuffs, taking them and hooking them into her waistband.

"I'm going to need you to get undressed," the woman instructed, a gentle tone in her voice. "You may keep your undergarments on."

"What?" I asked, eyeing the fabric in her arms.

"I'm sorry," she said, and I actually believed her.

I patted my pocket, feeling the Skeleton Key.

"I—" I stuttered nervously, attempting to concoct a plausible lie. "I can't get undressed in front of someone else."

"I'm sorry, ma'am. This is policy. It's why they have a female official in the room with you. It's protocol that prisoners are watched so they can't sneak anything that could be used as a weapon into the jumpsuit."

I felt my heart sink as I began to undress, leaving my clothes discarded on the dusty floor. The official handed me the orange jumpsuit, which I unfolded and held in front of me. The room felt cold and I shivered as I slid into the stiff garb.

"Hands, please."

I held out my hands as she cuffed them again.

She bent down, collecting my clothes before knocking on the door behind her a few times.

The door swung open and the male official reentered, roughly grasping my cuffs and leading me through another doorway and into a longer hallway.

This hallway was lined with barred cells on either side. The ceiling was at least five stories tall and there were stairs in front of me that led to each of the five stories of cells. The official pulled me up three flights of stairs before stopping at a cell where two other officials stood in wait. One of them clicked a key into the lock before sliding the bars open. The official who had been with me through the prison had then pushed me slowly into the cell. The bars slid shut as he looked me in the eyes, his face devoid of any emotion.

"Hands," he grunted in a gruff voice.

I slipped my hands through the bars and he unlocked the cuffs, taking them and leaving with the other officials.

I was completely alone.

"Eos?" I heard a timid voice call from the opposite side of the hallway.

I pressed my face against the frigid metal bars, squinting through the dim light, trying to make out the figure hunched over in the cell.

"Braylin?" I asked, recognizing Cindee's brother by his silvery hair, despite his young complexion.

"What happened?" he asked. "Why are you here? Where's Cindee? Is she okay?"

"She's fine," I answered. "We found Fortitude."

"You—" he breathed, trying to process my words.

I began to tell him how the group eventually found Fortitude. I told him about Club Belladonna, the shops, the café, and all of the positive things in Fortitude.

He doesn't need to know that Fortitude isn't entirely safe.

Then, I told him about what Zane and I intended to speak to Raine about, as well as what had happened.

"I'm so sorry," he sighed.

"How is it here?"

"It's not too bad," he grimaced. "They feed everyone twice a day. We get showers every other day. They have a collection of books, if you want to read. There's not much else to do here. I'm glad they put you across from me, though! I haven't had anyone to talk to since I got here. They haven't placed anyone in the cells near me until you."

"That's it, isn't it? Eat, sleep, maybe read. That's it?"

He nodded, a look of remorse creeping across his face.

"Alright. I guess this is it," I said softly, sitting on the edge of the thin mattress in my cell. The mattress rested on top of a rusty bedframe, and some of the springs were jutting out through frayed holes.

"I just sleep most of the time," Braylin admitted. "I prefer being unconscious. At least then, I can escape into my subconscious a bit, which may not be ideal, but it's better than this cell."

I need to get out of here.

"When do the officials come around?" I asked.

"Usually just for meals and to take us to the showers. They don't come very often. Why?"

"Just wondering."

I need to get one of their keys. If I can storm whoever comes to my cell, I can take their key and their gun, let Braylin out, and run.

"When's the next time one of them is coming?"

"Not until breakfast. We get breakfast and dinner."

I lay back on the mattress, feeling one of the springs pricking my side. I wiggled around, trying to find a comfortable position, but realized that my attempts were futile. The prison hall grew immensely dark by the late night. All night, I kept envisioning the moment when I turned to see Zane fall across Raine's desk. After a long night of fidgeting, sniffling, shaking, and squirming, I eventually fell asleep.

When the morning came, my back was stiff, and my mouth felt like it had been stuffed with cotton.

I need water.

I sat there on the edge of the bed, smacking my tongue against the roof of my mouth as I waited for an official to bring breakfast. When one finally came, she simply slid a bowl and a cup through the space between two bars. She did the same to Braylin's cell, as well as a couple others down the hall before retreating down the stairs without a word.

When I was sure the official was out of earshot, I called out to Braylin.

"Do they not come in the cells?" I asked.

"They do when they take us to the showers, but they handcuff you between the bars first."

Dang. They leave nothing to chance. I'll need to be more creative.

I picked up the cup. *Water.*

Thank heavens.

I chugged the water rapidly, dribbling a little down my chin as I downed every drop. Picking up the bowl, I slopped the brown mush around with the spoon, giving it a curious sniff. Scooping up a little in the spoon, I tapped the tip of my tongue against the goo to taste it.

The scentless, mushy substance had about as much flavor as it did color.

Hungry, but lacking an appetite, I managed to swallow a few spoonfuls of it before setting it down again.

A few days passed slowly, and every day felt the same. The only variety in the days was shower time, where two female officials cuffed me through the bars and escorted me to the shower, where I was hosed down with lukewarm water and then escorted back to my cell with sopping wet hair soaking the back of my jumpsuit.

One night, while laying on my death trap of a mattress, I was finally near unconsciousness when I heard a clinking sound at the bars of my cell. My eyes flicked open and I sat up instantly to try to make out the source of the noise.

"Hey," a dark figure said in a raspy whisper at the bars. "Skunk!"

"What?" I called to the figure, confused and unable to make out the source of the voice.

"Your hair. Skunk. It's suiting. Anyways—I'm busting you out."

Fortitude

"Skylar?"

"Bingo. You ready to get out of here?"

"More than ready. You stole a key?"

"In a manner of speaking," she said, holding a key up.

In the minimal lighting, I caught a glimmer of blue, purple, and green glass.

She has the Skeleton Key!

"How did you get that?" I asked, now standing.

"Let's just say Zane told me a few fun secrets. Speaking of—I couldn't find him. Any idea where they stuck him?"

I was silent for a moment, trying to decide the best way to tell her.

"He... um..."

"You forget? Or do you just not know?"

"He didn't make it," I breathed shakily.

"Didn't... what?"

"Raine Velora shot him. He's gone."

Skylar was speechless for a few seconds before collecting herself.

"So, are you ready to get out of here or not?"

"Uh—yeah. The guy across from me was from my group. He's Cindee's brother. We have to take him with."

"Sure. Whatever. Let's get moving."

She fidgeted with the Key until the lock made a heavy *thunk*. Skylar slid the bars open and I hurried out of the cell. She chucked my bag and my clothes at me as she

331

began to hurriedly unlock Braylin's door after I had called out to him to wake up.

"How did you manage to get this far?" I asked her as she led us, running to the stairs while careful to keep our weight on our toes so as not to create too much noise.

She kept running without giving me an answer, so I decided to follow her without further questioning.

I can figure the details out later. We need to get out of here.

We ran through some of the corridors, which were eerily empty until we reached the room full of chairs. Lying across the floor were three officials, soaking in puddles of their own blood. The officials writhed on the floor, two of them clutching their legs, and one grasping at his bloody shoulder.

Did Skylar do this?

Skylar squatted down beside two of the officials, batting away their hands as she unclipped their guns and handed them to Braylin and I without explanation before continuing to guide us out of the building, through the thick steel door.

"There are going to be more officials here in a matter of minutes—we need to hurry," she urged, sprinting toward the gate with Braylin and I trailing behind.

Just as we reached the gate, which was left cracked open— undoubtedly Skylar's work—there were gunshots coming from our right.

"Keep running!" Skylar hissed back at us.

We chased after her through the dark courtyard of the prison, nearing the gate when suddenly a flood of white light hit my eyes, disorienting me. I blinked rapidly, trying to blindly run straight. As soon as I could begin to see again, I noticed a glaring white circle of light surrounding us and exposing us to the alerted officials.

Skylar bolted out of the edge of the circle, slipping through the gate and into the dark sandscape without looking back, but as I tried to follow, I heard Braylin cry out behind me.

"Help!" he squealed as one of the officials snatched the collar of his jumpsuit.

The official then pointed her gun at me as I stared back, frozen in place. I placed my gun on the ground and began to raise my arms carefully in feigned submission, trying to decide how to get us out of there safely. Another official appeared beside the one holding Braylin, and there was a quick, rumbling bang. The second official crumpled onto the ground with a yelp, grabbing at a hole in his knee, and the official holding Braylin began to brandish her gun aimlessly toward the darkness of the desert. Before she could find her target, there was another bang. She fell with a thump onto the sandy pavement, her hands covering the gunshot wound in her calf.

"Come on!" Skylar growled from the darkness. "Grab your gun!"

I picked up the gun at my feet, and then Braylin and I locked eyes before taking off sprinting into the sand. There were more gunshots as I sped after Skylar, with Braylin at my side.

The sand sunk beneath our feet with every step, but we powered through, knowing this was our only chance.

My lungs were searing, and I couldn't see my own hand in front of my face, but still we ran forward. I could hear the heavy breathing of Braylin beside me, and I could feel the occasional puff of sand from behind Skylar as she ran. When we could no longer see the prison behind us, we slowed to a trot, and then to a complete stop.

"How did you know to look for us in Ironwood?" I asked, wheezing.

"I figured the plan wasn't going to go down without a hitch," she admitted. "When Zane came to say his goodbyes, I told him he was going to end up in Ironwood, he agreed, and he told me about the Skeleton Key and that you had it. It didn't take too long of asking around in Fortitude to find someone who knew about Ironwood's location until I had a general idea of where to go. Legend's brother came back to tell the group that you two had both made it to Fallmont, so I stopped him before he left and had him drive me within walking distance of Ironwood. I had to take down a few officials, but here we are."

"Thank you," I managed, my hands on my knees and my mouth dry.

"Zane would do it for me. I don't think you would, but I didn't anticipate having to rescue you without him. You've got Zane to thank for me saving your tail."

I nibbled on my lip, trying to swallow the lump in my throat with no success.

"Okay," I said, standing up straight and clearing my throat. "We should probably keep moving."

"Agreed," Braylin said.

"Why didn't you two use your guns back there?" Skylar asked as we walked.

"I've never held a gun before," I admitted awkwardly. "Let alone used one before."

"We're going to have to change that," Skylar said sternly.

"How?" Braylin asked. "I don't want to shoot anyone unless it's absolutely necessary."

"I wouldn't have you use a person as target practice," Skylar groaned impatiently. "Let's walk until we reach some ruins. Hopefully the sun will be up by then, and I can teach you two how to use a gun."

We continued in a straight line through the dark desert until we reached a cluster of crumbling buildings. The ruins were smaller than many of the others we had travelled through, but they would suffice for the night. We peered into one of the houses that still stood, checking each of the rooms for inhabitants. When we decided that the coast was clear, Braylin and I settled into a bedroom, taking the bed. Skylar insisted upon taking the couch, and Braylin and I decided not to bicker with her sleepy gruffness, letting her cozy up on a tan and grey chevron loveseat.

The night seemed to pass quickly, and I woke up to Skylar standing beside me.

"Up. Time for target practice," she commanded plainly.

"Shouldn't we eat breakfast or something first? Is there anything to eat here? I've got a bit in my bag, as long as the officials didn't take anything out."

"You can eat once you can hit a target with a bullet," she challenged, crossing her arms.

I groaned, throwing the dusty covers off and throwing my shoes back on.

Outside, I could see that Skylar had built a makeshift gun range out of rubble and some empty metal cans.

"Hit one of the cans and you can have breakfast," she said, pointing to the targets.

"Fine," I said, looking at Braylin as he joined us outside. "But we don't know how to shoot."

"Give me," Skylar said, putting her hand out and taking my gun.

She held out the gun, demonstrating how to load it and prepare it to shoot. Then, she held it at eyelevel, facing the cans.

"Line the little knob up in the sights, like this," she said, letting me take a look over her shoulder. "Take a deep breath and pull the trigger while exhaling."

She handed me my gun back and motioned to the targets.

"What's next?" Skylar asked. "In regard to the whole Raine Velora thing, I mean."

"Well," I hummed, holding the gun out in front of me. "We're going to prove to the cities that the exile system doesn't work, and that Raine Velora is not fit to be a city leader."

"And what do you propose we do in order to accomplish that?" Skylar prodded.

"Whatever it takes," I said, squinting my left eye shut as I pointed the gun at one of the cans, pulling the trigger.

Bang.

TURN THE PAGE FOR A SNEAK PEEK AT THE FINAL
INSTALLMENT IN THE EOS DAWN SERIES.

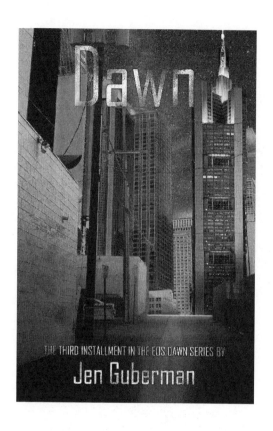

THE THIRD INSTALLMENT IN THE EOS DAWN SERIES BY

Jen Guberman

CHAPTER ONE

I lay there in the grass, my eyes squeezed shut, half-expecting and half-hoping I would wake up. All I wanted was to wake up and see Zane leaning against the tree beside me, peacefully eating breakfast. When I opened them, Braylin and Skylar sat at a pathetic fire, still half-asleep. Desperate, I quickly shut them again.

"She's been out for hours," I heard Braylin murmur to Skylar.

"Wake her up, then."

"She's been through a lot—"

"We all have."

It all started because I stole some expensive rum from a local bar with the hopes of selling it. From there, I was exiled to Avid, a town full of thieves. It was in Avid that I met Zane, and ever since then, each day had been a little brighter than the last—until Raine shot him and ended everything.

Skylar paused for a moment before speaking again. "You and I don't get to sleep in. Why should she?"

"We've been walking for hours, Sky, let her rest. You know as well as I do—she isn't handling it well."

"Handling *what* well, Braylin? Walking? She's walked all the way to Fortitude before. She's fine."

"You know what I meant."

"Zane's death? Is that what you meant?"

"You don't have to be so blunt."

I felt my heart sink at their words and decided to end their discussion immediately.

"I'm awake, guys."

"Oh."

With a groan and an exaggerated stretch, my eyes flickered open, blinking back the sunlight. Towering trees with thick, rough bark and yellowing leaves surrounded us like a complicated maze. In last night's remaining glow of sunlight, we arrived at the gates at the base of Clamorite— the exile town for the noise polluters and general nuisances of the New Territory. Considering we were in an exile town, Clamorite was the most beautiful of them—it was located behind a waterfall along the side of a mountain. The base of the mountain was full of trees and was the only place I have found wildlife in the New Territory.

"Your fire is stinking up the fresh air," I teased, fanning myself.

"*Someone* wanted toast this morning," Skylar said, her eyes flicking toward Braylin.

"My bread is stale, so I just wanted to make the best of a mediocre breakfast!" Braylin defended.

"Mine isn't," Skylar said. "You suck at keeping your food preserved, don't you?"

"I do not!"

"How do you store your bread?" she asked.

Braylin dug around in his backpack, his sleeve pulling up and revealing some of his simple black tattoos. He pulled out a loaf of bread, wrapped in a plastic bag that was merely tucked over on itself.

"You're lucky it doesn't have mold yet!" Skylar said, her petite nose crinkling. "You have to squeeze the extra air out and twist the end of the bag! You don't know the next time we can get more food, so we have to make this stuff last."

When we ran low on food, we had to steal from the cities or the exile towns. After the war years ago, the survivors rebuilt four cities: Fallmont, Eastmeade, Rockhallow, and Nortown. The population was a lot smaller than people were used to, and the government they once knew was destroyed with the rest of the country. Because of this, we ended up with the exile town system. In the past, if a citizen was caught committing a crime, he or she would be arrested, tried, and either fined or sent to prison. Now, people are given a trial that they have almost no hope of winning, and after they inevitably lose the case, they are shipped out to the appropriate exile town. Avid was created for the thieves and has also conveniently become the literal dump of the New Territory. Bellicose is located inside caverns, mocking the "caveman" qualities of the violent criminals. Delaisse, an abandoned industrial town, is where the leaders and government officials stick the drug addicts and the vandals. Equivox, my personal least favorite, is located at the bottom of what is essentially a huge crater where they keep the liars. Then, there's Clamorite. The "noise polluters" and rioters living in Clamorite are surrounded by beautiful, untouched greenery, and their camp is near a stunning waterfall.

"So, besides toast, what's for breakfast?" I asked, running my fingers through my hair and wincing when they tugged on a stubborn tangle. "Please don't say eggs."

"Eggs? Where would we get eggs?" Braylin asked, his head spinning around as if implying a market was hidden in the trees.

"The birds around here might've laid some eggs. Please don't eat them," I moaned, remembering when Zane and I were in Clamorite and I woke up to him preparing to cook a songbird's fertilized eggs over a fire.

"Birds? There are birds here?" Braylin's freckle-framed eyes widened.

I grunted in affirmation, forgetting that he wouldn't know about the wildlife since the birds had quieted by the time we arrived last night.

"How do you know?" He narrowed his gaze, as if expecting me to reveal a clever joke.

"I was here a while back. I found a key here that helped unlock the Skeleton Key box."

"You never did tell me much about that Key. Did you have it when you met me and the rest of the old group?"

"I did," I said as I picked at my split ends, never looking up to meet his eyes.

"Don't pick at your hair, Skunk," Skylar warned. "You'll make it look worse."

"Stop calling me that," I said, dangling a loose black hair over her. I was tired of Skylar calling me that stupid nickname because of my long, platinum and black hair.

"You had a key that could unlock anything, and you

didn't share with the group?" Braylin asked, fixated on the conversation at hand.

"I didn't know if I could trust you guys. Now I know, so now you know."

"How did you find it?" he asked.

"It's a long story," I said, finally turning to face him.

"I'll take the summarized version."

"I found some documents in Avid that mentioned that there was a single key in each of the exile towns that could open the box containing a key that could open any lock, so Zane and I found each of the exile town keys. Then, we found the box in Fallmont, unlocked it, stole *the* Key, and that's it."

Except it's not. I decided he didn't need to know that Raine Velora, the leader of Fallmont, the largest city in the New Territory, caught us and tortured Zane in order to get me to tell her everything I knew about the Key and how I travelled between exile towns.

"Huh," Braylin muttered. "Can I see it again?"

"Skylar's got it," I answered.

Skylar reached into a pocket on her bag and pulled out the Key, handing it to Braylin. He ran his fingers along its cool metal, holding it up to the light as the sun shimmered through the green, purple, and blue glass of the head.

"We need a plan," Skylar interrupted Braylin's trance.

"For what? Taking down Raine and the entire exile town system? Eh. No big deal," I said.

"Eos, I'm being serious right now. We can't just camp out here forever and hope this resolves itself."

"I'm aware of that, but we've also only been here for a few hours. We don't want to rush into this. I tried that already—clearly it doesn't work."

Skylar and Braylin shifted their gazes away from me and everything went silent.

"Guys," I said. "I'm fine. It's fine."

"That isn't something you just get over," Braylin said, his head hung low. "Does everyone who made it to Fortitude with you even know?"

"How would they?" I asked, my lip snarled unintentionally. "They're in Fortitude. I can't exactly mosey over and tell them."

I thought for a moment about my friends—the team that helped Skylar and I make it all the way to Fortitude. I hated that I never had a chance to say goodbye to Bexa before I left, and I wished Cindee was here to see her brother alive and well.

Upon seeing me sitting in silent thought, Braylin decided to throw in his two cents again.

"I think it would really help you to talk about it," he said.

I turned slowly to face him, staring dead into his eyes.

"Zane and I tried to convince Raine to change her mind. We didn't have a solid plan and we rushed things. Raine shot Zane. Zane's dead. Now we know better. What more do you want me to say?"

"Seriously?" Skylar looked back at me in dismay.

"You loved him, E. It's okay to grieve."

I turned away from them, my eyes locking on a tiny

crimson bird in a lush tree. When I locked eyes with the bird, it tilted its head at me, as if waiting for my response.

"Yup. I loved him, but I'm fine. Moping around isn't going to kill Raine Velora. Creating a rock-solid plan is going to kill Raine Velora, so believe me, I understand the importance of a plan, but for now? For now, I just want breakfast."

Without letting them respond, I retreated to my bag, lying at the base of a tree a few yards away. I dug out a walnut muffin and nibbled at it mindlessly. I looked up at the crimson bird, still perched in his tree, staring at me.

"What?" I mouthed to him, as if he could understand.

Just then, the little bird relieved himself, letting a small white puddle spatter against some rocks at the base of the tree before he flew away.

Nice talking to you, too.

My attention returned to my muffin, but I still felt Braylin and Skylar's stares on my back, so I turned on my heel and tucked off between some of the trees.

Truthfully, it didn't feel real. It was strange, not travelling with Zane—it almost felt as if he had gone on a supply run and would return soon. The few days I was in Ironwood, the only prison in the New Territory, were the worst of it. The city leaders only send criminals to Ironwood as a last resort because they don't have the staff to manage it. If it weren't for Braylin being in the cell across from me, I would have gone mad from the grief compiled with loneliness. *I made it*, I told myself. *I did my grieving, and now it's time to move on.*

When I finished choking down the dry muffin, I

wandered back to the makeshift campsite, walking in on an enthusiastic brainstorming session.

"It would work though!" Braylin said, his dimpled grin giving him a childish look, despite his silvery hair.

"But what about the officials? They were already all over the place, and if you think Raine doesn't have them on some kind of super alert after I broke you two imbeciles out of the only prison in the New Territory, you're delusional."

"Skylar's got a point," I said, sitting on a rock beside Braylin. "I didn't hear what the plan was, but whatever it is, we need to be mindful of the officials. We don't know what kinds of orders Raine has given them—whether it's to shoot on sight or to capture—but we do know they are definitely looking for us. That's why we picked here to hide out, isn't it? It's less likely they're going to check an exile town, so it at least buys us a little time."

Braylin crossed his arms defiantly. "You didn't even listen to my idea, so you can't discredit it!"

I motioned with my hands for him to present his case, and he straightened his posture, locking eyes with me before proceeding.

"Propaganda."

"What?"

Skylar jumped in. "He's got this crazy idea to deliv—"

"Hey! Don't steal my spotlight!"

"Okay, okay. Keep going," Skylar rolled her eyes. "Child…" she muttered.

"If we write letters that reveal the terrible, corrupt things Raine has done and how flawed the exile town system is, we can deliver them under people's doors, and maybe we can at least begin to convince people to stop supporting her. Maybe we could gain followers who can help us with supplies or give us shelter. If nothing else, we would be sneaky about delivering them, so even if it doesn't work, the only thing we lose is some time."

"Like I said, it's crazy—"

I hummed to myself as I visualized the logistics of such a feat.

It could go terribly wrong. Then again, when have we ever done anything that didn't have the potential to make everything worse? We always take risks—there isn't a safe route, but this one is about the closest thing we have. Like Braylin said, we just need to be sneaky about delivering the letters.

Skylar stared at me, head cocked to the side and eyebrows raised, waiting for me to speak.

"Actually, I think it's a good idea," I said.

"See?" Braylin straightened his posture proudly. "I told you!"

"There are at least a hundred ways this could go wrong! Do you really want me to count them off?"

"Sure," I said flatly, arms crossed. I blinked impatiently at Skylar.

Her mouth hung open for a moment before she composed herself and began to speak.

"One... We could get caught and sent to Ironwood. If we're all arrested, you can forget escaping this time. Two... they might just save themselves the time and kill us. Three... even if we aren't caught by officials, residents might see us and send search parties after us all over the New Territory—"

"You think they aren't already all searching for us? We escaped the only prison in the New Territory, I killed an official, and we've escaped exile towns. Even just escaping Avid before the rest of this mess started— that alone gives them a reason to be hunting me down. I took just about the only rule of the exile towns and made a mockery of it by breaking into and escaping from every single exile town. They have plenty of reasons already to be scouring every foot of sand in this hellhole," I responded.

"Fine. You know what? You want to try Braylin's propaganda idea—we'll try it. If I even catch wind that we've been spotted, I'm leaving you two behind, and I'll be gone so fast you—"

"You'll be missed," I teased.

"Damn," Braylin muttered, his eyes darting between Skylar and me.

"So, how do we start these letters?" I asked, turning to him and ignoring Skylar's stunned expression.

"There aren't any printers in the exile towns, and it's far too risky to break into one of the cities to try to casually print off thousands of letters. So, first we need paper and pens."

"Sounds simple enough," I said.

"Not exactly. I don't know about you, but I doubt the exile towns have much of a paper and pen supply, so we might have to really scavenge."

"Avid has pencils and paper," I said, remembering the closet under the stairs in my building in Avid. Early in my stay there, after finding the Skeleton Key documents, I had asked Lamb if she had paper and a pencil—I had intended to take notes on the documents, but I refused to tell her what I needed them for. Little did I know at the time that Lamb would join Zane and me in the hunt for the Key, ultimately leading to her death in Equivox at the hands of a deranged exile.

I felt my stomach burn, dragging me from my thoughts.

"What? Really? Alright—I guess we'll go to Avid. About how far is it from here?" Braylin asked.

"It's on the other side of Fallmont."

"Crap. Is there anything closer?" he asked.

"Delaisse and Fallmont," I said. "Everything else is just as far or even farther."

"You were from Delaisse, right?" Braylin turned to Skylar, who already had her arms crossed and eyes narrowed at him.

"Yup."

"Did they have pens and paper?"

"No pens. And not paper for writing."

"Paper for wh—"

"Nevermind," Skylar cut him off, rolling her eyes with a subtle smirk.

I snickered under my breath.

"All jokes aside, no. Not as far as I ever saw," she said.

"Fallmont has to have pens and paper," he thought aloud.

"Yes, they should," I said. "And officials. Probably some citizens who would love to turn exiles in to those officials as well."

"Touché."

"So, Avid is our next best option?" Skylar asked.

"I think Bellicose is just about as far, just a different direction. It's also a lot harder to break into and out of, and I don't really know if we'd find what we need there."

"I also don't really want to be surrounded by murderers, thanks," Braylin said, his leg twitching.

"That's a generalization," I corrected him. "They aren't all murderers and you know that."

"I know," he grumbled. "Still don't want to go there."

"It sounds like that wouldn't be logical anyways, so stop whining about it," Skylar snipped.

"Well, I guess we should be on our way?" He stood and adjusted his socks around his ankles, which had become uneven as he sat.

Skylar and I groaned in unmotivated unison.

"It's nearly lunchtime already," Braylin observed. "*Someone* decided to sleep in, so we've already lost a few hours, and it took us about a day to get here from the last ruins we stayed in. It'll be a couple days before we reach Avid, so I'd rather get going."

"I hate that we came all this way just to turn around and go right back in the same direction," Skylar said.

"I know," I agreed. "But this was just the best option for the time. I think they're less likely to check the exile towns for us first, and this one was close and seemed like the best option at the moment."

"But why not just make this our permanent camp?" Skylar asked. "It's so much better than the desert for so many reasons, and like you said... who's going to look for us in an exile town?"

"Eventually they might think to, and in the event that someone was to spot us, there aren't limitless escape routes here like there are out in the ruins. There's one exit. If they find us here, we might not have a chance to escape."

"Let's get moving!" Braylin called, already walking toward the gates.

"You heard the man," I signaled to Skylar, sarcastically saluting Braylin with a teasing smirk.

Braylin beamed at me as he spoke, throwing his bag over his shoulder.

"Darn skippy."

JEN GUBERMAN-PERRY

Jen Guberman-Perry isn't a New York Time's bestselling author, and she has no critical acclaims, but her mom thinks her books are pretty good. She graduated from Gardner-Webb University with her Bachelor's in Communication & New Media, and she was a member of three honor societies. Jen lives with her husband and their cat in Charlotte, North Carolina.

Made in the USA
Columbia, SC
16 May 2021

38039520R00217